The Demarcation

of

Jack

The Demarcation

of

Jack

by

Dana & Blakely Bennett

TandemWriters

The Demarcation of Jack

TandemWriters

Cover Design by Patricia Maia of Maya's Teasers & Design
Logo design by Olivia E. Bennett
Edited by Todd Barselow

ISBN: 978-0-61591-097-0 (Trade Paperback)
ISBN: 978-1-62890-399-7 (eBook)

We dedicate this story to long abiding love, like we have found with each other.

ACKNOWLEDGMENTS

Thank you to all our friends and family who have been so encouraging and supportive in our publishing endeavors. It's been an amazing journey so far and we've learned a ton along the way.

Special thanks go to our beta readers Stephanie H., Brenda L., Heidi S., & Serena K., and a special shout out to Shannon P. for proof reading.

We have amassed a great crew for our first independent publishing project. Finding our great editor, Todd Barselow, our incredible cover artist, Stephanie Higgins, and logo artist, Olivia E. Bennett has been priceless.

Tandem writing has been an amazing adventure and we look forward to writing more stories together.

CHAPTER ONE

Jenna stood next to her bed, staring at the suitcase as if it might spontaneously up and finish packing itself. She should have been excited to be getting away, going to Jamaica, but instead wished she could stay home, alone, without Jack. She glanced around their bedroom, still in love with the paintings and sculptures he had created. She wasn't sure, though, if she still loved the man behind the art.

As she lifted the lid of her battered suitcase, she thought of the life she had lived before marriage, the baggage she brought to the relationship and the new issues that currently weighed her down. She could hear her fellow traveler in the next room, whistling as he packed his toiletries into his cosmetic bag. *Ten days in Jamaica*, she thought. *Fuck!*

Her ire reared its ugly head again. "I can't believe you asked them to come along without asking me," Jenna shouted to Jack. "You should've at least discussed it with me before approaching them."

Jack winced at the disappointment evident in Jenna's voice. He entered the bedroom with the shower bag in one hand and his coffee cup in the other. He approached her with caution and said, "Please, let it go and try to relax; we're going to Jamaica. Catch some rays, drink some rum, it's all gonna be fun."

He peered through an opening in the curtains at the drizzle swirling under the south Florida wintery sky. The temperature had fallen another five degrees in the last hour brought on by a cold front lumbering its way toward Key West.

"Can't we get past this and have a good time anyway?" Jack said smiling a silly grin, hoping to elicit a positive response. Jenna's dour look caused him to heave a sigh as he zipped up his garment bag.

"But ten days with two more people than I expected," she said, flumping down on the bed. "I want to know why you think spending time with them is going to help us." She bounced back to her feet, reached into her drawer for another bathing suit, and flung it into her suitcase.

"Well, what do you want me to do about it now? They're already coming and I'm not exactly expecting them to help us." He strode over and picked up the phone. "Look, how's this? I'll call and tell them we can fly together, but once we arrive, they have to stay on one side of the resort and we'll keep to the other." He held up the telephone in an impudent gesture of question.

"Don't be ridiculous. You're not listening to me." She turned to look directly at him. "I don't know if we should even take this trip."

"Please, let's not argue about this," he said, holding out his palms in front of him. "Jen, come over here and give me a hug." He opened his arms wide to receive her, wishing to melt some of her anger.

"No," she said, holding up her hand. "Jack, this is exactly what I'm talking about. This is the kind of stuff we need to work on."

"Okay, okay … I'll try to do better and it won't happen again. Until the next time," he mumbled under his breath. Jack grabbed his mug and hefted the garment bag.

"I heard you, you son of a…" she shouted, hurling a pair of running socks at his head.

"Just kidding," he yelped, recoiling and blocking his face with the coffee cup. "We're going to Jamaica, mon. Ya mon? Everyting gonna be all right," he said, putting on his wrap-around sunglasses and straw hat as he bounced out the door headed to the kitchen.

"I'm not so sure about that," she grumbled. Tramping from the room, she wheeled her suitcase to the front door. "Did you call the taxi as I asked?"

"Yes, dear," he called, rinsing his coffee cup in the kitchen sink.

"Don't mock me, Jack. I'm upset, and I think rightly so, because this is supposed to be *our* time to focus on *us*." She pulled open the curtains and looked through the rain for the lights of the taxi.

"Hey, I'm excited about this trip. I'll clean up my act and we'll have plenty of time to spend together. Okay?" He smiled as he joined her at the front door.

After nine years together, Jack's short stature, dark eyes, and his messy short black hair still stirred passion in Jenna. She loved his flirtatious nature but it frustrated her to know that she would yet again succumb to his charismatic charm.

He exuded infectious energy and only seemed to find stillness while he slept or in utter exhaustion after sculpting. In the beginning, his child-like enthusiasm in almost every situation fascinated her, but recently, that fascination had morphed into a constant irritation.

"Alright, let's hit it," Jack said as he opened the front door of the house. A wave of cold, humid air engulfed them as they stepped onto the screened-in porch to await the taxi. The rain had pelted the coast for the last few hours, underscoring their desire for the warm tropical beaches awaiting them in Jamaica.

"Are you sure you called?" she said. "I don't want to be late. Here, take the umbrella, please."

"Here he is, right on time," Jack said. He pushed open the screen door and opened the umbrella. "I'll take the bags out and then come back to get you. Wait here."

Jenna held the screen door open as Jack shouldered the bags. He swayed slightly under the weight of the luggage as he sloshed through a couple of puddles to the back of the bright yellow cab.

"Good morning," Jack said as he approached the driver. "Glorious day, aye?" He handed the driver the stuffed garment bag and the large suitcase.

Rain had soaked the cabbie's turban causing droplets to cascade down his forehead onto the tip of his nose. "Yes sir, beautiful day," he said, in a decidedly Indian singsong accent. "Where would you be going?"

"Fort Lauderdale Airport. Going to Jamaica, mon," Jack said with a big smile.

"That's fine then. In a few hours, you'll be lying on a hot sunny beach. That's a good thing," he called to Jack who had headed back to get Jenna.

"Are you ready?" Jack asked as he held up the umbrella. "Please forgive me, so we can have a good time. Okay?"

"I'll try," she said, ducking underneath the canopy and high stepping to the taxi attempting to avoid the puddles.

Jenna thought that the taxi was clean enough. The odor of musty leather and the faint smell of whiskey reminded her of sitting on her father's lap as a child while he read to her.

The wipers swung just slightly out of rhythm causing a downbeat that reminded Jack of Sting when he played bass with *The Police*. He watched the rain stream across the window as they approached the airport. Homeland Security had raised their alert to orange, and to ensure everyone's safety, they randomly stopped cars to check for bombs.

"Do they stop cabs often?" Jack asked surveying the scene as they drove passed.

"No, sir, wouldn't be good for business."

"I see," Jack said.

"That doesn't make any sense," Jenna said. "You could be carrying a terrorist. You could even be a terrorist."

"Excuse me?" the cabbie said, his face close to the

rearview mirror.

"No ... sorry. I didn't mean you, as in you in particular," Jenna stammered.

"Way to go champ. Now he's going to drop us at arrivals," Jack whispered into her ear.

"I didn't mean anything by it," she said. She leaned to the side trying to engage the driver in the rearview mirror with her innocent smile.

"Air Jamaica, next stop," he said, looking into the backseat with a scowl on his face.

"What's the damage?" Jack asked.

"Thirty-five for you, sir. Seventy for your companion." He broke into a grin and winked at Jack.

"Oh man, where's my wallet?" Jack asked. He reached into his back pocket and checked his jean jacket.

Jenna glowered at Jack and then checked the front pocket of the backpack. "Here it is." She handed over his wallet, got out of the cab and waited on the curb.

"Here you go, my man, and thanks for your patience," Jack said to the driver, handing over the fare including a large tip. He moved toward the far door to exit and said to Jenna, "Get a skycap to check the baggage, will you?"

After they took care of their luggage and entered the security line, Jack wrapped his arms around Jenna. "Honey, look ... let's try to have a good time. I really didn't mean to piss you off."

"Jack, thank you for saying so. No more surprises, okay?"

"Right, sure. I'll do my best. Seriously, I promise," he said as he squeezed her against his body.

They joined the sea of people winding their way through the maze, stripping off their shoes and filling square plastic buckets with their travel paraphernalia.

"I wonder where Marc and Summer are?" he said,

peering over the crowd.

"She tends to run a little late," she said. "At least when it comes to her yoga classes."

"No worries, I'm sure we'll see them at the gate then."

"So what's the first thing we're going to do when we arrive?" Jenna asked, finally giving into the adventure before them.

"We're going to purchase a little cannabis," he whispered. "Like only enough for personal use, you understand."

"Are you nuts? I'm not spending time in a skanky Jamaican prison," she whispered back.

"It's legal."

"Then why are you whispering?"

"Because, it's legal—there. You never know who might be listening to our conversation here," he said. He then pulled up his jean jacket collar to cover his face.

"You're weird," she said, chuckling while she tugged on his sleeve.

"Like you didn't know that about artists when we met. Van Gogh, Picasso … wine, women, parties? Are we getting the painting here?"

"Is that it? You're working your way to crazy?" she teased.

"I am crazy, baby. I live in my own world, every day."

"Hey, you two," called out a familiar voice from within the crowd behind them.

"They're here. Right over there," Jenna said, pointing through the profusion of colorfully clad travelers.

"I'm going over to speak to them. Save my place," he said.

"No, Jack. Let me find out what's up. I don't trust you—you'll tell them everything and I'll be uncomfortable the whole trip."

"Fine. Go, but be nice. It's not their fault."

"I've not forgotten whose fault it is," Jenna said over her shoulder as she jostled through the crowd.

Jack felt an unexpected rush of emotion as his eyes followed Jenna threading her way through the labyrinth of stanchions and passengers. She appeared more beautiful to him now than she did as a younger woman. He recalled her arresting smile when they first came face-to-face as she walked out of the local pub. She had agreed to model nude for him that night.

Recently, Jenna had let her brown waves cascade a little past her shoulders and when pulled away from her face, it highlighted her bright green eyes. Her hips had widened slightly to give her a more womanly figure and her straight nose, high cheekbones, and the overall symmetry of her face made her a pure and refined natural beauty.

As Jenna disappeared from Jack's view, he felt a lurch in his heart. He realized he missed her ready smile and the way she used to gaze at him with awe. Unfortunately, in the past several months, the strained conversations and her palpable dissatisfaction had become the norm.

❋ ❋ ❋ ❋ ❋

"Oh my gosh, you look so ready for Jamaica," Jenna said as she approached Marc and Summer.

"You like? I bought this outfit just for the trip over," Summer said, swinging from side to side.

She wore a multi-colored floor-length sarong with a slit up the side exposing her sexy, toned leg. The yellow fitted top and Panama straw hat completed her island look. She had creamy caramel skin and jet-black curly hair she let grow wild—a perfect blend of her Jewish mother and African American father.

"I love it and you look stunning as always," Jenna said.

"Are you excited yet? I'm beside myself," Summer said, moving in close to Jenna to give her a peck on the cheek. "For a minute last week I thought we wouldn't be able to make the trip. Marc's partner gave him a hard time about taking an impromptu vacation. He is such a worrier sometimes. Marc had to promise to have his cellphone with him to allay Rich's concerns."

"Marc, how are you doing?" Jenna asked, turning to give him a hug. "You look great as well. I can't get Jack to wear a sports jacket to save his life." She thumbed the edge of his lapel. "So is it true you've given up head shrinking?"

He laughed. "Yes, it is. I finally decided to lay off the mind and focus on the whole body. Rich and I sold our private practice and bought two wellness centers. He handles the books and I handle operations, so he thinks the gyms will fall apart without my constant attention." Marc placed his bag in front of him and slid it forward with his foot. "I left work behind yesterday when I started packing."

They moved up the line a few steps and as they stopped, Summer skimmed Jenna from head to toe and said, "I don't know about you, but I can't wait to get out of these clothes and into a string bikini."

"Me, too," Jenna said, looking down at her blue jeans and sneakers. She tugged at her FIU sweatshirt. "I don't know what we were thinking; Jack and I dressed for the weather here. We're going to look ridiculous when we arrive and I expect we'll be peeling off a few pieces of clothing pretty quick."

"I sure hope so," Marc said as he scanned Jenna up and down. He winked and put his arm over her shoulders.

Jenna felt a hot blast flush her cheeks and quickly said, "Jack's farther up in the line now and it looks like we're next," she said, rising up on her toes. "Got to go. See you at the gate."

She waved goodbye as she quickly moved away from Marc. "Excuse me … sorry … I'm already in line toward the … sorry … excuse me," she said, making her way back to Jack. "God, you would've thought I was committing a capital offense and the looks—"

"Honey, do you have the tickets?"

Jenna felt the blood drain from her face and shot Jack a furious look.

"Just kidding. We're almost there," he said, fidgeting with his identification. "You did wash your feet this morning didn't you?"

"What?" she asked, tilting her head.

"You know—the foot fetish people they hired as part of the security team—they make you take off your shoes? You're safe unless they actually start touching your feet," he said, gesturing as if he cradled a foot in his hand. "Most of them are only foot voyeurs, but some of these guys are the real thing—madmen, I tell ya."

"Shut up, you fruit loop. You're such a weirdo sometimes," she said, attempting to hold back her laughter.

"Next." A TSA agent motioned them forward.

"Okay, it's happening," Jack said excitedly. "We're going to Jamaica."

"Down boy, we're not even on the plane yet." Jenna turned to look back toward Marc and Summer. "You know if I were a betting woman, I would say that Marc made a pass at me back there."

"Nah, I doubt it. Right in front of Summer? No way," Jack said as he untied his shoes.

CHAPTER TWO

"What time do we land?" Jack asked, as he placed Jenna's backpack under the seat in front of him.

"Eleven and the sooner the better," Jenna said. "Where are Summer and Marc sitting?" She pulled herself up high enough to see over the headrest of the seat in front of her. "I don't see them. They must be toward the back."

"Once we're flying you can get up and find them," he said, pulling a barf bag from the seat pocket. "Is this yours?"

"Don't be mean, I'll be fine," she said, forcing a smile, but could already feel the butterflies whirling in her stomach.

"You seem to be relaxing. I like this attitude. Does this mean you're ready to party?"

"Yes, as long as we commit some time to talk about our relationship." She flipped mindlessly through the in-flight magazine from front to back.

"That's why we're going to Jamaica. I think it's in the doing, not the talking, but I'm willing to talk about it as well," he conceded.

"Glad you added that last part," she said. She felt the sudden revving of the engines and reached over to clasp Jack's hand.

The jet engines effortlessly propelled the winged giant onto the tarmac where the pilot maneuvered the nose of the plane toward the east. Mottled streaks from the heavy rains formed on the tiny oval windows as the plane waited its turn to depart. The engines whirled with increased power, causing the jet to swell with energy—suddenly, the pilot released the brakes and the jet dramatically sped up.

Jenna felt the forceful flow of adrenaline through her

body as the buildings and in-coming planes whizzed past in the opposite direction. She closed her eyes tightly against the dire images in her mind, feeling her stomach sink right at the moment the plane lifted from the ground.

"Are you doing all right?" Jack asked.

Jenna felt out of control and squeezed his hand as the nose of the plane angled toward the sky. She finally felt the jet gently leveling out, seemingly suspended in the ocean of air. Her fearful experience gave way to excitement the moment she opened her eyes to her new surroundings. She peeked cautiously out the window at the earth moving slowly beneath. The expansive blue sky, coupled with the churning white-capped waves in the Atlantic, and a few white wispy clouds calmed her nerves.

"So picturesque," she whispered.

The plane titled to the right, then, leveling out again, began the one hour and forty minute flight to Montego Bay. The seatbelt light dinged off just as a flight attendant suddenly appeared.

"Yes, can I help you?"

"I pushed the button," Jack said, pointing to the overhead. "I thought it might help if she got some cold water."

"Good idea," Jenna said.

"Well, here's to good friends and new adventures." He raised his hand as if holding a drink.

"Speaking of which," Jenna said as she hesitantly stood, "I'm going toward the back to see if I can find those two."

"Okay. Send Marc back here when you find them. Tell him I'll have a Red Stripe with his name on it."

Jenna made her way to the end of the aisle and slid by the service cart. She looked back down the rows, and spotted Summer and Marc huddled together.

"What're you reading?" she asked as she drew near.

"Hey there. Wow, there's so much to do at the resort.

We're just trying to figure out how to fit it all in," Summer said, holding up the brochure for Jenna to take a closer look.

"Oh cool. We didn't get one of those or at least I don't think we did."

"They're tucked into the…" Marc rummaged through the seat pocket. "Right here. Here you go, take this one."

"Thanks. Jack wants me to send you back to our seats for a beer. He was just about to order one for you."

"I'll leave the beer to the boys," Summer said. "I ordered a mimosa for myself. What did you get?"

"Water," Jenna said meekly. "Way too early for me to start drinking. Besides, my stomach is never very happy on planes."

"Hey, don't worry about it. I ordered water too, but somehow they spilled some scotch in mine," Marc said, glancing up at Jenna with a smile on his face. "I was upset at first," he continued, "but Summer reminded me that we're here to have a good time and it's not right to get upset over such trivial matters." He lifted his drink in her direction. "It's good. You should try one."

"Get out of here and go see Jack," Jenna said, chuckling at his humor. "Let Summer and me have some time together and we'll come up with a plan."

"Guaranteed to blow your mind," Summer said, winking at Marc.

"I like the sound of that." He leaned over and kissed her fully on the lips and then Jenna on the cheek. "I'll see you lovely ladies, in a bit," he said, raising his eyebrows to Jenna and making eye contact that she felt in places she'd rather not think about. "I'm going to leave my drink here."

* * * * *

"Hey, mon. Have a seat," Jack said, patting the cushion

next to him.

"Is this your first time to Jamaica?" Marc asked, ducking under the overhead compartment to sit next to Jack.

"Ya mon. This be me first time." He held out a Red Stripe.

"Nice. Thanks," Marc said. "I've been a couple of times, years ago."

"Where did you guys stay the last time you were there?"

"I was with a bunch of guys from med school. We had a crazy time."

"Oh, so not you and Summer?"

"No, a long time ago. We stayed in this dive at the end of the island, not far from Negril. The beds were horrible. No phones, no TV, not even a radio. The first shower I took there was in light brown water. It was wild," he mused, stroking his chin. "We found this little bar on the beach—we practically lived there. We went from the water to the bar and then back into the water. We'd smoke up and go scuba diving or sailing until around three o'clock and then pile into hammocks for a nap. If we hadn't run out of money we'd probably still be there."

❋ ❋ ❋ ❋ ❋

"I'm so glad you invited us along," Summer said.

"Yeah, ah … me too," Jenna said.

"Is everything okay?"

"Yes and … yeah it's going to be fine," Jenna said. "We were supposed to take this trip alone—kind of a second honeymoon—to reconnect, but Jack … you know how men can be. First-time couples get a huge discount if they bring another couple along and Jack can't pass up a deal."

Summer held up the brochure. "Listen, we can schedule everything so you two have plenty of private time. We certainly don't have to hang out together."

"I know I'm just being silly. It's just that so much has happened recently, I feel like I need a break."

"A break from what?" Summer asked, shifting in her seat to face Jenna.

"A break from life."

"A break from life? That sounds serious. You seemed fine in yoga class. Is it something you want to talk about?"

"I don't know. Part of me feels like I'm being dramatic and another part of me—a bigger part of me—feels overwhelmed."

They sat quietly for a few moments, Jenna lost in her thoughts.

"I thought my mother was going to die," Jenna said, breaking the silence. "She had a mild heart attack and while in the hospital she contracted an infection. I'm not particularly close with her, but it made me feel like life is too short. You know what I mean?"

"That must have been very scary."

"And then there's the fact that I can't get pregnant. I found out about a month ago." Jenna leaned her head back against the seat. "I thought if we had a baby, Jack and I could work out our problems. I thought if Jack became a dad, he might grow up and be more responsible. Instead of being devastated like I am, he's relieved. I think that's why Jack decided to plan this trip, as a sort of pick-me-up for me. On top of all of that, I don't like the person I've become and— I'm sorry," she said, shaking her head, "I don't—"

"Don't sweat it. However, I do have to say that having a baby rarely works to bring a relationship back into focus. If anything, most of the time, it adds to the stress. This vacation sounds like the very thing you need."

"That's what Jack says."

"If you don't like who you've become, maybe opening yourself to new experiences is exactly what you need."

"Yeah, try something new. I was a lot more liberal in college." Jenna slapped her thighs with both hands. "Enough of this morose crap, let's see what adventures we can plan."

"Are you sure?"

She leaned over toward Summer to share the brochure. "Yeah, I'll be fine. So what shall we schedule for the next ten days?"

"Look at this list," Summer said, running her French manicured fingernail down the page. "I have no idea where to begin."

"It says here we need to make dinner reservations for Le Gourmet as soon as we arrive," Jenna said. "Must be popular. Oh my, it's stunning. On the other hand, we could go to the Bayside. That looks yummy, too."

"The Bayside is Italian. I don't eat out a lot, so when I do, I want it to knock my socks off," Summer said. "But I imagine you must be the same way. By the way, how'd you get ten days off from the paper? Are they having you critique the restaurants at the Couples Resort?"

"No, the paper's only interested in local fare. Nah, it's not too hard to get time off there. I write for the Sunday paper and my intern is going to write for the next couple of weeks. She's very excited and besides, I had some vacation leave saved up," Jenna said and then looked back at the brochure. "This is going to be a task working out our schedule. Should we get the boys involved?"

"No, I don't think so," Summer said, laughing. "We should take care of it and tell them when and where to show up."

"Right. Let's see ... we can go snorkeling, but I've always wanted to try scuba diving."

"Marc would probably be into that but not me," Summer said. "I prefer being above the water. Too many Jaws movies, I think. Oh look at this, a sunset cruise, I definitely want to do that." She placed a check mark next to it.

"They also have tandem bicycles," Jenna said. "Oh my gosh … the horseback ride through the plantation sounds wonderful. Put a check mark for us."

"Do you mean us as in you and me or you and Jack?"

"Hell, whoever wants to go," Jenna said, finally giving into the excitement of the vacation. "Did you check out the Couples website? The place looks incredible."

"Like this?" Summer asked, turning the page to show her the pictures in the brochure.

"Exactly," Jenna said. "Listen to this—"

> *Couples Ocho Rios resort is nestled in a cove of shimmering cyan waters on the shores of the Caribbean Sea in front of a beautiful pristine beach peppered with sun worshipers. West of the main building, a wooden dock extends a third of the distance to the nude island offshore. Broad-leafed banana trees, tall grasses, and shady palms provide a sense of privacy as the island lies directly in view of everyone on the big island beach. The large brick buildings, painted brilliant white, reflect old English boarding school architecture with windows and balcony doors flung open to allow the Caribbean breezes to caress sunbaked bodies while they enjoy an afternoon nap.*

"I didn't realize the resort would be so huge," Summer said, expanding the brochure to its full size.

"Excuse the interruption," a male voice announced. "The captain has turned on the 'fasten your seatbelt' sign because of upcoming turbulence."

"I need to get back to Jack," Jenna said nervously. "We can finish the schedule later."

"Okay. But let's definitely check out the resort tour and see if it's worth our time."

"Yeah. Okay. I really need to get to my seat." Jenna quickly made her way to Jack and sent Marc on his way.

"I hate this," Jenna said, snapping her seatbelt around her waist and pulling it tight.

"Try to relax, honey. We're probably halfway to Jamaica," Jack said, lightly touching her hand. "Not too much longer now."

✳ ✳ ✳ ✳ ✳

"That's Montego Bay," Marc said, pointing out the window.

"Oh, I can see the ocean," Summer murmured. "I can't wait to take the bus. I like the idea of seeing the country-side up close."

"I can't wait to get you alone in our hotel room," Marc said, and then captured Summer's lips in a salacious kiss.

When they broke away to catch their breath, Summer said, "Too bad this isn't a longer flight. I have always wanted to join the Mile High Club."

✳ ✳ ✳ ✳ ✳

"We're not landing on that little strip down there, are we?" Jenna asked.

"Honey, close your eyes and I'll let you know when we're on the ground," Jack said, taking her hand in his. "We're taking the bus to Ocho Rios. It's supposed to be a very interesting ride from what I hear."

"Okay. I can do this," she whispered, aware of the pounding of her heart as her hands moistened. She could hear every sound and sensed even the slightest change in altitude. The whirl of the engines slowed and the jet seemed to float momentarily, and then nosed down slowly to descend. The plane rolled to the left, which exposed Jenna to a full view of the runway and the Caribbean Sea. She felt the urge to jump into Jack's lap, but then the wings leveled out again.

"It's sunny and mild today in Jamaica, as it is most days," the pilot said in his thick Jamaican accent. "Thank you for flying Air Jamaica and have a wonderful stay." The pilot paused and then said, "Mon."

Laughter broke out throughout the plane.

The giant wheels of the jet touched the runway with a rumble, the nose of the plane fell dramatically forward followed by the loud rushing of the reverse thrust. Moments later, the jet taxied lazily toward the terminal. Anxious tourists filled in the center aisles in an orderly fashion and shuffled forward to disembark.

"This is awesome," Jack said. "How much trouble do you think you can get into on this tropical island, mon. Wait, that didn't come out right. I mean, how can you get into trouble on this beautiful island? That's not right either."

"Just don't," Jenna said.

CHAPTER THREE

"Hey, customs is over there," Marc called out.

As Jack and Jenna stepped from the plane onto the tarmac, a man wearing dark sunglasses and dreadlocks asked, "Do you need anything, mon?"

"No. I'm fine for now," Jack said. He turned to Jenna. "Can you believe they would hit me up before going through customs? Do I look like a pothead?"

"They're asking everyone who departs the plane. And I refuse to answer that question on the grounds that it might incriminate you," Jenna said, laughing. "Besides you said it's legal here."

"Right. I did, didn't I?"

"Jack, forget it. Let's catch up with Summer so we can sit together on the bus."

Buses had gathered from various locations around the island and sat ready to transfer the tourists to their respective destinations.

When leaving the lobby of the airport, after a customs check, a dark-skinned man wearing black sunglasses, a crisp white buttoned down shirt and khaki shorts sauntered up to the group and asked Summer, "Would you be going to Couples or Ciboney in Ocho Rios, my lady?"

"Yes, we are. Couples," Summer said.

"Not to worry. We will take care of everything," he said.

"How long of a ride is it?" Jenna asked.

"It all depends on how you feel about riding in a bus through the countryside of Jamaica." He smiled. "We will be making a stop for refreshments about halfway to the hotel. If you'd like, I can keep letting you know how far it is until we get there, but I want to encourage you—this is not a time to worry, my lady. Irie?"

"It's Jamaican time … kind of not time," Marc said. "No matter the circumstances 'it's no problem, mon.' Even a problem is considered 'no problem'."

"Well then, that is no problem. Oh my gosh, this weather is fantastic," Jenna exclaimed as she reveled in the sunshine and blue skies. "I wonder if I have time to change. Hang on a sec, Jack, I'll ask." Jenna caught up with their bus operator. "Sir, excuse me, do you think I have time to make a quick change of clothes?"

"We have all the time in the world, my lady, but if you can do it in the next ten minutes or so, that would get us to your destination in plenty of time for you to have lunch. Which is your bag?"

After changing into blue shorts and a fitted pale blue tank top, Jenna settled into her seat and stared out the window at the people walking by from all over the world. She could relate to their smiles and looks of joy to be on the island at last. Jenna glanced at Marc and again wondered if he had indeed made a pass at her or as Jack said, she'd only imagined it. Her stomach twisted at the fact that Marc's flirtation still occupied her mind. In an effort to stop the direction of her thoughts she blurted, "I thought he said we would be leaving in ten minutes? All those buses are pulling out. What do you think is going on?"

"Or so…" said the bus driver as he sat down across the aisle from them. "My cousin works at the hotel and needs a ride. He should be here any moment. In the meantime, can I get you anything?"

"No thanks," said Jenna.

"What's the chance of a cold Red Stripe?" Jack asked.

"Ya mon. No problem," he said with a big pearly white smile. "You in the spirit of the islands now. I'll be right back."

The other passengers seemed oblivious to the delay. Twelve strangers gathered on a bus for a ride from Montego Bay to Ocho Rios, Jamaica, bound by island time. After another five minutes, the driver and a young man boarded the bus and greeted everyone, apologizing for the slight delay. The driver delivered the cold beer to Jack and graciously accepted five dollars with no way of making change. Jack smiled.

The bus bolted into traffic with abandon, joining a caravan of other buses and local drivers in a chaotic scene of speed and lane changes. On the island, if a bus is full of tourists, it's up to the local drivers to yield. However, that small bit of information failed to register to some whose cars skimmed so close that the group collectively gasped each time at the near misses.

"It'll be better once we hit the highway," Jack said, clutching Jenna's thigh reassuringly as she bounced in her seat.

"No it won't," Marc said. "In fact, it's going to get a lot worse. You'll find yourself contemplating insurance policies and beneficiaries." He looked directly at the three who stared back at him to see if he would break into laughter. Not even a chuckle or a smile showed. "You'll pray before this trip is over," he said.

"Then why are we doing this?" Jenna asked.

"Because I've always survived … so far," Marc said with a wink. "The other option is a small plane, but you still have to take a bus from the landing strip to the hotel."

"That wouldn't work for me. I don't do small planes, can barely tolerate the big ones," Jenna said. She consciously avoided looking directly at Marc.

The route out of town offered a sense of relief, but only briefly, as the tour bus left the city streets for the main highway around the island. The chatter started between couples but soon enveloped everyone on the bus, with the exception of one. He was driving like a madman.

"Oh my god! Did you see how close we came to that Rasta man standing on the side of the road?" Summer exclaimed, pointing out the rear window.

"I swear I don't see him back there anymore. Oh there goes another," Jack said nervously. "That was close. This is nuts," he said, laughing.

"Why do they keep blinking their headlights?" Jenna asked.

Marc scooted toward Jenna. "Well, it could be family or friends or a warning that they plan to make a pass," he said with a wink. "I meant cars passing. They usually won't challenge the buses, but I've seen them snake between a bus and a car."

"I see," Jenna said. She looked away to hide the slight smile that Marc's double entendre had evoked.

The bus careened off the road, heightening the apprehension of the passengers. The tourists glanced wild-eyed about the coach when a young Jamaican driver rapidly blinked his lights as he changed lanes and sped past. In only a few hundred more feet, the road narrowed over a bridge. As the small car slid into its lane, pedestrians seemed to place their faith in their ability to remain steady and undisturbed by the closeness of the passing vehicles.

"Oh, I can't take it," Jack said. "How many people are hit and killed each year, besides the twenty or so we're responsible for?"

"I don't know," Marc said.

"Thank god," Jenna said, looking out the large side window. "We only have eighty kilometers to go." She turned to Jack and asked, "How far is that?"

"I don't know," Jack said. "I'm guessing too far for my

heart, though."

Arriving at the midpoint in the drive to Ocho Rios, the clicking of the microphone drew everyone's attention to the front of the vehicle where the big burly man spoke into his one hand while spinning the large steering wheel with the other.

"Okay then, we will be stopping for refreshments for twenty minutes," the driver announced as he slowed and turned down a road that led to a marketplace. He pulled in next to ten look-a-like buses and parked. "I would be suggesting you write down the number of our bus. Twenty minutes," he said over the loud speaker. "This is the only stop until elegant Couples and Ciboney, Ocho Rios."

Jenna walked toward the front of the bus. "How much longer? Oh, never mind," she said, holding up her hand. "I know, I know. Just relax, right?" She turned, grasped the handrail and shook her head as she descended the three steps of the bus to stand amongst the others.

Their shoes crunched along the gravel path to a shanty shack. Upon stepping through the open doorway, they were pleasantly surprised at the cleanliness of the market. Jenna perused the general store filled with trinkets, Red Stripe beer, and local art. Questionable sandwiches wrapped in what appeared to be plain plastic repelled most tourists, while toward the back of the market, on a dark wood paneled wall, hung paintings from local artists. Each artist captured the essence of Jamaica in colors that vibrated with warmth; the art elicited a shared invitation to play and bask in the romance of the island.

"This is lovely," Summer said, lightly touching one of the oil paintings. "Let's buy it, Marc."

"Are you sure?"

"Yes," she said, staring at the painting of a starry Jamaican sky above a huge bonfire on the beach where drummers and dancers moved to rhythms of the night. "I think it's lovely."

"How much do you need?" Marc asked, admiring the artist's work.

"Thirty-seven." She took the money from his hand. "Thanks, honey."

Jack and Jenna, backlit by the vast blue sky, stepped into the doorway of the shanty, each holding two Red Stripe beers.

"Had to," Jack said, shrugging his shoulders. "I have a feeling we'll be needing these for the second leg of this trip, it may be the only way my heart will survive the rest of this ride. I figured you might like one as well." He handed a beer to Marc and offered the other to Summer. "Whoa. Nice painting. Summer, you've got a good eye."

"Thanks, babe." She moved shoulder to shoulder with Jack and held the painting up in front of them. "It's kind of sexy don't you think? I can almost feel the drum beat." She tossed Jack a come-hither look that he easily caught but straightened up, feeling Jenna's stare.

"These cats can put some paint down, ya mon? Inspiring," he, nodding his head.

The four strolled back in the shade of Banyan trees through a small herd of goats that paid them no notice, and climbed the steps to the aisle, flopping back into their seats.

"Two minutes until the race for Ocho Rios is on again. Are we ready?" Marc asked.

"Let's all hold hands," Jack said, reaching for Summer's hand. "Shall we pray?" He joked.

Summer smiled at Jack and gave his hand an extra squeeze. Jenna kept her hands in her lap to avoid clasping hands with Marc.

The bus driver suddenly appeared, taking the mic in hand—not necessary for a bus that size—and said, "Okay then. We're halfway, ya mon." His voice echoed over the loudspeaker. "Let's get started and finish this trip up. Remember, bus drivers don't make a great deal in Jamaica, so tips are well appreciated. I'm sure you'll feel a great appreciation when we arrive safely at the beautiful Ciboney and Couples, Ocho Rios." He cranked the bus and backed out carefully and slowly. He then slid into first gear with a slight resistant grinding and sped out as if he had robbed the place.

"He didn't even count heads. Is everyone here?" Summer asked, glancing around the bus.

"Ah, I'm sure we're all here. So what have you girls decided we're doing first?" Marc asked.

"There's a resort tour—whoa, what was that?" Jenna called out as the passengers all bounced in unison when the bus hit a huge pothole. "Somebody needs to fix this road," she said, rubbing her behind. "Anyway, there's a tour at the hotel when we arrive, so I'm thinking we should go and get a feel for the place. We'll have time to unpack first."

"That's a good idea," Jack said.

"Can that be right?" Jenna asked. "That sign said we have 65 kilometers to go. Is that possible? Are kilometers that small?"

"I always thought a kilometer is similar but shorter than a mile, but not that much smaller." Jack shrugged and slid over to the window to gaze out over the countryside. "Marc, what's with all the goats?"

"They eat them. They roam free throughout the countryside."

"Yeah, I'm noticing. They're everywhere," Jack said.

"Oh my god! You've got to see this! That sign says 80 kilometers to Ocho Rios. How can that be?" Jenna said, pointing out the window as the sign whizzed past. "Is he taking us in circles?"

Marc laughed boisterously. "Maybe they should lay off

the ganja when they're hanging signs. 'Eighty, sixty-five, eighty? No problem, mon! Hey, they still gonna get there, mon,'" he said, continuing to laugh.

"Frankly, I don't find it funny," Jenna said, scanning the scenery. "Are we ever going to get there?"

"Don't make me pull this bus over," Jack said, trying to lighten the mood.

"Kiss my ass!" Jenna said, pushing playfully at Jack.

"So, what else did you guys plan?" Marc said.

"Holy shit, that's either the largest cigarette or the biggest joint I've ever seen in my entire life," Jack said, holding his fingers in front of him about six inches apart. "Did you see that guy on the side of the road?"

The driver pointed out the cruise ship ports and different resorts along the highway in an effort to help pass the time. After twenty minutes of silence, the mic clicked on for an announcement.

"Welcome to Ocho Rios," they heard over the loudspeaker. "We'll be making one stop at Ciboney Resort and then we will make our way to Couples."

"I can't wait to get off this bus," Jenna said.

"I can't wait to see the resort," Summer said.

"Wow, check out this Rasta man … bathing in the creek by the road," Jack said.

"Where? Aww, I missed him. Was he naked?" Summer asked.

"He was naked and I think you would've liked him," Jack said, grinning.

"Damn, let's turn this bus around," Summer said, giddy with excitement.

"That's my girl," Marc said. He leaned in close to Summer and whispered, "There'll be plenty of boys for you to flirt with once we get to the resort."

The bus abruptly pulled into the roundabout for the

Ciboney Resort. The husky driver accompanied two German couples off the bus to extract their bags from the luggage compartment and then lingered ready and waiting for a tip. After receiving his gratuity, he returned to the bus and said, "Okay then, Couples is right up the road. Now doesn't that make you happy? Irie."

"Makes me very happy!" Jenna shouted.

"And you look great when you are happy," Marc said, raising his eyebrows as a grin played across his lips.

"Really? Aww, thanks, Marc." Jenna felt a blush run through her entire body at his compliment. She moved closer to Jack and leaned her head into his shoulder.

The white and red coach shimmied into a driveway lined with tall tropical palm trees swaying gently in the ocean breeze and heliconia in full bloom on either side of the road. As they moved along the route toward the resort entrance, they discovered 'COUPLES' embossed in the grass with bougainvillea rosenka shaping the letters. A red tile roof rose dramatically above as they approached the front steps and landing to the grand entrance of the resort. The driver maneuvered the bus in front of the hotel stairs bringing the vehicle to a sharp halt. Everyone breathed a sigh of relief for having simply survived the trip. Suddenly the air filled with excited chatter while the passengers noisily retrieved their belongings from the overhead racks.

"Do you guys happen to have any small bills?" Jack asked.

"No problem," Marc said. He handed Jack a five and the foursome shuffled to the front of the bus.

"Thank you, sir. We appreciate what you do," said Marc, handing the driver a ten.

"Irie, mon, you have yourself a fine vacation."

"That was a most interesting ride," Jack said as he extended his hand to the driver. "I do appreciate getting here alive."

"Thank you, sir … and my lady, I hope you enjoy your stay more than the trip from Montego Bay. This is Jamaica, mon. Irie?"

"Thanks," Jenna said. "I'll do my best."

Jack took Jenna's hand and followed the group towards the stairs.

With a beaming smile on her face, Summer looked back over her shoulder straight at Jack and asked, "Are you ready to play?"

Jack glanced at Jenna and said, "You know, if I were a betting man…"

CHAPTER FOUR

The foursome ascended the stairs into the hotel lobby where the vaulted ceilings and massive wooden columns dwarfed everyone and everything.

"Hello, and welcome to Couples. Please enjoy a complimentary glass of champagne while you wait your turn for check in," said a hotel host. "As soon as the front desk is ready for you, you will be called. Thank you."

The open French doors that lashed to the outside brick walls allowed the ocean breeze to swirl among the huge clay pots that rested on the terracotta floor interspersed with colorfully hand-painted tiles. Overstuffed couches and dark wood chairs filled the foyer, with no more than four seats in any one grouping. The colorful primitive art that adorned the monolithic walls encouraged everyone to slow down, take a moment and enjoy the slower pace. The newly arrived vacationists strolled to the rear of the lobby and perched at the window ledge to see Tower Island.

Tanned bodies, glistening in the sun, paraded chaotically among the hubbub of activities below the windows. The rope hammocks strung between and in the shadows of palms, cradled couples of all shapes and sizes—one couple in a hammock waved and Jenna instinctively waved back.

The four sidled up to the large dark-wood front desk to wait for the doling out of room keys.

"Have a seat and relax. We'll have you all in your rooms in no time," the receptionist said cheerfully. "Hi. What's your last name?"

"Harper, Jack and Jenna Harper," Jack said. He smiled and picked up their carry on.

"It'll be just a few minutes, sir," she said, writing on a clipboard. "We only have a certain number of baggage handlers and we want to walk you to your room."

"How about I take my own bags and go to the room?" Jack said.

"Jack, knock it off," Jenna said. "You need to chill out."

"Look at those two. Hey, you two, get a room for god's sake," Jack called out to Marc and Summer. "Ha! I made a joke," Jack said, laughing at himself.

"It's nice to see them so in love," Jenna said.

"You still love me don't you?" he asked, but didn't wait for an answer. "Can we get another glass of champagne for my wife and I?"

"Me."

"What?"

"It's 'me'."

"What about you?" he said. "What are you talking about?"

"Never mind," Jenna said as she walked over to the front desk and asked, "How much longer do you think? He gets grumpy when he hasn't eaten."

"One second, please," the desk clerk spoke into her walkie-talkie. "Do we have a bellman for—what's your last name?"

"Harper," she said, smiling.

"For the Harpers?"

"Yes, just now, he'll be heading your way in a few moments," the voice squawked on the walkie-talkie.

"Oh, okay. We'll just be right over here."

"Dr. Beckum, your room is ready, sir. Right this way, please."

"Call us and we can meet up for the tour," Summer said, looking back as they followed the bellman to the north end of the property.

"So cheerful she is," Jack said sarcastically. "Sorry, I'll behave. In fact, I don't care when we get into our room because we're on Jamaican time. We're here to enjoy the fruits of our labor," Jack said, drawing attention to himself.

"Don't be so loud. You're being obnoxious," Jenna whispered to Jack. "Trust me, he's safe," she said to the host.

"Mr. Harper, right this way, sir," said the clerk from the front desk.

"Crap, I hate it when I get ahead of myself," Jack said. "Now, I've shown my ass for nothing."

"Is there a time when you show your ass for a legitimate reason?" Jenna asked.

"Hmm … you are a clever woman, certainly not to be trifled with," he said in a mock English accent.

"If anyone was offended, I apologize. Please be so kind as to forget our last name." She flipped her backpack over her shoulder and joined Jack.

Jack picked up his champagne flute, pulled on his shades and hat, and fell in behind the bellhop.

"Wait. What's this place?" Jack said, pointing to the open door.

"It's the resort store, sir."

"You guys go ahead. I'm going to buy a pack of cigarettes," he said, slinking down as if on a clandestine mission. "American, of course."

"Jack," Jenna called out. "You're not going to buy smokes are you? Really?"

"Just for here, Jen. I would never smoke in the states. Only for a few days. It goes well with drinking and cavorting with everyone."

"We'll wait for you sir, no problem," said the bellman.

After Jack came out of the store, their escort led them down a carpeted hallway decorated with brocaded pineapples and floral patterns. He pushed the keycard into the slot and said, "We want you to enjoy your stay, so if there's anything we can do for you, my lady and sir. Would you be needing anything special today?"

"No. At least not at the moment," Jack said. He had the impression that the bellhop meant marijuana and not food or drink.

"When you do, it would be good to speak to the gardener."

"Maybe you guys could take this up later," Jenna said, pushing in between the men.

"Yes, my lady."

"Oh cool. This is excellent," she said. "Check out the towels shaped into two swans kissing. That's so cute. The bed looks nice. Oh Jack, this is great. Wow, look at the view we have from our balcony." She threw open the French doors and walked out onto the mezzanine. "What's that island, Jack?"

"That's the nudie place," he answered. "Doesn't seem like something you would want to do."

As she reentered the room, she responded to Jack, "I don't know about that." She walked over to her suitcase and unzipping it she said, "I might just try it."

"Yeah … and I'm going to ride the rollercoaster at Boomer's, too," he said, hanging up the garment bag.

The soft, warm Caribbean winds whipped the chiffon liners of the window treatments out onto the balcony where they waved like flags in celebration. The bright colorful patterns and the rich dark furniture wrapped them in the warm Jamaican culture. The airiness of the room combined with the array of yellows found in the curtains, bedspread, and tile floors inspired romance and relaxation.

"Did you see the gazebo? We can watch weddings right below our balcony," she said, placing her shirts in the bottom drawer.

"Honey, surely we can find better things to do here than watch other people's weddings."

"Like what," she called to him in the bathroom.

A naked Jack came dancing out from the bathroom singing, "I feel like making love."

"You're so weird. Go sculpt something."

"You mean use my hands—yes, manipulations—like this?"

"Don't be so barbaric," she said giggling, pushing his hands away.

"Don't be such an ice queen," he said.

"I'm not an ice queen, fuck you. We only have a half hour and I don't want to take the time right now."

"So much for fucking Jamaican time."

✻ ✻ ✻ ✻ ✻

"I love it here," Summer said, running over to Marc and throwing her arms around his neck.

"The resort is remarkable and I love being able to look out over to the island, and to the beach right below us," Marc said as he swung her around. "I hope we get at least one really good thunderstorm so we can lie in bed listening to music and making love while the storm comes in," he whispered in her ear.

"Dr. Beckum … I was wondering. We don't have a lot time before the tour, so can I get a short treatment for my oral fixation?" she said, pushing him onto the four-poster bed. She pulled her clothes off while he freed his shorts and kicked them off to the floor.

He lay back and gave into Summer's playful antics while admiring her toned body in the mirror on the closet door. That's all it took to make him erect. "Kiss me first," he said and she quickly obliged by crawling her lithe, fit body over him. He clutched her aggressively against his chest and kissed her full lips. "Hmmm, you taste so good."

He tugged on her bottom lip with his teeth and she groaned just before he stole her breath with a deep, penetrating kiss. He swirled his tongue about hers, creating the stir that always seemed to connect and arouse them both. He'd never known another lover like Summer, so very available and receptive.

She pulled away to catch her breath and said, "My turn." She swiveled down Marc's body and eagerly lowered her mouth to his erection, taking in his smell and taste. "Yummm," she groaned as she came up for air. She palmed his testicles, and gripped the base of his shaft to protect her throat from gagging on his long phallus. She sucked hard on his head, knowing the best way to make him come quickly.

She didn't mind being late for the tour, but she eagerly anticipated seeing Jack again.

She lightly massaged his balls, and pumped her fist rapidly up and down over his length as she circled her tongue around the head.

Marc clutched her hair just as his orgasm started to fire, releasing several squirts down her throat. "Summmmer," he called out as he came. As he lay there recovering, he muttered, "Damn, girl."

"You can pay me back later," she said with a laugh and then scooted off the bed.

"No doubt I plan to. I love you so much," he moaned.

"I bet you do," she teased.

❋ ❋ ❋ ❋ ❋

An upsurge of excited voices in the open-air lobby aided Jack and Jenna in locating the tour group huddled adjacent to the steps that led down to the beach.

"Hi, how are you?" Jack said to a couple on the couch. "First time?"

"Third, but it's been awhile since we were last here."

"Got it," Jack said. "First time for us. We plan to come back every year for the next ten years. Right, honey?"

"Yeah, maybe," she said and took a seat next to a couple speaking Spanish.

Jack dealt with his impatience by pacing back and forth while awaiting the tour to get underway.

"Sorry guys, we're running a little behind schedule," Summer said as they approached the group.

"Not really. Apparently on time isn't that important here. We were supposed to start like ten minutes ago," Jenna said, standing to give them a hug.

"I'm getting hungry," Jack said. "Can I at least get some coffee?"

"Go grab a cup and catch up with us," Marc said.

"Yeah, I think I will," Jack said. "Honey, I'll be right back."

"Okay. We'll probably still be here."

"So did you get settled in?" Marc asked, sitting down in the seat next to Jenna.

"Yeah, we unpacked and Jack changed his clothes and then…" Jenna said, quickly looking away when the intensity of Marc's stare rattled her. "Did you guys unpack?" she asked, looking around at all the people waiting for the tour.

"No," he said.

Jenna glanced back at him and he winked and said, "We used our time in a different way."

"Oh," she said, quickly facing away again.

A few minutes later, a strapping young man with a broad smile, bellowed, "Okay then. Good morning to you all." He glanced down at his clipboard and scribbled something. "My name is Jonathon, and I will be your tour guide this afternoon," he said as he handed out maps of the grounds. "Now that you know my name, you may seek me out at any time during your stay should you have any questions. Each of you has been supplied with a map, but sometimes it's easier to find your way around if you're familiar with the resort."

"About how long does the tour take?" Summer asked.

"Probably will take about one hour and a half," he said. "No problem?"

"Wow that might be," Summer said. "Just kidding. No problem."

"Okay then. First thing we must go over are a few terms that you will be hearing a lot of while you're here: the first is 'Ya mon.' Okay now let me here you say it."

"Ya mon," said a few people in the group.

"Ya mon," he said. "That was terrible."

The group laughed, quickly sharing glances.

"Next term: 'irie.' Do you know what this means? It means like 'alright' or 'that's good.' It can also serve as a greeting to someone as in 'Irie, mon.' So let me hear you say 'irie.' This time say it together. Ready?"

"Irie," the group droned in chorus, with the exception of a laggard who followed in a lonely voice. "Irie," he said and laughed at himself.

"Irie, mon. You caught up with the rest of us by now," he called out to the man in the back of the group. "Last term: 'No problem.' This is the most important term you can learn. It has magic embedded in it. The old men say it adds ten to fifteen years to your life. No problem? No problem. Ya mon."

The group laughed and began to move forward to follow the tour guide.

"Okay then. Right this way," Jonathon called out, bidding his sheep to follow.

"You know what?" Summer said quietly as the guests began to shuffle forward. "I think I would rather explore with the map than do the tour."

"Let's follow them out onto the patio and then we'll stop at some point and they can go on," Jenna whispered to Summer.

"What are you two planning now?" Marc asked.

"A defection from the tour." Summer laughed and playfully pushed against Jenna.

"That sounds good to me. I hate tours. We can keep asking questions as we go," Marc said.

"Yeah, I can hear it now: 'Ya mon, you should've done the tour, irie?'" Summer mocked the tour leader's voice and they all chuckled.

They ambled with the throng as far as the all-night grill and then parted ways. Strolling up the stairs to the open bar, Summer discovered Jack sitting nonchalantly sipping a Red Stripe as he enjoyed the buzz of multilingual conversations around him. Marc and Jenna stopped to watch a local hat maker weave a sunhat from palm fronds.

"You bad boy," Summer baited. "Drinking a beer for lunch, too? Where's your coffee, huh?" She climbed onto a barstool next to Jack. "Do you really think you should be drinking a beer for lunch?" Summer raised her hand toward the bartender. "Can I get a rumrunner, please?" She turned to Jack for a high five and then looked back at the bartender. "You are so cute," she said to the voluptuous woman on the other side of the counter. "How do you pronounce your name?"

"Ko-ki, as in house key and la as in tea doe. Kokila," she said, smiling, as she darted back and forth like a hummingbird from blossom to blossom.

"Wow, that's so pretty. Sounds Hawaiian. Is it?"

"Yes. Good guess," she said, smiling in Summer's direction. "My father's in a reggae band. He was in Hawaii playing at one of the hotels, where he met my mother. They fell in love and they came back to this island to live. A lot of couples come here to marry, you know? There's a lot of wooing in these islands." Kokila left to take an order at the other end of the bar.

"That's so cool and romantic. Don't you think so, Jack?" Summer asked.

"Sure. I guess so. I'm thinking I'd like to sculpt her." He put his hand to his chin. "She's so curvy and firm."

"Right," Summer said, taking a sip of her rumrunner. "Is that what you and Jenna call it—sculpting?" She winked at Jack.

"Oh god, don't even go there. Talk like that can get me into all kinds of trouble," Jack said, placing his finger to her lips.

A steel drum quartet began to pound out the rhythms of the island near the Calabash Grill to the left of where they sat.

"Ah, I love this music," Summer called out. "It makes me want to get up and dance right here, right now," she said laughing, tugging on Jack's arm.

"Oh, hell no. Not me, I don't dance." Jack squirmed to free himself from Summer's strong grip.

"Come on, Jack," Summer pressed. "Move your hips like this."

Jack laughed boisterously as he pulled away and sat back onto his bar stool. He visually consumed her gyrations as the synchronized steel drummers performed their own glorious dance.

Marc and Jenna sauntered up to the corner of the shack bar and took their places straddling two bar stools next to Jack. Jenna rested her chin on one hand and waved over the barkeep.

"What can I pour for you?"

"Could I get a piña colada?" Jenna asked.

"Coming right up and you, sir?" she asked.

"I'll have a scotch and soda," Marc said.

"Wow, check out Summer. Now that girl can dance," Jenna said.

Summer rejoined the group at the bar after the song ended. When Jack and Jenna weren't looking, Marc stole Summer's attention with a glance. His eyes then shot in the direction of Kokila and back to Summer, greeting her with a mischievous smile. Summer winked and lifted her drink slowly to her lips while watching Kokila prepare Jenna's piña colada. "Delicious," Summer announced, smiling even broader at Marc.

"Thank you," Kokila said. "But be careful. We make them strong here."

"I'm feeling this drink already," Summer said. "Jack," she asked secretively, "what do you think of her—that long black hair … that bronzy skin tone and that nice round butt?"

"I've been sitting here imagining what it would be like to sculpt her in marble. She is exotic. So Gauguinesque," Jack said. "She could've modeled for his paintings of the island women."

"Totally."

"Wow, this looks fantastic, but this must be for Jack," Marc said as Kokila set a plate of Jerk chicken and corn in front of him.

"I ordered two plates," Jack said.

"Help yourselves to some," Marc said to Jenna. "I'm not going to be able to eat all of this. I'll be hitting the gym every day for a month."

"I'll still love you," Summer said, leaning over Jack and patting Marc's flat stomach. "Listen, after you finish we should take a walk down to the dock and find out when the dinghy to the island is going over again."

"I think I'll stay here on the beach and get some sun," Jenna said casually.

"Public nudity isn't Jenna's cup of tea," Jack said.

"I understand," said Summer. "It took me two years to go to Haulover Beach the first time. Got naked with five hundred people and I still felt like they were all looking at me. After the first time, shoot, you don't even think twice about it."

"I'm willing to try it," Jack said. "This'll be my first time in front of a bunch of strangers … right out in the open."

"I think you're going to be very surprised," Marc said, wiping his mouth with a napkin. "People have this idea that it has something to do with sex. The only thing I can say about that is—after you see some of these people, you may never want to have sex again."

"Marc, cut it out. That's not true at all. I think it's great that you get to see all different shapes and sizes," Summer said, winking at Marc.

"I don't know. I think it would feel strange," Jenna said and took a bite of chicken. "Whoa. Spicy, and kind of messy."

"Well, we won't know until we've tried it," Jack said. "You want some of this, Summer?" he asked, holding out a piece of roasted corn, dripping butter.

"Maybe you could try going topless on the beach," Kokila suggested, wiping down the bar in front of Jenna. "Wow, you have the most extraordinary eyes. They look like golden flowers with green around them," she said, moving in closer.

"Oh … um … thank you," Jenna said, turning away toward the beach. "Topless would freak me out. The beach is worse because people could see me from all over the resort."

Kokila leaned forward onto the bar. "Well, why don't you come to the island on Wednesday? I'll be tending bar for Cornelius. Tell you what, you come over on Wednesday and your first two drinks are on me," she said, smiling.

"Very funny. I'll think about it, but a lot would have to

happen between now and then."

"We'll definitely be there," Jack said, smiling broadly at Kokila.

Jenna rolled her eyes and took another sip of her drink.

"Marc, are you ready to head out to the island?" Summer asked.

"Sure. The chicken was excellent," he said, pushing away his plate. "I need to go back to the room to get our sunscreen. Do you want to wait here?"

"Sure. I'll finish my drink. See you in a bit."

"Do you mind if I go with them?" Jack asked Jenna.

"Do what you want. I'm going back to the room to change into my bathing suit. I'll be on the beach," Jenna said, holding out her hand for the room key.

"Where's your key?"

"I forgot mine."

Jack laughed. "No problem, mon," he said.

"Hope to see you Wednesday," Kokila called as Jenna walked away.

✳ ✳ ✳ ✳ ✳

Marc rejoined Jack and Summer. The trio meandered toward the dock through the maze of sunbathers glistening in the hot Jamaican sun and the shadowed hammocks brimming with napping sun worshipers recovering from the previous night's frivolities. Marc's sandals picked up the hot sand, laying it adroitly between his toes, which caused his rather rocky gait. He had to pause to shake out the sand and cool his burning feet.

They hiked down the long dock to the dinghy that lay tied up for the next group heading to the island, willing to shed their clothes and fears of nakedness.

"Would you be wanting to go to the island?" asked a tall sinewy Jamaican wearing a white tank top, long red and white basketball shorts, and sandals.

"Yes, thank you," Marc said.

"You, where's your lady?" the boatman said to Jack, lifting his sunglasses as if to get a better look at him.

"She's going to the beach. She's still a bit shy," Jack said.

"Sorry, mon, no lady, no go." The tone of his voice made it clear there would be no compromise.

"What?" Jack said.

"No lady, no go," he said, while blotting the beads of sweat from his forehead with a white hand towel and then rearranging it atop his head to provide cover from the sun.

"He means—" Summer began to say.

"Yeah I get it. Man, I was really looking forward to checking out the island," Jack said, turning around to walk back to the beach.

"Hang on a sec," Summer said. "Do you mind if he goes with me," she whispered to Marc.

"Can he go with her?" Marc asked.

"If it's okay with you, mon, it's okay with me. No problem."

"Jack," Summer called after him. "How would you feel about going over with me?"

"Are you sure?" Jack asked, looking from Marc to Summer.

"Have a good time. I'll go down to the beach and keep Jenna company," Marc said and then kissed Summer goodbye.

"I'll see you later," she said with a big smile. Then she winked and shouted, "Have fun and don't do anything I wouldn't do."

CHAPTER FIVE

"What are you doing here? I thought you were going over to the island with Summer and Jack," Jenna said, gazing up at Marc who stood with his towel draped around his neck.

"Apparently only couples are allowed to go over. I guess they think it'll eliminate any chance of problems," he said, shrugging his shoulders.

"Oh. So why Jack?" she asked, using her hand to shield her eyes from the sun as she glanced over toward Tower Island.

"He seemed really excited about checking it out and we have plenty of time here. I also thought it would be a good opportunity to spend some time with you, if that's okay?"

"Oh. Sure, okay," she said.

Marc spread out his towel on the lounge next to Jenna's and said, "Can I get you anything from the bar?"

"I've seen a couple guys taking orders."

"Takes too long. I can run up to the bar and be back before they get to us."

"In that case, sure. A bottle of cold water would be great. Thanks."

"Water coming up." He tramped to the far side of the beach and up the stairs to the Calabash Grill.

Jenna turned onto her stomach awaiting Marc's return. She noticed several older women, sunbathing topless, conversing loudly, laughing and carrying on as if it was the most natural thing in the world. She envied their carefree manner. Then, out of the corner of her eye, she caught a glimpse of Marc stepping back onto the beach. From behind her shades, she secretly observed him as he traversed back over to her.

He stood taller and straighter than Jack. He exuded a relaxed confidence and a friendly demeanor. His body appeared strong and lean as his legs came closer, obstructing her view of the island.

"Here you go," he said, handing her the bottle of water. He carefully balanced his drink on the lounge and proceeded to peel off his t-shirt, pulling it over his head, exposing his fit upper torso and taut stomach. "I can't believe I had forgotten how hot the sand can be. I have to do a little shuffle now and again to save my toes."

Jenna appreciated the graying at his temples and his piercing steel-blue eyes. His broad face and distinctive features inspired her to take notice. She expected him to be a hairy man because of the hair on his forearms, but it turned out that his chest was smooth, hairless, and tanned. Realizing she was staring, she quickly looked away. "Thanks for the water." She took a long drink, placed the bottle in the holder on the armrest and asked, "So what are you drinking?"

"Iced water for me, but no splash in it this time. I don't really like drinking alcohol when I'm lying in the sun," he said, filling the palm of his hand with sunscreen.

"Same here."

"So if you don't mind me asking, why don't you want to go over to the island?"

"I don't like the idea of a whole bunch of people looking at my body."

"I see. I think you have an attractive body."

"Well, it doesn't look like it did when I was in my twenties, but thank you for the compliment. Jack hasn't said that to me in a while." She turned on her side to face Marc.

"Well, it's unfortunate, but people tend to get complacent in their relationships," he said. "They sometimes forget the importance of making the other person feel wanted and special."

"That doesn't seem to be a problem for you and Summer," Jenna said, sitting up and pulling her hair into a ponytail. She lay back against the lounge and felt the heat of the sun.

"That's true, but I'm older than Jack and I've learned a thing or two along the way. By the way, Summer tells me this was supposed to be like a second honeymoon and she gave me the impression that you're upset with Jack for inviting us along."

"I wish she wouldn't have said anything. It's not like I have anything against you guys, it's that—"

"I didn't think you did," he said. "Summer and I talk about everything, so if you say something to one of us it's like saying it to both of us." He slid off his sunglasses. "It's completely understandable that you would be upset with Jack for inviting us without discussing it with you."

"I feel so embarrassed," she said. "I don't want you to feel uncomfortable and I don't want to feel uncomfortable either." Jenna paused for a moment. "Besides, I'm now thinking it'll be more fun this way."

"Excellent. I think so, too. Don't worry about Summer and me; we have no problem entertaining ourselves. If you need some space, just tell us."

"You're being very nice about all this. Thank you for that."

"I hope you give the island a try before you leave," he said. "It can be a very liberating experience. After a few minutes, you forget all about being naked." He looked at Jenna over the top of his sunglasses with a toothy smile. "No, seriously."

"Yeah, right. I find that hard to believe. I've never felt comfortable with the idea of just flaunting around. I could model nude when I was younger, but not now."

"Why is that, do you think?"

"I'm not sure. My parents were fairly conservative when I was growing up. I can only recall seeing them fully clothed. Nude modeling was more avant-garde for me, but acceptable," she said, turning over and sitting up. "Would you like to go in the water? I'm getting hot."

"Sure. Did you put on sunscreen? Because you're going to need it here."

"I put some on my face but I don't usually burn."

"We're a lot closer to the equator here," he warned. "Why don't you let me put some sunscreen on your shoulders and back? How does that sound?" He held up the sunscreen.

"Umm ... well ...okay," she said as she flipped onto her stomach and anxiously awaited the first touch of his hands.

"It's okay, I'm a doctor," he said with a lilt of laughter in his voice. He placed his large, strong hands on her shoulders and applied the sunscreen using a gentle massage that left her tingly.

"I'm unfastening your top, if that's okay?" he said.

Jenna felt the straps drop next to her sides.

"Now that's a lovely back. You have a beautiful 'V' shape that I find very sexy."

"I think I need to lose some weight," she said, leaning her head on her crossed arms.

"Not at all. If anything, you need to put on some weight, in my opinion. Summer needs to put on some weight as well. I like wholesome women."

Needing desperately to interrupt the moment, she asked, "Are you ready to go into the water?"

"Are you going topless?" he said, teasing her.

"No. Don't even go there." She looked around at the half dozen or so women sunbathing topless. "Maybe a little later when I get up the courage," she said as she hooked the clasp of her bathing suit top. "Let's go." She jumped up from the lounge and ran toward the ocean.

"I'm right behind you," he called out.

The hot sand inspired a quick jaunt toward certain relief in the tepid, azure Caribbean waters. Marc caught up with Jenna, taking her hand firmly in his as they ran together, romping into the clear water. They dove into the ocean, gliding smoothly and arching to the surface meeting face to face. Jenna dropped back into the water to make her hair lay uniformly against her head. She wiped the salty sea from her eyes and face, pausing to gain her bearings.

"You're eyes are amazing," Marc said, pulling her gently toward him.

"Hey," she said as she pushed him away. She splashed water toward him in an attempt to gloss over the awkward moment. She peeked up at him and their eyes locked as a surge of energy passed between them. She quickly faced Tower Island and blurted out, "I wonder what they're doing over there."

"We can go see for ourselves or wait for them to come back and get the low down."

"I think I'll wait … but, maybe Wednesday."

✳ ✳ ✳ ✳ ✳

Jack and Summer coasted in the small dinghy over the shallow water toward the island. The silver metal bottom of the boat scraped the rocky shore and slid to an abrupt halt. As the ferryman stepped out, he steadied the boat and reached for Summer.

"Watch your step, my lady," he said, holding her hand unwaveringly.

Jack climbed out of the boat without assistance and awkwardly stood waiting on the small platform.

"Thank you," Summer said as she stepped out. "How do we get back?"

"All you need to do is step out here—with your clothes on—and I'll come pick you up," he said as he pushed the boat away from shore.

"This is a bit weird. Where do you drop your clothes?" Jack asked in a whisper.

"You're killing me here, Jack," Summer said, laughing. "Why are you whispering, can you tell me that? You would think that nudity wouldn't bother you at all."

"It feels illegal," he said, dropping his head feigning shame. "Alas, other people's nudity, I should say women's, doesn't bother me at all, but my own, now that's a different story."

The duo traversed the path from the island beachhead up through the palms. They arrived at the pool area, which was already populated by several hotel guests.

"She's so cute," Summer said, as they laid claim to two open lounge chairs.

"Are you allowed to say that sort of stuff?" Jack asked in a hushed tone, stepping close to her side, watching a sexy woman sit down on the pool edge.

"You need to loosen up." Summer turned to Jack and said, "Prepare thyself, I'm going to disrobe." She casually dropped her Hawaiian print cover-up onto the lounge, and then untied her bright yellow top, letting it drop onto her wrap. She slid her matching string bikini bottoms over her sandals and added them to the clothes haphazardly thrown in a pile.

"Maybe I should go wait for the boat," Jack said as he awkwardly averted his gaze from her. His attention panned across to the resort hotel and traveled around to the swim-up bar, and back to Summer who stood naked in front of him. She was even more stunning than Jack had imagined and he couldn't pull away his gaze. Her well-proportioned lean body and wild hair caused his artist's hands to twitch, wanting to see her in marble. "Oh man. Wow," he said, stammering.

She slipped out of her sandals. "Sit down, Jack, and pull in your tongue," she said with a sexy grin. She strolled over to the pool, hopped in and swam up to the bar. "Hi there. I'm Summer."

"Cornelius, my lady. What can I get you?" he said, as he wiped the counter in front of her.

"I would like a rumrunner and a Red Stripe for my friend," she said, coyly smiling and pivoting to check on Jack's progress.

Jack waved, frozen in the same position, still wearing his clothes.

"Tell him, my lady, he has about thirty more seconds to remove his clothing or he must leave the island."

"Jack," she called out. "The naked police are on their way here to arrest you for not disrobing. Get out of your clothes, *now*."

People within earshot at the bar laughed and started shouting encouragement.

"What's the bloke's name?" asked a red-faced, light-skinned man with an English accent.

"Jack," she said.

"Is he sensitive?" he asked, displaying a mischievous grin.

"Depends," she remarked. "I can't vouch for anything."

The Englishman, along with five others, climbed out of the pool, strutted over to Jack and bellowed, "We're not leaving until you're naked." They started singing in chorus the stripper's anthem, "Ta duntduntdunn … ta duntduntdunn."

Jack recoiled into a standing fetal position on one leg, but then acquiesced. He pulled off his shirt and swung it around a few times, letting it sail down to the lounge chair next to him. He was more reticent taking off his shorts and quickly jumped into the pool, once fully disrobed. He swam over to Summer and his new friends at the bar.

"Man, it takes a lot to get you out of your clothes, doesn't it? It must be hell getting you to take a shower," Summer said, shaking her head.

"Depends on who's showering with me," Jack said, raising his eyebrows and holding her gaze.

✳ ✳ ✳ ✳ ✳

Jenna approached Jack who sat at the table just inside the French doors, drinking a Red Stripe. "I can't believe you went to the nude island and let Marc join me at the beach," Jenna said, flinging her hands out in front of her in anger.

"He offered and seemed fine with me going. Did he do something that made you feel uncomfortable?"

"That's totally not the point." She marched over to the table and sat down.

"What is the point?"

"Jack, I swear, do you listen to anything I say to you? Do you recall saying to me that you wanted to take this trip to rekindle the romance in *our* relationship—to work on letting go of the past? I think that's a direct quote. What it looks like to me, is that this trip is about you having fun. I'm not against fun, but I thought it was supposed to be us having fun together." She lumbered over to the bed and sat. "I'm not sure it's worth it anymore. I'm so tired of fighting."

"So let's not fight."

"Right. You know what?" she asked, peering around him out the French doors. "Do what you're going to do and leave me alone."

"I was the one who wanted to have sex when we first got

50

here."

"That's just it. It's always what you want. What about what I need? When does that take a priority for you? You brought me here under false pretenses. You thought if we went somewhere fun and exotic, all our problems would miraculously vanish. It doesn't work like that."

"And why not?"

"Oh grow up," she said, slapping the bed. "This is not about a skinned knee, or the messes left in the kitchen after your artist friends leave. It's about the fact that you don't hear me. If my concerns or needs don't seem rational or important to you, you dismiss them. I'm tired of living my life accommodating your artist whimsicalities. Being talented doesn't give you the right to put yourself above everyone else."

"I don't know what to say," he said, walking over and sitting next to her on the bed. "I didn't realize the situation sucked so badly for you. I'm not sure what you want from me. We used to have such great fun together. Why can't we get back there?"

"I'm tired, Jack. I'm tired of wrapping my life around yours and putting your needs first. I won't do it anymore. I want equal standing in this relationship or I want out. That's it."

"You do have equal standing in this relationship."

"I know I'm as much to blame as you. I've let you live like a kid all these years. What are your responsibilities? Sculpting and playing. I do everything else. I'm ready to have someone take care of me for a change."

"Honey, I love you. If there are changes that have to be made, I'm willing to make them. You're the most important person in my life and I don't want to fuck this up. Come here," he said, opening his arms to embrace her.

"No. I'm very angry with you right now."

Jack stood and continued to hold open his arms toward Jenna. "I swear, you will begin to see a new Jack starting right now." He reached and took her by the hand, pulling her to a standing position. He held out his arms again and she finally acquiesced. "What do you want to do about tonight?" he asked, holding her and swaying back and forth.

"Can we have dinner alone, without Marc and Summer?"

"Sure, let me call them," he said. Jack picked up the phone and dialed their room.

"Hey there," Summer said, lazily. "What's up?"

"We're going to beg off for dinner tonight, but we're still on for the falls tomorrow."

"That's fine. We may hang out in bed for the rest of the night anyway. You guys have fun, ciao."

"Bye," Jack said, and hung up. "So where would you like to eat?"

"Let's see if we can get into Bayside. They have Italian food."

"Sounds excellent to me."

"Let me change into a dress. I'll be ready in a minute."

"You know, I like the feel of this," Jack called out toward the bathroom. "It feels like we're dating."

"I know you may not believe this, but I really want this, our relationship, to work out," Jenna called back.

"Oh man, me too. I really don't think I could live without you, Jenna." *Fuck, maybe that's the problem.*

"Ready?" Jenna said. She then pranced back into the room in a formfitting, purple and blue flower, ankle-length dress. Strung around her neck was a handsome wood bead necklace that accentuated her décolletage.

"One of yours?" he asked, thumbing the necklace.

"Yep, I made it for the trip. What do you think?"

"I bet these would sell like hot cakes around here."

"Hmmm. Maybe." She shrugged.

"Shall we?" Jack pushed their hotel room door securely closed and took Jenna by the hand. They began weaving their way through the hotel maze to the far side of the resort. The darkness of the night softened as they approached the pin-lighted elevated dock meandering along the edge of the shoreline to where the Bayside restaurant seemed to hover above the golden shimmering water.

The maître d' touched his black Panama hat as they approached and informed them that there would be a short wait.

Jack turned back to Jenna, wrapping his arms around her and said, "It's an awesome night, isn't it?"

"Yes, and thank you for having dinner with me alone," Jenna said, nudging her way under his arm. "It means a lot to me."

"You're welcome," he said.

They hugged as they watched the brightly lit fishing boats pass offshore, brimming with tomorrow's delicacies. The subtle combination of the ocean breeze, the waves lapping against the pilings and Jack's warm, affectionate embrace left Jenna feeling more at ease than she had in a long time.

"Your table is ready, sir."

Jack and Jenna followed the maître d' to a small, round, wrought iron table with a glass top and rustic matching chairs that sat near the water's edge. He handed them large menus covered in Leonardo Da Vinci drawings.

"Jenna, how would you feel if I pulled my chair around next to you?"

"Sure. That would be nice. Might be a little crowded after I order," she laughed. "But yes, scoot on over here."

Jack dragged his chair around and sat. "Listen, I've been thinking about what we're going through. I don't know where we got off track and I don't know if we can get it back together, but I do want—" he took her hand and said, "—to ask you to marry me again."

"You can be so sweet sometimes," she said to him. She sat up straight. "I'm not as anxious to marry you this time as I was the first. We've got to work on our relationship so that I don't feel so angry all of the time. You've got to show me more respect. It was funny in the beginning when you would piss me off and then come skulking back, but not anymore. I want some stability, Jack."

"With an artist? I don't know. We're a pretty crazy lot."

"But I don't think you have to be. Can't you sculpt without having to be a Pablo Picasso?"

"I wish I was Pablo, minus the abuse, of course, and the philandering of women, but most of the rest."

"Well, you're getting closer every day that we don't get this worked out."

"What do you mean?"

"I believe he had six wives didn't he?"

"Nah, two wives, but nine women in his life," he said quietly. "Eh, should I move my chair back around?"

"No. But thanks for asking," she said softly.

The waiter approached and took their orders.

The aroma of roasted garlic melding with rich tomato sauce and diced green onions flowed to every corner of the Bayside. The restaurant placed a great deal of importance and reputation on creating authentic Italian meals based on the different regions of Italy. The delicate ambience came alive as local fishing boats glided silently past, their running lights casting reflections on the water. Light mandolin music played softly, cradling the diners in an atmosphere of old Tuscany.

"The food is spectacular," Jack said.

"I totally agree— it's superb. I think I'd have to give this place five stars. Would you like to try a bite?" she said, holding out her fork toward Jack.

"Mmm," he said, chewing. "Delicious."

"We have to do this again and invite Marc and Summer along," she said.

"Summer and Marc are sitting right over there," he said, pointing over her shoulder.

"How long have they been there?"

"A while," he said, and shrugged. "Should we go over and say hi?"

Jenna hesitated and then said, "Okay."

As they approached their table, Jack said, "Weren't you staying in bed all night?"

"Yeah well, when his stomach starts grumbling, it's time to feed him," Summer said, looking affectionately at Marc. "Plus he reminded me we have plenty of time to be horizontal, if you know what I mean. It's that Maslow thingy."

"You have a wonderful view from your table," Jenna said, scanning the ocean and avoiding eye contact with Marc.

"Would you guys like to join us for a drink?" Marc asked.

Jack glanced at Jenna. "Not tonight but we'll definitely be in the mood at the beach party tomorrow night. I'm looking forward to watching the girls dance. Me, I've got two left feet. I guess I got all the talent in the hands," he said, shuffling back and forth. He took Jenna's hand and said, "You guys have a great dinner and we'll see you tomorrow morning."

"Not too early," Summer said with a playful side-look.

"Not to worry, we plan to sleep in as well," Jenna said, never quite bringing her gaze up to connect with Marc. "I don't think we leave for the falls until around ten."

Marc waited until Jack and Jenna were out of earshot and asked, "What do you think about those two?"

"We've talked about them as a possibility before and the

more time I spend with him…" Summer said, watching Jack stroll back to his table. "I like his energy and his humor. I'm not sure though, still feeling him out. What about you?"

"I'm thinking that they may have some issues to sort through before I would consider them as potential. I have no interest in causing them more problems or bringing drama into our relationship."

"I understand but—"Summer stopped speaking when the waiter approached with their salads.

✳ ✳ ✳ ✳ ✳

"I'm going to get out of this dress and into my night shirt. Today was a long day … but overall a good one," Jenna said.

"I could use a drink. Why don't you throw on some shorts and we'll take a walk down to the bar," Jack said, sitting down on the bed.

"You know, I'm so tired, can we order something in?"

"That's fine. What would you like?"

"A piña colada would be great," she said, hanging up her dress. "Dinner was nice. I would definitely eat there again."

"Same here," he said, picking up the telephone to place the order.

Jenna came out of the bathroom in her night t-shirt.

"Come here," he said, grasping her hand and pulling her onto his lap. "I knew this was what we needed. Spending time in a different place and breaking out of the rut that our life has become. I love you, you know," he said and then he kissed her.

Melting into the connection they so desperately needed, they lost themselves in the kiss. The familiar dance of their tongues and lips guided them to a place of comfort. His mouth swept her up in a fire of passion he could easily ignite if she just let him in.

She sighed as she broke off the kiss and said, "I love you, too." She cradled her head in the crook of his neck, and said, "So, tell me about the island."

"It's really cool. There are like four or five gazebos around the perimeter and a pool and swim-up bar in the center, which was fun. That big tower, that's where the bathrooms are, and I'm going to tell you a little secret. When I first got there I freaked a bit." He pointed to his chest and contorted his face.

"Oh yeah? And you think I'll be able to—" Jenna started to say but a knock on the door distracted her.

"I'll get it," Jack said, pushing her from his lap.

"Good evening, Jack." The bellhop entered and placed a tray on the table next to the French doors. "Enjoy your night," he said as he strolled back out.

"Ah, thanks," Jack said.

"Irie, mon," he said. He exited the room, closing the door behind him.

"They gave you three Red Stripes, honey," Jenna said. "I think these people like you."

He took her in his arms and kissed her again with an abandon they had not shared in a long time. He moved her toward the bed and they fell back together.

"Do you want to take your clothes off," she whispered to him.

"You don't have to ask me twice!" He rolled to the side and threw off his shorts and t-shirt.

"I guess not," Jenna said, lying back and watching him quickly disrobe. His intense interest was immediately apparent.

Although Jack stood only slightly taller than Jenna, his muscularity from constant movement coupled with his expansive personality made him seem much taller. She loved that he still got aroused simply at the idea of having sex with

57

her. It had been way too long since she had let her guard down enough to let him in.

After positioning himself next to her on the bed, he rolled Jenna halfway on top of him and resumed his penetrating kiss.

"Hmmmm," she said.

He lifted her shirt revealing her pendulum breasts, her nipples already hard in anticipation. Lowering his mouth, he sucked her right nipple into his mouth and tugged with his teeth and lips. He fondled her other breast, slowly working his way down the side of her body. They had been together so long, he knew all the right buttons to push. It had been a long time since she had allowed him to go down on her, and he decided to take the chance.

Spreading her legs wide, he repositioned himself, massaging his hands up the inside of her thighs until he used his thumbs to finger her wetness. "Oh, babe, I love to feel you so wet."

Jenna glanced down into Jack's eyes and saw the desire there, flaring her own. She needed this. They needed this.

Jack lowered his head, taking in her smell just before tasting her. "So good," he said.

Jenna pulled a pillow under her head and relaxed into the sensation. As her libido climbed, her thoughts traveled to earlier in the day and her time on the beach with Marc. She could not deny there seemed to be mutual attraction and his flirtatious nature left her feeling far more attractive than she had in a long time. "Mmmm," Jenna moaned. She wondered if Marc's cock might be longer than Jack's or as thick? Once her orgasm hovered close, her mind quieted.

Jack used his knowledge from his history with Jenna to keep her just at the edge of the precipice for a while, making her strain and groan for fulfillment. He finally softened and slowed the pace just enough to send her soaring into blissful release.

She practically purred as she came down from the high of her orgasm. Jack always loved her best in these moments, when all the stress of their lives seemed to disappear. She rolled to the side and breathed a big sigh. "What can I do for you?" she mumbled, not yet fully back from her excursion.

He lifted up onto his elbow. Looking down at her, he said, "I know this is going to sound crazy coming for me, but let's spend some time talking and getting to know each other again. Okay?"

"Oh … yeah, sure, okay," she said, sitting up in the bed. "So shall we take this outside?"

"Sure," he said, kissing Jenna's forehead as he shifted to get up.

He threw on his shorts and Jenna pulled her nightshirt back on. She opened the French doors for Jack and he carried the tray of drinks onto the balcony.

After opening his pack of cigarettes, Jack lit one. "I think I was a happier person when I smoked," he said, inhaling deeply.

"I have to tell you, I like the way you smell now, that is, after you quit. Don't you remember?"

"Yeah, I remember, and I don't plan to take the habit back with me, so you can relax. I just thought I could let it all go for the time we're here. What happens in Jamaica stays in Jamaica."

"But you do realize that you'll smell again, right?" Jenna said.

"That's not completely true is it? You can handle it for a few days can't you?"

"I guess I can live with it for a few days. So … finish telling me about the island."

"Right, okay. So at first, I was freaking out, frozen, looking around, but you can't be on the island with clothes on. So they give you enough time to get settled but then you have to get naked or you get thrown out. So I'm standing there with all these naked couples around me—"

"Were you by the pool?"

"Yeah, near a lounge chair by the far side. The swim-up bar was across the water from me. Summer pulled off her clothes the second we got there. She jumps in the pool and swims up to the bar where apparently the bartender tells her if I'm not naked in thirty seconds, he's personally going to kick me off the island. Right? So now, all these people around the bar are staring at me. I stood there, frozen, looking kind of stupid, I'm sure. This Brit, I think his name was Cliff, and several of his friends got out of the pool and walked over by me and started cheering me on. You know, don't you, they started doing the striptease song and of course, I had to oblige. I stripped for the entire pool, so don't be surprised if I get a whistle or two around the hotel lobby."

"I can so picture it. You're such a goof sometimes," she said. "Now you've sufficiently scared me out of going over there."

"Why? It was a lot of fun," Jack said enthusiastically. "The people that hang out there are great and the bartender completely entertained us. You can get food brought over from the resort. If you can get past being naked, I'm sure you will love it and the people."

"What if I get there and change my mind? What if I don't want a bunch of people watching me?" she said, shifting uncomfortably.

"If you get there and change your mind you can go back out on the dock, wait for a few minutes and they come and take you back. That's all."

"Oh, I see."

"Plus there are gazebos that are more private," he said, staring out over the water toward the island. "What about you?" He turned back to Jenna. "How was the beach?"

"It was alright. The water felt wonderful and Marc was nice enough. She looked away and added, "Nothing that interesting happened." But as she said it, she could still feel the rush of Marc's first touch.

"I wonder if I can get a hold of some clay. I would love to find the kind I use back home but I doubt they have it here."

"You can ask the concierge if they can get it for you."

"That's a great idea. I'll do that tomorrow."

"So what has you so inspired? You haven't been sculpting much lately."

"I told you before that I was interested in sculpting Summer in a yoga pose. I'll use clay first but ultimately I see it as a marble piece. And Kokilay would be interesting to sculpt. She looks so Renaissance."

"It's Koki*la*."

"Right," Jack said.

"Well, I'm tired. I think my drink and that wonderful orgasm put the finishing touches on me," she said, standing and bending over to stretch her legs. "Are you coming?" she asked, crossing the threshold into the room.

"In a minute. I want to finish my beer."

She returned to the balcony and passionately kissed Jack, a little thank you for the earlier play. As she headed back inside, at the last second she glanced back and said, "I'm looking forward to climbing the falls tomorrow and thanks for tonight. Sweet dreams."

"Night, Jenna." He watched her saunter into the hotel room, remembering the good times in the past. He felt melancholy about their current problems but more encouraged than he had in a long time. He propped his feet on the balcony rail, closed his eyes and wondered what tomorrow might bring. He knew he would be seeing Summer again.

CHAPTER SIX

"**O**h my god … that dream again," Jenna uttered, sitting up in bed. "Jack, Jack, wake up!"

"What? What's the problem?" he said softly. "I thought we were sleeping in today." He propped up his upper body on his elbow.

"I hate having that dream," she said, burying her face in her hands.

"What was it about?"

"I dreamt about you letting Tina give you a blowjob. It was terrible. Why do I keep reliving this crap?"

"Why are you dreaming about that?"

"I don't know," she said flipping onto her side. "Maybe it was because you went over to the island with Summer. What do you think?"

"Oh yeah, sure, like something is going to happen between me and Summer. Well, go back to sleep," he whispered. "It was a dream. We can talk tomorrow." He adjusted the pillows under his head.

"I can't," she said. "Why did you have oral sex with Tina? And why in god's name did you tell me about it afterwards?"

"Damn it, not this again. It's been seven years," he groaned into the pillow.

"If you would explain it to me, I would be able to let it go, but every time—and it's not very often that I bring it up— you don't answer my questions. I can't let it go because I don't understand it."

"There's nothing I could say that would satisfy you," he said, turning away from her.

"An answer for a change would go a long way. Why did you have sex with her when you were in a committed relationship with me?"

"Look, this is your issue. It has nothing to do with me."

"What? Are you serious? So you're saying if I let my ex-boyfriend, or anyone for that matter, go down on me, and you had a problem with it, it would be your issue?'

"Yes, it would be my issue."

"That's really fucked up, Jack. Why did you let her go down on you? You guys were on such bad terms. She totally screwed you over and yet you let the bitch give you a blowjob. And why in the world did you tell me about it? Were you angry at me?"

"I truly regret telling you about it," he said, pulling his pillow over his head.

"But you don't regret doing it?" she asked.

"God, Jenna, why can't you let this go. It was a long time ago. You can't understand because you're not a guy," he said, rolling back and glaring at her.

"So should I be worried that there are other women out there wanting you and you might comply?"

"Don't be ridiculous. I was a different person then. That would never happen now."

"You know, I might be able to let it go, if you weren't such a jerk about it. You never apologized," she said, flipping the switch on the bed lamp. "I remember when you told me. It was *so* matter of fact. It was like, 'Honey, I folded the clothes in the dryer.' Not even: 'It was a mistake.' Not a: 'I don't know what came over me.' How can I ever let it go when you're such an ass about it? Maybe I should find someone to play with and see how you deal with your issue!"

"Look, I'm going back to sleep. I'm tired and we have the falls tomorrow—today—in a little while. You should go back to sleep as well," he said, pivoting onto his side, facing away from her.

"Yeah, right," she mumbled. She roughly got out of the bed, being sure to jostle and shake it as much as possible for spite, then retrieved her laptop from her pack and began typing her anger into the computer. After she had typed in her feelings of disappointment and frustration, she quietly dressed and left the room.

A steady early morning ocean breeze playfully cast aside her sarong exposing her thigh and tossing her flaxen hair. She tiptoed down the quiet hallway to the stairs and made her way out onto the lawn where the dew formed a shimmering watery blanket on the grass. She ambled slowly to the beach and sat down in the soft sand. She laid her head on her knees, wrapped her arms around her legs and wept, releasing months, perhaps years of pent up anger and frustration.

After she felt spent, she turned her head to the side and drifted off to sleep. She was startled from her half-sleep state by a figure stalking toward her in the dark. As he came closer, towering over her, she could feel her heart begin to race. She could barely make out his features as she felt the urge to jump up and run.

"Jenna? Is that you? What are you doing out here all by yourself?" Marc asked, moving in closer to her.

"You scared the hell out of me."

"Sorry, I definitely didn't intend to. Do you mind if I sit? I was hoping to catch the sunrise," he said, sitting cross-legged next to her.

"Doesn't the sun rise on the other side of the island?"

"Hmm ... now that you mention it," he said, looking back over his shoulder. "No matter. I don't know what I was thinking. And I sat out on our balcony watching the sunset last night. I guess ... I'm just so used to watching the sunrise on Hollywood Beach. Of course that's on the east and not the west." He laughed. Looking back at Jenna he said, "You look upset. What's wrong?"

"I don't want to be the downer on this trip."

"Jenna, we're becoming better friends, right?" he asked.

"Of course, but this is really between Jack and me."

"Look, I'm concerned," he said, "and we have plenty of time before the rest of the resort wakes up, so if you want to, you can tell me about it."

"Well, it's Jack … it's me…" she said and then paused. "Hell, I don't know who it is. We had a nice time at dinner and all, but I had a dream early this morning and we ended up in a fight. Yeah, I know," she said as she held up her hand. "It's an old argument that never gets resolved. I'm sure I'm making a big deal out of nothing but I can't help it." She looked down, playing in the sand with her toes.

"The fight was about the dream? I'm confused."

A cool breeze floated in off the water causing Jenna to shiver. Marc moved in closer and put his right arm around her shoulders.

Jenna leaned against him and said, "I dreamt that Jack let an old girlfriend give him a blowjob while he and I were together. This actually happened many years ago."

"I see, so it's not a dream. You happened to dream about it again last night, because you haven't reached a resolution regarding the situation. And the argument?"

"Same one we have every couple of years or so. I want him to explain to me why he let her do it and why he told me about it. He never answers me," she said, tears filling her eyes again.

"What do you want him to say?" he asked, soothing her back with his big hand.

"I want him to explain it so I can at least understand."

"Maybe there's no explanation. Maybe he doesn't know why he did it."

"Give me a break," Jenna said, slightly shifting away

from Marc's touch. "I don't believe for a minute he doesn't have a reason for what he did."

"Men do stupid things sometimes," he said, forming a mock gun with his hand and pointing it at his foot.

"He never apologized for it either. Not over all these years. He says it's my problem and I need to work it out with myself. He's so incredibly frustrating sometimes. I'm a non-violent person but I swear I could've hit him."

"Do you think he should've told you about it?"

"I think he told me to hurt me."

"That doesn't seem logical. Maybe he's not very bright. Maybe he doesn't understand how he impacts others and sometimes, people don't know where their lines of demarcation lie until after they've committed the act."

She shrugged her shoulders and shook her head. "Like I said, he never apologized. He told me in such a matter-of-fact way that I was completely stunned. I couldn't understand it then and I don't understand it now. The woman was a complete bitch. He told me how he hated her. I understand why she did it though."

"Why?"

"She knew we were happy and she wanted to prove she could still have him if she wanted him."

"Do you think you could let it go if he apologized?"

"I don't know. If it were sincere, it would certainly help. I'm starting to wonder what keeps us together. I feel like I've turned into this bitchy, unhappy person. I never used to be like this. It's been so long since I've felt like he's listened to me, actually heard what I've said." She glanced up at Marc and said, "Sorry and thank you for letting me rant."

"You're welcome," he said, embracing her close, as if trying to keep her warm against the sea breeze. "Why do you think you dreamt about it now?"

"Same reason it usually comes up from the depth of my

subconscious. Well, and this is a little embarrassing, but I think it was Summer and Jack going over to the island together."

"Oh? I see. I think I understand. So this is an ongoing issue for you, but not for Jack. That makes it very tough on you. He's finished and you're not. I can see why you might be asking yourself why you stay together. Do you think Jack could say why the two of you are still together?"

"I doubt it."

"I think you have a right to be upset. But remember, not everyone is in touch with why they do what they do. It's been awhile so maybe he's not clear about what motivated him. Maybe he doesn't remember why he did it in the first place."

"Why are you defending him?"

"I'm not. I'm trying to help you let go of the need for an answer. He never did it again, did he?"

"No."

"So he must have seen it as a bad choice."

"That's all great, but this is not the only issue we're dealing with. Frankly, I don't think about it until something triggers the memory."

"Understood, but it does keep coming up. How are you going to resolve it with yourself? What're your alternatives? You could get counseling with him, you could leave him, you could get counseling without him or you could cut your losses and let this go. You have to decide for yourself, which option is going to meet your most important fundamental needs. Is there anything worth salvaging in your relationship?"

"I don't know these days. God, that's scary to say, but it's true." She felt a hard lump rise in her throat.

"Tunnel vision can be a dangerous thing. We focus on one thing to the exclusion of everything else and pretty soon nothing seems right."

"The dream is what's up for us today. Last week it was that he didn't ask me about inviting you guys. The week before it was something else but it wasn't always like this. I'm not sure what happened between us, but we used to have fun no matter what we were doing. Now it seems we find conflict at every turn instead," she said, peering down at the sand.

"It seems you guys have a lot to work through."

"Yes, it would seem we do."

"Would you like to go for a walk?" Marc asked as he released his arm from around her shoulders and stood up.

"Yes, that would be nice," she said, holding out her hands so Marc could pull her to her feet. She brushed the sand from her backside, noticing that dawn was breaking. "The sky looks so incredible right now."

"And so do you," he said, wiping a remnant tear from her cheek. He cautiously lowered his mouth for a kiss and Jenna did not rebuke him. The kiss lingered for a moment and then she slowly pushed him back and looked away.

"I think I need to go," she said.

"Okay, I'll walk you there," he said, placing his hand on her back.

"I'm fine making it there by myself," she said, stepping out of his reach.

"It's not that far and I don't mind. It's still fairly dark out and I'd like to see you safely back to your room." He started across the sand.

"If you insist," she said, trailing behind.

They strolled silently through the lobby and down the long hallway to Jenna's room. She didn't know what to make of his kiss or why she gave into it.

"Thank you for being such a good listener, but the kiss—"

"Was I being too forward?" he asked.

"Let's just say it took me completely by surprise. I'll have to think about it." Jenna entered her room feeling stimulated yet confused by Marc. She lay down on her side of the bed but could still feel the gulf between her and Jack.

CHAPTER SEVEN

"What time is it?" Summer asked, sitting up and stretching her arms above her head. She looked over at Marc on the balcony and called to him, "Good morning, Marcus, how'd you sleep?" She rolled over into Child's pose and stretched her arms forward.

"I actually had an interesting experience early this morning," he said, walking back into the room.

"Oh, do tell."

"First, let's snuggle a bit," he said, sitting down on the edge of the bed. His cellphone rang interrupting the moment. "It's work. I'll take this on the balcony and only be a minute."

"Marcus, it's Rich. One of the Jacuzzis stopped working and had a smell of … like something was burning. Robert called Jim to come fix it, but I'm not sure when he'll get here. The line to the other Jacuzzi is getting long."

"Well, we've used this guy before and he's very reliable. Sounds to me like you're handling this very well. Nothing more I can do from here. Relax, buddy and have a good day."

"Okay, just keeping you in the loop. I'll call if I need you for anything."

Marc walked back into the room and said, "I'm leaving this here." He opened the top drawer of the end table and tossed the phone inside.

"Well, now that you've got my curiosity piqued about this morning, you can't keep me waiting any longer. We'll snuggle and talk at the same time," she said, pulling him back toward her. She turned over, letting him spoon her from behind. "So what happened? Did you leave the room?"

"Yeah, I went downstairs to watch the sunrise."

"The sunrise?" she said.

"Yeah, I don't know what I was thinking. Anyway, I went down to the beach and who did I run into? None other than our Jenna."

"Really? How early was this?" she asked, caressing his arm that wrapped around her torso.

"I think it was around 5:30."

"What was she doing on the beach?"

"She and Jack had a fight—"

"At 5:30 in the morning? Jesus, those guys start early."

"Well, sweetie, if you would stop interrupting, I could explain," he said, and then shared with her what happened on the beach.

"Wow. That doesn't sound very good," she said, sitting up in the bed.

"It seems like they have a lot to work through and on top of all of that, I impulsively kissed her."

"What were you thinking?" She stood up and turned to face him. "Did the little head take control of the big head?"

"Obviously. Are you angry?"

"Not for me but it seems unwise to kiss a woman who is upset and doesn't know about our open lifestyle. Now she's left to decide if she'll share the news with Jack and that could make this all much more complicated. I mean, they are already fighting and I'm not sure I would tell him about the kiss if I were in her shoes."

"You tell me everything."

"That's different, Marc. Their relationship isn't like ours."

"Yeah, it was *not* one of my finer moments, that's for sure," he said, moving to the end of the bed and touching her leg.

"If they came to you for counseling, hypothetically, what

71

would you think their chances are?" she asked.

"I don't know. I haven't heard how he currently feels about the relationship, but I know it was great for them at one time. She has a lot of built up anger she has to deal with. I don't get that sense from him, do you?"

"Hmmm … no, not anger, but there's something there. Disappointment maybe or it could be sadness. He covers it well so it really isn't very evident. I can't be sure." She climbed back onto the bed to do her morning stretches. She opened her legs, lying forward between them.

"I apologize for being so irresponsible in my actions. I hope this doesn't make things awkward between us all."

She climbed into his lap and he wrapped her in his arms. "You must really like her. I haven't known you to be impulsive like that with other women. I still love you, you know," she said, and hopped off the bed. "Do I have time to do my sunrise set before breakfast?" she asked, kissing him on the cheek.

"I ordered breakfast in. It should be here in a half-hour or so."

"Great. Will you keep me company while I do my yoga?"

"Sure," he said, getting up from the bed and sitting in the chair by the table. "So do you think they're a longshot now?"

"At this point, probably. I guess we'll have to see how it all plays out. Do you think Jenna likes you?" she said, lying on her stomach with her arms lifting her upper body.

"How can you talk and hold that posture?"

"Lots of practice," she said, her voice deeper from the sustained pose.

"She did kiss me back … but then she pushed me away," he said, uncrossing his legs and leaning forward. "So I'm not sure, but it's clear to me we may need to take things slower."

"You mean you do, big boy. I haven't accosted Jack yet."

✳ ✳ ✳ ✳ ✳

Startled awake by knocking, Jenna glanced back and forth as she became oriented to her surroundings. Her eyes trailed Jack as he strode back into the room from the balcony and over to the door. She quickly pulled the sheet up to her neckline when a man entered the room carrying a large tray filled with several covered plates.

"Over here," Jack said, pointing to the table out on the balcony.

The attendant placed the breakfast down and hoisted the tray with last night's emptied drinks. As Jack followed the attendant toward the room door, Jenna could hear a muffled conversation between the two men. Given the opportunity, she lunged from the bed, snatched her nightshirt off the chair and slipped into the bathroom. She glanced in the mirror, noticing her puffy eyes. *Great, that's just perfect*, she thought. She washed her hands and face, brushed her teeth, and then pulled on the robe that she had hung on the wall near the shower. She took a deep breath and opened the bathroom door. She didn't make eye contact with Jack as she made her way onto the balcony and sat down looking out at the ocean.

"Jenna," he said, pleading as he approached.

She didn't want to look at him. She didn't want him to see the guilt on her face. She felt incredibly vulnerable.

"Jenna, please," he said softly as he took a seat next to her.

She willed herself not to turn but she did nonetheless. She peeked up into his eyes and saw deep sadness.

"I would so love to be able to undo so many things in my past," he said, raking his fingers through his hair. "Make better decisions, undo some wrongs. The one thing that I know I wouldn't undo is you. You mean the world to me. I love you very much and if I could wipe out that memory for you, I would in a heartbeat. I hope we can move on from here. I am truly sorry. What is happening between us is really starting to scare me. I don't want to lose you."

"Uh … I'm stunned. This is not how I thought the morning would start." She hid her emotions behind her hand. "Wow. Jack," she said, fanning her face. "I think that's the sweetest thing you've ever said to me."

Tears welled up in her eyes and she rose up to reach for him. He stood and embraced her as she laid her head on his shoulder. "I love you," she said as the hot tears fell down her cheeks. She didn't know if this would change anything in the end, but in that moment, she felt incredible relief, a weight lifted from her shoulders.

Jack sighed. He pulled back so he could see her face. "Let's have a good time today," he said with renewed energy. "Let's forget all the issues and everything that's happened in the past and just be together, you and me, one on one like we used to. Please, I need it. *We* need it."

"Yeah, I think so, too," she said, angling her face to him. She fell into his kiss, losing herself in his feel and taste. Enlaced in each other's arms, she rocked back and forth, unable to purge the thought of Marc's kiss.

After a few minutes Jenna's stomach growled and she said, "What did you order? I'm starved." She chuckled, pushing against Jack's chest to break their embrace. "Food is such a great distraction."

Jack laughed and began lifting the covers of the plates.

"Wow. There's a lot of food here."

"I didn't know what you would be in the mood for, so I wanted to make sure you had plenty to choose from," he said, sitting back in his chair to pour a cup of coffee.

"Hmmm … where to begin," she said, finally putting a cheese Danish on a small plate and placing it in front of her.

"That's it? That's the extent of your feast? Would you at

least drink some juice?" he said as he moved from plate to plate, sampling the colorful and exotic dishes.

"I've already brushed my teeth. Is there water?"

"Water?" He squinted at the thought, but poured cold water into a glass. "I thought I heard the door open during the night, but I must have been dreaming because you were in bed when I woke up."

"I left the room shortly after our fight."

"What?" he said. "No way. Where did you go?"

"Just down to the beach."

"Alone?" he asked, his voice raised slightly.

"Well, I wasn't alone for that long," she said, shifting in her seat.

"What does that mean?" he asked.

"Marc showed up a little while after I got there."

"Marc? Am I missing something?" he said, leaning forward in his chair. "Is there something I should know?"

"No. He thought he would be able to see the sunrise. He forgot it sets here."

"So it was really early morning," he said. He rested back in the chair and forked a large piece of jerk chicken.

"Yeah, I guess. Does it matter?"

"I don't like the idea of you walking around alone in the middle of the night. Or in the early morning for that matter," he said, adding more coffee to his mug. "How long were you gone?"

"I'm not sure. An hour or so, I guess."

"So Marc was with you for an hour?"

"Honey, I don't know. I think I dozed off for a little while."

"Jenna, please, *please* don't do that again. Who knows if it's safe here? You wouldn't do that back home."

"I was angry and wasn't thinking straight."

"Yeah. Good thing Marc was there. Did you tell him

what was going on between us?"

"Well … yeah, sort of. I had been crying and he could tell," she said, furrowing her brow. "Are you mad?"

"No. Just make sure you tell him we've worked it out," he replied. He rose and went back into the room.

"Okay," she said, taking an apple from the tray and following him inside. "I'll tell him as soon as I see him."

✳ ✳ ✳ ✳ ✳

"Hi there. Are you wearing a suit underneath?" Summer asked as she approached Jenna. "Yeah. I have a feeling we're going to get wet," she said, feeling nervous seeing Summer and Marc again. "I think we walk up the actual falls, don't we?" Not making eye contact, she placed a baseball cap on her head and pulled her ponytail through the hole in the back.

"We climb them?" Summer asked. She leaned in closer to Jenna. "Are you and Jack all right?"

"We're doing much better I'm happy to say. Did Marc fill you in about last night?" Jenna asked, tension filling her stomach.

Summer didn't answer right away, instead she scrounged in her tote bag for lip balm. When she found it, she looked up at Jenna and held it out it to her. "Yeah, he told me about it."

"Uh, no thanks," she said. "Everything?

Placing her arm around Jenna, Summer said, "Yes, everything."

Jenna's stomach dropped and she didn't know what to say.

"Don't worry about it. Hey, I'm glad that you guys are feeling better. That leaves me feeling better."

Jenna breathed out a sigh of relief and said, "Could you do me a favor in case I don't get a chance to talk to Marc alone?"

"Sure, what?"

"Please tell him that we're alright and … well, thank you.""

"Yeah, he's a keeper." She hugged Jenna and winked at Marc who stood next to Jack outside the French doors. "Is this our bus pulling in now?"

"Yeah, that's right," a familiar British accented voice answered.

"Oh hi, Cliff, how are you?" Summer asked.

"Bloody well, considering. By the way, this is the lovely wife, Becky." He tilted his head toward Summer and whispered, "What a bleeding hangover." He rubbed his forehead and shook his head. "I love this all-inclusive idea, but I don't have the discipline for it."

"Hi Becky, I'm Summer, this is Jenna and Jack and my husband Marc, short for Marcus," she said, pointing to each of them.

"Yeah, we remember you," Cliff said, shaking hands with Jack.

Jack furrowed his brow and said, "Uh … it's you, ha, didn't recognize you with your clothes on."

They laughed and Jack began to side step, back and forth, waiting for the go ahead to board the bus. He stopped moving briefly and then walked over to the check-in desk. He spoke to the woman behind the counter and Jenna could see her pointing across the lobby. She watched Jack go through an open door. A few minutes later, he strolled back to Jenna, smiling.

"What was that about?" she asked, shifting her bag to the other arm so they could hold hands.

"It's a secret," he whispered. "You'll be the first to know when it happens, my love."

Everyone shuffled aboard the bus, finding seats with their circle of friends and settling in for the ride to the falls.

"Here we go again," Jack said, taking a seat toward the back.

"Aye mate, can I ask you a question?" Cliff asked, turning around in his seat. "Did you happen to catch the barmy highway signs coming in from Montego Bay?"

"Yes. Tell me what you saw," Jenna said, moving in close to Cliff. "I thought I was losing my mind. I saw 80, then 65, then 80 again," she said laughing.

"You know what, she was starting to freak me out, man," Jack said, chuckling. "She looked like a person on the edge."

"That's the Jamaican D.O.T," Marc said. "They put the 'high' in highway."

"You're so funny sometimes," Summer said, squeezing his thigh.

"So, 'ow long you lot here for?" Becky asked.

"We arrived yesterday and we're here for ten days," Marc said. "We haven't decided whether or not to spend time at Couples Negril."

"We spent a week there," Becky said.

"And a small fortune," Cliff interjected.

"Oh shut up, it was lovely. There wasn't much to do. At least it seemed that way. Wish we had come here first. We were married over there though, and it was stunning."

"It was lovely, wasn't it? Still, I would've rather been here. We practically live on the island. Good people over there," Cliff said, looking over the back of his seat.

"Wow. You got married in Jamaica. That's very cool," Summer said, leaning back against Marc.

It wasn't long before the bus bounced into an unpaved parking area lined with similar buses that had already dropped tourists from other resorts.

"Bet he says, 'I'd be writing down the number to this bus, mon,'" Jack said, staring out the window at the dizzying replication of buses passing before his eyes.

The microphone clicked on. "There are areas to the right for shopping. Your guide will pick you up in a few moments. I would be writing down the bus number and remembering where we've parked."

"What does he mean, a bloody guide?" Cliff asked.

"To guide us in our climb up the falls," Summer said.

"Doesn't sound right to me a' tall," Cliff said, his eyes darting and his head bobbing as he looked out the large side window. "Judas Priest, I've done it this time."

"What's up?" Jack asked.

"I thought we were coming to take pictures of a bloody waterfall. Balls, I had no fucking idea we had to climb the bloody thing. Christ, what've I done to myself?" he said, shaking his head.

"We'll all be together," said Summer. "I'm not sure I understand."

"It's quite simple really. I'm so fucking hung-over, I can't see a black cat on a white wall. It's your fault, isn't it ducky," he said, turning to Becky.

"Yes, of course it is, love. You don't have to climb, you know," Becky said and turned around to look at the foursome. "I can go with you, can't I?" she asked, searching their faces for approval.

"Sure, no problem, mon," Jack said, looking over the top of his sunglasses at Becky's ample bosom, straining her bathing suit top.

"Sure you can. We'd love to have you," Summer said.

"Fine by me," said Jenna.

"Fine by me as well," Marc said.

"Lovely then. You can stay here and we'll come get you when we get through," Becky said, holding Cliff's hand.

"Oh god. I can't fly all this way and not climb the falls, can I? Bollocks, no more drinking for me," he said and then added, "Until I recover from this hangover." He looked up and struggled to smile.

A loud, energetic voice at the front of the bus pierced the quiet mumbling and caused Cliff to crouch for cover, holding his ears. "Gooood mooorrning," he said, smiling and bowing. "I am Ramous. I am responsible for getting you up the falls in one piece." He laughed as he bent backwards. "Eeee … Eeee … Eeee." His laugh went into his body instead of out and repeated the same sound each time he drew in air. "You need not worry, mon. I am the best and I know exactly where to take you so you don't come tumbling down to the bottom again," he said, flashing his infectious smile.

"Ya gotta love that Eddie Murphy laugh. This is going to be a trip," Jack said.

"I love the shorts and shirt," Summer said. "What is that print?"

"Marijuana leaves," Jack whispered. "I'm sorry, marijuana leaves," he restated in his normal volume.

"Okay. Follow me to the bottom of the waterfalls and we'll take a group photo so you'll have a picture before any injuries," Ramous said. "Eeee … Eeee … Eeee."

The group off-loaded the bus, chattering their excitement and filing in behind the guide for a hike into the rainforest. At the bottom of the trail, a sugar-white beach turned into small rounded pebbles that led to a view of the Dunn's River Falls. The group stood shoulder-to-shoulder, admiring the magnificent volumes of water and spray rolling over the big boulders and bouncing in slow motion to the next step on its way to the Caribbean Sea.

"Everyone say 'ya mon,'" Ramous said and took a group picture. "Eeee … Eeee … Eeee," he laughed. "You are a fine-looking group." He then instructed them to divide into teams of three couples.

Summer locked arms with Marc and Jenna. Jack reached for Jenna's hand and grabbed Becky who had her arm around

Cliff's waist.

"You must stay together," he called out over the roar of the falls. "Gentlemen, there are places where you must help your ladies. If you have cameras and want pictures, give the cameras to me. I will keep them dry as a skeleton bone in the desert."

"Is the water cold?" Becky yelled over the sound of the roaring water.

"Oh no, my lady, it's as warm as a jaquizzy. Eeee … Eeee … Eeee," he said, leading them into the merge of freshwater and sea.

"This isn't so bad," Summer said.

"I thought it would be colder than this," Jenna commented.

"You'll be climbing 960 feet to the top of the falls. You will have to climb even farther if you slip," he yelled, using his hands as a megaphone. Ramous then displayed a pearly white toothy grin.

He motioned for them to come forward. He used gesturing to communicate with them over the rushing sound of the river seeking its resolve at the foot of the sea. He gave them instructions to pair off as couples and to stand underneath the first waterfall for their beginning shot.

Jack and Jenna were the first to plunge underneath the flow of the clamshell shaped fall.

"Ah fuck … it's freezing!" Jack yelled as Jenna wrapped her arms and legs around his body. Jack lunged with Jenna, struggling forward, to free them from the icy rush.

"It's so cold. Oh my gosh. I'm numb," Jenna squealed.

Ramous approached the group putting his hands on Jack and Jenna's shoulders.

"No mon, warm like a jaquizzy," he said, finding their plight amusing. "Who'll be next?"

"Maybe it'll cure my hangover … or give me a heart

attack. Either way, here we go," Cliff shouted over the thundering of the falls, pulling Becky by the hand. They made a charge at the wall of water and disappeared for a moment only to scramble out wide-eyed like two children running in fear.

Ramous clicked away. "You're going to love these shots," he said.

"That's not possible," Cliff yelled. "People could die from that! It's so bloody cold, mate. What, they got an ice machine at the top?"

Becky stood next to Cliff, holding her legs together with her hands folded in front of her crotch, bouncing up and down.

"Let's go, baby. It's our turn," Marc said to Summer. They joined hands and looked at one another. "One … two—"

"Well, there goes the hair! Wait!" Summer hollered. "Look at me in case this is the last time we see each other."

Marc let out a monstrous, "Yahoo!" as the two of them ran into the cold shimmering pool boiling from the weight of the torrent. They stopped just short of the waterfall, turned around, and walked slowly back toward the group, smiling. "Sorry, I detest cold water," Marc said.

"Same here," Summer said.

"It's not fair, then. At least you could get wet," Cliff said in his British singsong.

"Go on then. Give it a go," Becky called out.

Marc looked at Summer. "Alright?"

"What the hell."

The two plunged into the pool of ice water screaming obscenities.

"Ya mon. Strong," Ramous said, pointing at Marc and flexing his biceps. "Follow that path and I'll meet you at the next level."

When they rejoined hands, Marc took Jenna's hand trailed by Summer, Jack, Becky, and finally Cliff bringing up the rear. Making a human chain to assist in scaling the boulders, they fought against the powerful onslaught of the rushing current.

Jenna couldn't help but notice that the feel of Marc's hand in hers had somehow become familiar. The electric current that entered her palm caused her nipples to peak.

Upon arrival at the next plateau, Ramous said, "Irie, mon. No problem. Everybody still with us! Eeee … Eeee … Eeee."

They safely scaled to a place where the river swirled quietly in a pool surrounded by large dark stones and boulders highlighted by a fortuitous shaft of sunlight. Jenna quickly let go of Marc's hand and trudged through the water to Jack. Each couple took a turn having their photograph taken while kissing.

"Wow. This is so unbelievable," Summer said as she slowly turned in the pool.

The placid island rainforest hung thick and lush with a towering canopy that barely allowed the hot Jamaican sun to filter to them. The environment inspired an unspoken reverence.

"Welcome to the other Jamaica, mon," Ramous said quietly. "Listen carefully and you can hear everyone who has been here in the past. Don't pay any attention to the screams of people sliding back down the falls. No one has ever died from the slide," he said, wagging his finger toward the group. His jolly laughter echoed throughout the forest.

The steep climb required the vine of people to assist those below them, up the tenuous rock shelves and over slippery patches of fungus growing on the river stones. At different stops along the climb to the top, Ramous had the couples strike a pose for a picture.

"Why don't we swap partners for this picture?" Summer

said, her eyes locked on Jack.

"Great by me," Jack said, not waiting for Jenna's response. He moved closer to Summer, pulling her into the falls.

"Okay?" Jenna said, more like a question.

"I don't bite you know," Marc said, sidling up close to Jenna. She glanced up, swallowing hard and then tried to laugh it off.

Ramous positioned each couple so that the men stood behind the women, wrapping their arms about their waists.

Jack, barely taller than Summer, perched his head on her shoulder.

"Cute shot," Marc said. "Our turn," he said to Jenna, pulling her along to the edge of the falls.

Marc, much taller than Jack, stood a head above Jenna. He laid his large palms across her belly. He slanted his mouth near her ear and whispered, "I shouldn't have kissed you, but I can't make myself regret it either."

They smiled for the picture just as the chill of his words cascaded down her neck, firing all her nerve endings. She wondered what her expression would look like when they transferred the photos to the computer. Part of her wanted to linger in his arms but another part wanted to run away as fast as she could.

They all ascended to the next stopping point.

"Oh my god, I can't believe how far we've come. Look down there! Look how tiny the beach looks. This is so amazing," Summer said, waiting her turn to have her husband scoop her up in his arms for the next picture.

"Wow, I love the way the canopy of trees creates a cave effect all the way down to the beach," Jenna said.

"Bloody hell, this is high up. How are we to get down?" Cliff asked, taking Becky's hand and moving away from the edge.

Once all the pictures were taken, they all clasped hands again. The line of friends approached another terrace with each person helping the one behind them over the top of a jutting rock.

Jack slipped as Becky pulled him from the ledge below her. He immediately growled, "Owww! Oh man, that hurt!" Struggling up and hopping on one foot, he reached out for Marc who ducked underneath Jack's arm to give him stability. "There's a goddamn hole over there," he said, pointing to the edge. "Someone needs to fill that."

"Honey, are you okay?" Jenna asked, carefully mounting the rock next to him.

"That looked like a brutal slip," Marc said. "Let me take a look at it."

"Oh mate, are you okay?" Cliff asked.

"Jack, I'm so sorry," Becky said. "I didn't mean to lose you. It frightened me. I thought you were going to fall all the way back down."

"I'm okay, I think." He stood and put pressure on his foot. "It hurts a little but I'm thinking—"

"If you can stand on it, we should keep moving," Marc said. "It'll probably swell anyway, but the water's so cold in here, it should keep the swelling down for now. Ramous, how much farther to the top?"

"It's not far now, about two hundred feet. We can transfer over to the side walkway, mon. It's stairs that run along the edge of the falls."

"Blimey," Cliff said, looking in the direction of the side of the river. "You mean to say that I could've walked up the stairs?"

"Did I fail to mention that?" Ramous said, scratching his head. He looked back at Jack and asked, "Can you do this, mon, or should I get a rescue team up here?"

"I'll be alright if it's only two hundred more feet. Let's

go," Jack said, looking up the incline and steadying his stance. "I can do this. Somebody needs to get me a couple of emergency Red Stripe beers when we get to the top." He grimaced and then laughed. "Ah, man this is going to hurt like a bitch later, I can already tell."

The group managed to make it to the top of the falls and decided to skip walking through the makeshift marketplace. Instead, they picked up a few beers and meandered back down to the bus with Jack in tow. Jack hobbled next to Marc while Summer and Jenna walked in front of them. Cliff and Becky brought up the rear, debating which of the two should bear the blame for Cliff's hangover.

"When we get back, you may want the hotel infirmary to take a look," Marc said. "If you broke something you may have to go into Ocho Rios to the hospital."

They arrived at the bus and assisted Jack to his seat. He stretched his leg across Jenna's lap and tried to get comfortable.

"It looks like it's swelling. Sorry, man," Marc said, examining at Jack's foot. He returned to his seat next to Summer.

"How's your hangover?" Summer asked Cliff.

"I feel better. I must, because I was thinking I should've gotten a beer as well."

"Here take this one," Jack said, reaching over Jenna to pass the beer. "We're not that far from the hotel."

"Thanks, mate. I'll buy you one when we get back."

"I love how everyone offers to buy people a drink at an all-inclusive resort," Jenna said.

"Makes it easy, doesn't it? I could buy him a pack of fags instead," Cliff said, smiling over at Jack. "Those aren't included."

"Oh, no. That's definitely not necessary," she said, looking over at Jack. "How's it feeling?"

"Not great," he said.

"If nothing else, ice and an ace bandage will fix you up," Marc said. "Stay off your feet as much as possible in the first twenty-four hours and don't worry, we'll come see you."

"We can all sit on your bed and watch the closed-circuit TV." Summer reached back and patted Jack on his leg.

The group rode in silence until Becky turned to Jenna and asked, "Are you coming out to the island this afternoon?"

"Tomorrow. Well, I have until tomorrow to make up my mind. I hadn't thought about it really," Jenna said. "Besides, it's couples only and Jack's—"

"And single women," Becky chimed in. "You should join us. It's lovely, and the people on the island are a great deal friendlier than those sticks-in-the-mud on the beach."

Jenna felt her face flush. Glancing at Marc, she said, "I'm not a single woman." She saw him raise an eyebrow, and then she quickly looked back at Becky. "Besides, I can't even think about that right now. I'm too stressed over Jack's ankle and what that means for the rest of our stay."

She could still feel Marc's gaze, but dared not raise her eyes to meet his.

CHAPTER EIGHT

"**D**o you need a wheelchair, sir?" the hostess asked as they got off the bus.

"No, thank you. I think I can make it."

"They radioed ahead. The doctor is waiting to see you. It's right this way."

"If you won't be needing us," Summer said, "Becky and I are going to get something to eat."

"Where will you be?" Marc asked.

"The patio bar. Kokila should be working today," she said over her shoulder and winked.

"Okay," Marc said.

Jack hopped on one foot, supported by Marc on one side and Cliff on the other. Jenna trailed behind. They made their way down a hallway off the reception area into a fifteen-foot square room adorned with numerous tacky pharmaceutical ads and a paper-covered patient examination table.

"Well mate, it looks like you're all sorted. I'll just take my leave then," Cliff said.

"Thanks for all your help, buddy. I appreciate it," Jack said, reaching out to shake hands.

"Thanks for the beer, and I'll keep a cold one ready for you when you're out of here and in fighting form again."

Jenna, Jack and Marc introduced themselves to a handsome older man in a long, white lab coat.

His handshake was firm and reassuring, his smile genuine and warm. He examined Jack's foot with the gentleness normally afforded newborn babies. After a few minutes, he looked at Jenna and said, "I don't see any reason to send you into Ocho Rios." He looked back at Jack and said calmly,

"I'll have the nurse wrap your ankle in ice. Keep it elevated and by tomorrow, you should be feeling a lot better. You can use these crutches to assist you back to your room." He placed the crutches against the doorjamb. "Take two aspirins and call me in the morning." He grinned.

"Thanks, Doc."

"No problem. And at the request of your wife, our staff has forgotten your last name. So I will simply say it was nice meeting you—Jack." Smiling at Jenna, he reached out to shake Jack's hand. He picked up his clipboard and patted Jenna on her back as he walked toward the door. "Do try to stay off your foot for at least twenty-four hours," he said as he exited.

The nurse wrapped Jack's foot in an ice pack and ace bandage. "Is that comfortable?" she asked.

"I guess," Jack said. "At least as comfortable as a swollen foot can be. You did great."

Marc helped him to his feet while Jenna brought over the crutches.

"Here, take this," she said, placing it under his arm.

"I'll help you back to your room," Marc said, "but Jenna's going to have to take it from there. We'll miss you tonight at the beach party."

"I might be able to make it," Jack said.

"Oh, no you won't," Jenna retorted, narrowing her eyes. "We need to take care of your foot so it doesn't get any worse."

"Don't be silly. At least you can go to the party. Marc and Summer will take care of you."

"I'll think about it," Jenna said as she glanced in Marc's direction.

"Look, I'm only saying you should go and have a great time. I'm going to be fine, and besides, I can watch the festivities from the balcony and if you come over and flash me, I'll throw you some beads."

＊ ＊ ＊ ＊ ＊

Marc delivered Jack and Jenna to their ocean-view room on the south end of the resort.

"I'm going to catch up with Summer. Can I get you guys anything?"

"No. We'll be fine. Thanks, Marc," Jenna said as she walked him to the door. "I may join you guys for lunch in a few, but don't wait on me."

"Summer went to lunch with Becky, so maybe you should join me?" His smile lit up his blue eyes.

Jenna made a quick glance back at Jack before responding. She smiled but said, "I don't think that would be a good idea." Her hearted pounded heavily and she tried to get it together before she reentered the room.

Marc made his way back up the hallway, strode through the airy lobby and out onto the terrace, walking past the Calabash to the terrace bar.

"So how's Jack doing? Are they going to join us?" Summer asked.

"I hope the bloke's okay. That was a nasty spill," Becky said.

"He seems like he's going to be fine and no he won't be joining us. Jenna will, well, maybe later. It's bad to have this happen here in Jamaica when there's so much fun to be had," Marc said, straddling a barstool. "I hope he follows the doc's advice."

"Hi, Kokila. How are you today, lovely lady?" Marc asked.

"I'm great all the time. I'm blessed that way," she said as she walked away.

The smell of coconut sunscreen lingered and mixed with

the jerk chicken smoke floating on the light, warm Caribbean breeze. The beach teemed with partially nude bodies, capturing the irresistible tanning rays of the sun as a medallion to show off to their envious cohorts back home.

"We should run up and take a shower." Summer pushed her glass forward on the bar.

"And a nap," Marc said as he slid from the barstool.

"That's a good idea," Cliff said enthusiastically.

"I'm assuming you mean with me," Becky said, placing her hands on her hips and pivoting to face him.

"But, of course I mean you, love," he said and winked at Summer and Marc.

"You better." She hugged Cliff's arm and said, "Let's forgo the shower and catch the next ferry to the island, shall we?"

"Alright then, that sounds good. Catch you later," Cliff said, strolling away with Becky in tow.

"Hey, are you guys leaving?" Jenna asked as she approached them.

"Yeah, we're going over to the island but Marc and Summer were still at the bar just now," Cliff said.

"Have a good time," Jenna said. She quickly turned around decided to avoid Marc and Summer when she heard Summer call out, "Hey Jenna."

"Oh, I didn't see you," she said, walking up to the bar.

"We're headed to the room for a shower and a nap."

"That sounds good," she said quietly.

"So are you coming with us?" Summer asked, enthusiastically. "I mean to talk about the plans for tonight— or to shower with us, I wouldn't mind."

Jenna wrapped her arms around herself and said, "Stop it. You keep teasing me."

"Maybe, and then again—maybe not," Summer razzed as she and Marc gathered their things to return to their room.

"I think I'm safer here," Jenna said, laughing uneasily.

"Call us and we'll make plans," Marc said.

"Give us a couple of hours," Summer said.

"Okay."

Jenna climbed onto the stool. "How are you today, Kokila?"

"Hi there. Good. Nice of you to drop by," she said, grinning. "What can I make for you?"

"Can I get a rumrunner?"

"Going adventurous today?"

"A little something different. I think I need a change," Jenna said.

"Change is good," Kokila said, scooping ice into a glass and expertly filling it up with the requested concoction. "Here you go. I took it easy on you this time. Next time, the real thing."

"Can't wait," Jenna said. She took the first sip. *Holy sh— damn, this is strong.* She cleared her throat and wiped her mouth with a napkin. "Wow, I wasn't expecting that first shot to be so harsh." She sat back for a minute and watched Kokila work the tourists with incredible ease. As soon as she finished with a customer, she migrated back to Jenna. "So will I see you tomorrow on the island?"

"I'm still debating," Jenna said, swirling the straw in her drink.

"That qualifies as something new, right?"

"Yeah, that's true."

Kokila crossed to the other side of the bar again and Jenna called out, "I'll see you later. I need to get back to Jack."

✳ ✳ ✳ ✳ ✳

Summer entered their room, dropping her clothes as she approached the bed. "Everything seemed to go fine today. I mean, other than Jack's foot. I don't think Jenna told him about the kiss."

"That's my impression, too and she did seem a little tense at times. But overall I think it went really well."

Summer playfully jumped right in the middle of the mattress and flexed her buttocks three times. She stretched her arms above her and turned over onto her back.

"If you think that's going to arouse me," Marc said blandly, "you are so right." He sauntered over and lay on the bed next to her. "Come here my little naked nubile nymphet. My beauty." He enveloped her in his arms and said, "Can you believe we found each other? I have no idea what would've happened to me."

"I do—and it ain't a pretty picture," she said, snuggling into his chest. "I'm the best thing that's ever happened to you. And I will confess, you're the best thing that's ever happened to me, too," she said softly. "Kiss my neck, you fool. Make me a screaming banshee. Go on, I dare you. Make the neighbors call security."

"That's a lot of pressure."

Summer laughed and pulled Marc's mouth to hers. They both groaned as he deepened the kiss and their connection. Sitting up, he brought her with him. They sat facing each other in the middle of the bed, breathing each other in.

Marc ran his hands along her neck, down her sides, and around to her peaks. As he pulled on her nipples, he dipped his head down and nibbled and suckled her neck. Summer tilted her head to the side, giving him easy access.

"Ohhhh," she moaned.

"You smell so good. I would love to taste you, but only if that's okay with you," Marc said as he kissed his way down her body, pushing her legs wide apart.

"Oh I think that is very okay," she muttered as she adjusted her body to accommodate him.

Summer inclined back on her palms, and watched him take in her naked lips and trimmed bush. She could see his blue eyes dilate just before he lowered himself onto his stomach, his legs hanging off the side of the bed.

"Oh, yes, please," she said as soon as he touched her swollen bud with his tongue.

He spread her labia with his thumbs and with a soft, flat tongue, flicked her clit repeatedly, occasionally dipping down to taste her essence.

Just as he brought her to the edge, she stopped him, and said, "You know what I want."

He quickly responded, situating himself in the middle of the bed reaching out for her. She settled herself on his lap, her legs over his, and slowly lowered her hips down with his help.

"Oh god, always so wet," he said. As soon as he was fully seated within her, they both resumed their kiss and held each other tight as they rocked back and forth.

"I'm so close, so so close," Summer whispered.

"Lean back for me," Marc said.

She angled back on her hands as he wrapped one arm around her lower back, keeping up the pace. With his other hand, he circled around her most sensitive place, causing her first explosion.

"Yesssssss," she yelled, throwing her head back as the convulsions ripped through her. She fell onto her back as she enjoyed the high of her release. Her hips still rested on Marc's lap.

He waited patiently for her to recover.

"Again," she said, a big smile lighting up her face.

He chuckled and said, "My pleasure."

"I'm pretty sure it was all mine. Come with me this time?"

"Absolutely."

Summer grabbed the comforter in both hands, using it as leverage to gyrate against Marc. He resumed his delectable assault as he continued to manipulate her clit.

"Oh, yes, so good, my favorite way to come. I love how you fill me! I'm so close."

"I'm following right behind. Go for it," he said. Back and forth he plunged, kicking off their climaxes and sending them flying up to the heavens. "Oh babe," he grunted.

"Oh yessssssss," she yelled, finally crumbling back into the mattress.

Marc collapsed next to her, both of them breathing hard, floating on the ecstasy of their own making.

❋ ❋ ❋ ❋ ❋

Jack heard a soft rapping on the door and went to answer. When Jenna entered, she saw clothes strewn everywhere and towels draped over the backs of chairs. Her irritation flared over the state of their room.

"You never remember your key," Jack said, hopping back to the bed.

"I need to wear it like a dog tag," she said. "Sorry you had to get up to let me in. What would you like to order for lunch?"

"I thought you were picking up something when you went downstairs," Jack said with a furrowed brow.

"Yeah, well … I stopped for a drink and then decided to check on you. I figured we could order food in just as easily. So what would you like?"

"I want some kind of fish."

"Do you want me to get you some ice? Beer? Do you need another pillow?"

"Honey, I'm fine. Stop worrying about me, okay? The beer would be great, though." Jack grabbed two pillows for his foot and plopped on the bed. "Ow! That hurt," he moaned.

"Be more careful, please," Jenna said, walking over to the telephone. While placing their order, her eyes inspected the room. She concluded it needed immediate attention. As soon as she hung up the telephone, she picked up the dirty clothes from the floor and placed them in a laundry bag, and collected the towels she'd hung outside.

"Honey, the maid will take care of that when she gets here," he said, straightening his pillows.

"I know. I don't mind doing it. I can't stand it when it's a mess," she said, walking past Jack to the French doors.

She grabbed the breakfast tray from the balcony table and placed it outside their door in the hallway for pickup.

"Jenna, why don't you sit down with me for a sec," Jack said, while attempting to find a comfortable position.

"This won't take but a minute."

"Would you just relax, please?"

"One more thing…" she said and walked into the bathroom. She straightened the vanity and picked up the dirty towels, replacing the top of her bathing suit that had fallen off the towel bar. "You know, since we can't go anywhere," she said, joining Jack on the bed. "Maybe this would be a good time to talk about our relationship."

Before he could answer, they heard a knock on the door.

"I'll be right there," she called out as she jumped up. She looked back at Jack and said, "I know what you're thinking, saved by the bell or, in this case, a knock."

He broke into guilty laughter.

She opened the door and directed the man carrying the tray to the inside table.

"Please excuse the mess," Jenna said, escorting him back to the door.

"My lady, this is no mess. You would not believe some of the other rooms."

"Thank you," she said as she closed the door. She removed the cellophane from the plate of Mahi-Mahi and brought it, along with a beer, to where Jack lay in the bed.

She looked over at him and said, "So are you willing to take some time, now, to talk about our marriage?"

"Not sure I have much choice, do I?"

"Well, that's true. You are my captive audience and I find it somewhat delightful that you can't run. But I still think we should set down some ground rules."

"Such as?"

"Well, we've had a really good twenty-four hours … mostly."

"I agree. It's been wonderful. Notwithstanding, no pun intended, Dunn's Falls," he said as he pointed to his foot.

"True. Okay, so 'wonderful' is a relative term. Anyway, let's try not to be too defensive and if we start getting a little crazy we can stop and take a breath to relax."

"Okay," he said. "You know I don't like to fight."

"I can't stand thinking that this is all my issue, but apparently it is because I'm the one who's angry. I'm the one who's going through changes, and I guess over the years, Jack, I've grown up. I mean, that's not to say anything negative about you. I mean what we had in the beginning was wonderful. It was crazy and wild and it was Parisian and artistic, but I can't keep going on with the same behaviors, over and over and over again."

"What behaviors?"

"The rollercoaster ride with you. One day you're up and you're manic and everything is great and you're totally optimistic and then a piece of your art doesn't look the way you want and you take a dive. Then you start partying and your friends come by. It's crazy, Jack. I can't deal with it. I need more stability. That's all I can tell you," she said, shaking her head.

"But I'm not sure I can be any different than I am."

"I'm not sure you can be, either," she said sadly.

"You know, I'm enjoying my life. I like my life. Even when I'm down and pissed off about a sculpture, I'm enjoying my time. I enjoy my friends. I like to have them come over. You know, it's not like I'm hurting anybody nor doing anything fucked up. You know, I'm … I'm not sure what you want … other than for me not to be who I am. What do you really want from me?"

"I guess what I'm saying is that I can't stay with you the way you are. And you're right, it would be wrong for me to ask you to change."

"But you haven't said, other than me not being how I am, you haven't said what it is you want. What is it that you want? You want me not to have my friends over anymore? If I'm in a bad mood, how does that affect you?"

"I think it's an accumulation of years of the rollercoaster. I'm not willing to put up with it anymore," she said, straightening her back. "The craziness, the—"

"I don't think you're being fair, Jenna. I mean you still haven't said what you want. What is it I could do to make your life happy?" he asked, taking a swig of beer and placing it a little too hard back down on the end table.

"Ideally, I would like you to have a real job," she said as if saying the words pained her.

"Why? We don't have any money problems. You don't have to work if you don't want to."

"It's not that. As an artist you … you … it's emotionally draining to have to take care of you."

"But you don't have to take care of me."

"Well, that's how I feel," she said, moving from the bed to the rattan chair next to the table and crossing her arms in front of her.

"Jenna, you … but you're the one who's changing. I

mean, I don't know what to say to you. I mean still, you want me to get a different job? That's the one thing you want and you know it's the one thing I'm not going to do."

"No. You know what? I've said this from the beginning, this is about me, and this is not about you. I'm angry with you because I've changed. And that's not fair. I'm the one that's made the changes," she said, glancing away.

"Yes, but I've never asked you—"

"I've changed away from you."

"This is ridiculous. I've never asked you to take care of me. I mean, those are choices you made for yourself and now you're holding me responsible for them," he said, pointing at her and then back at himself.

"Well, I don't know how to reconcile the two. I don't know how to be who I am and you be who you are and stay in this relationship. I don't know how to do that right now, Jack."

"I don't want this relationship to end," he said, dropping his shoulders.

"I know you don't," she said, sitting rigid and clenching her teeth so hard the muscles in her jaw flexed and ached.

"I love you so much," he said.

"You know what? I believe that, I really do," she said, uncrossing her arms. She stood and began to pace.

"Why don't you take some time to figure out who you are or whatever it is that's going on with you? I mean why is this … you know, I don't understand why you're angry all the time."

"I'm … I'm not as angry as I am afraid. I don't want this relationship to end, Jack, but I'm afraid that's the direction it's heading and I don't know how to stop it." She stopped in front of the TV console and rested her elbow on top of the cabinet.

"Sounds to me like you do want it to end. I mean—that's

what I'm hearing."

"Then I don't think you're listening. If I wanted to end it, I would walk away. I wouldn't have come on this trip," she said, crossing her arms again. "I wouldn't have put up with your crap for the last couple of months."

"Well—"

"I think my behavior indicates I want this relationship to work, Jack. I just don't know *how* to make it work."

"Well, what do you want to do?"

"I don't know. This may be our last hurrah," she said, looking him straight in the eyes.

"See? But again you're talking about the relationship ending and yet you say you don't want it to end," he said, staring back with a pained expression on his face.

"You're not listening again Ja—"

"You're confusing me. This is our last hurrah?" he said, holding the sides of his head as if to keep it from exploding. "What the hell is that supposed to mean?"

"I didn't say it was the last hurrah," she screamed back. "I said it may be."

"That's a pretty pessimistic attitude, even coming from you," he said, turning away.

"Well, you can keep pushing my buttons, Jack, and you're going to get what you say you don't want," she said, glaring at him.

"I don't want it to be over but you—the only thing you can tell me is that you don't want me to be an artist anymore."

"No. I want you to listen to what I'm saying and you're not."

"I am listening," he said, raising his arms in the air with his palms up. "I asked you what you wanted from me," he said, slapping his legs with both hands. "And you said you want me to have a normal job. And you know that's not going

100

to happen. It's not in my makeup and I still don't get what that will change—"

"You don't listen—"

"It's not like you're even giving me the chance to do anything different."

"Jack, you are who you are. This is so beyond—maybe you can't hear what I'm saying," she said as if an epiphany had revealed itself. "Or maybe we're going to end up being the best friends two people can have for the rest of our lives."

"Well, that won't work for me," he said sadly, holding his arms in close.

"You can close the doors in whatever direction you want to but—"

"You know, you say you don't want it to end and everything out of your mouth is its ending."

"I'm going for a walk," she said, getting up and stalking toward the door without looking back.

She tried to slam the door hard enough to make a statement, but the door resisted and quietly shut behind her.

CHAPTER NINE

J enna trudged down the carpeted hall carrying the weight of
the argument on her mind. It seemed inevitable she would
have to make a serious decision in the near future. At the end
of the walkway, she saw a courtesy telephone. She
contemplated calling Marc but hesitated because of her
growing attraction to him. She ambled around the resort for a
while trying to clear her thoughts. She finally picked up a
phone and dialed his room.

"Hello," Summer said.

"Hi Summer, is Marc available?"

"He's not here at the moment. He went downstairs to the
lobby to confirm dinner for Le Gourmet on Thursday night.
Can I help?"

"Sure. I wanted to discuss a couple ideas about Jack and
me with Marc."

"Well, that's his forte and for good reason. I'm not very
good at listening to the whole story. I hope you find him. Tell
him you talked to me and I won't expect him back for a
while."

Jenna went straight to the concierge's office where Marc
had just received an envelope confirming his reservations.
She pushed through the glass door and stood next to him.

"Hi. This is a nice surprise. What are you doing here?" he
said, shifting in her direction.

"I need to talk with you if it's okay," she said, looking
down at the floor.

"Sure. What can I do for you?"

"By the way, I found you because I spoke to Summer,"
she said, peeking up at him. "She said to tell you that she

would see you later or when you get there or something." She lowered her voice and asked, "Anyway, if you can spare a few minutes, can we talk about my relationship with Jack?"

"Sure. No problem," Marc said. "Let's take a table at the back of the Calabash."

They walked through the nearly empty open-air restaurant and sat at a table in the far corner away from the pool.

"I'm not sure what's going on between *us*, but that's not what this is about," Jenna said. "I need to sort out what's going on with me and Jack."

"I completely understand and will endeavor to keep my lips to myself."

"Good," she said, holding back a smile.

"I should tell you up front it's really important to think over what you're about to do. Once the talking has started, there's no turning back," he said, tilting his head slightly forward and raising his eyebrows. He waited for a reply that didn't come.

She sat across from him, staring toward the pool area.

"Are you sure I'm the person you want to do this with? I don't want this to cause any problems between us."

Jenna turned back to him and said, "That's the last thing I would want. I really want to bounce some things off you and get an idea of where I want to go and what I need to do to get there."

"Okay, that's fine," he said.

"It's Jack, or should I say, it's our relationship. Things have changed, and we seem to be having so many arguments these past few months," she said, flipping a napkin back and forth. "I feel like I'm pushing him away and there's nothing I can do about it. The end of us seems inevitable." Jenna grimaced at having said the words aloud and began tapping her foot against the leg of the table. After regaining control, she continued, "I'm very confused about all of it and Jack's not making it any easier."

The two sat in silence for a minute with Jenna's body speaking volumes: her foot bobbed up and down while she bit the end of her fingernail.

"You seem very much like a volcano that's been letting off steam once in a while, but now you feel like you might blow."

"That's a good description. I'm ready to erupt and I don't know how to stop it once it's underway. I'm terrified of the results."

"That's understandable." He sat forward, placing his forearms on the table. "I'm hearing a couple of things that I would like for you to help me understand more clearly. It seems to me that this is not about Jack, but about you."

"I hear what you're saying but you don't know what it's like being married to him. He doesn't listen when I talk. Shit, our whole lives revolve around him."

"And whose fault is that? If you look, you'll see that you've been making choices for yourself all along. You're at the point now where you want to start making different choices. I think you can do that and still be with Jack."

"Maybe this was a bad idea," Jenna said, angling her body away from Marc.

"Maybe, but I think you have the strength to take a good look at yourself. It's easy to focus on Jack and his problems. As you've said, you've been doing it for years. Why not take the chance to dive into you, find out what's making *you* tick?"

"Because I feel like ... if he would just do certain things, everything would be fine, that I would be fine."

"You can't be fine based on someone else's behavior. You've lost the most important part of any relationship—the feeling that you're staying in the relationship through your own choice."

"Maybe I do have a choice, but not one I like," she said, folding her hands on the table. She paused. "Yeah, okay, I can see how you would say that. So how do I get my choice back?"

"That's an interesting question. You never lost your choice—you only drew that conclusion because you perceived yourself as trapped. But you're not trapped at all, except by your own devices. You've concentrated so heavily on Jack that you may have missed your own solution."

"My solution to what?"

"What's the bottom line for you right now? What's driving this anger about who you are or who you're becoming? This is about how you feel about yourself in this relationship. Jack has his own issues, but they belong to Jack. When you think about *you* in this relationship what comes to mind?"

"I mostly think about how Jack is still where he was ten years ago. He needs to grow up," she said, folding her arms in front of her.

"And you? Are you satisfied with your 'growing up' at this time?"

"I don't know."

"Are you more grown up than Jack?"

"Yes. At least I'm responsible," she said, coming forward in her chair.

"Does Jack cheat on you, beat you, or lie to you?"

"No. He doesn't clean up after himself. Sometimes he gets into a funk and doesn't produce anything for weeks on end."

"And you don't know if he will again?"

"Yes, exactly," she said, uncrossing her arms.

"And that leaves you feeling vulnerable and dependent on Jack, but you don't want to be independent because, you

105

would have to—what?"

A silence fell and the two sat quietly for a few moments.

"Grow up," she said, chuckling at the realization. "This *is* about me. Damn."

"Listen, take it easy on yourself and on Jack, if you want," he said, smiling broadly. "It seems to me what you're going through is a very healthy part of the growing and evolving. It's good for you to clarify your values every few years." Marc sat back in his chair allowing his legs to slide under the table. "We aren't static beings, you know. We change. I suspect even Jack has made a few changes along the way, imperceptible as they may be to you.

"I believe it will be difficult to clearly see what's going on in your relationship until you can clearly see yourself. It seems it's time for you to get to know yourself again and make the changes you need. Three weeks from now you may still want to kick Jack to the curb, but at least you'll be clear about your motives."

"Whoa, that's a lot to take in. I've got so much to think about," she said as she reached over to touch his arm. "Thanks ... thank you. I think it's time for a long walk on the beach."

"Sounds great. We'll see you tonight, I hope."

"Yeah, maybe."

Jenna stepped to the edge of the terrace and inclined against the wall. She looked out over the beach and decided to find a more secluded area to meditate on her new revelations. She walked back through the lobby and asked at the front desk where she could go for a quiet retreat.

Jenna meandered to the garden, where she hoped to spend time thinking about her conversation with Marc. The Couples garden left nothing to Mother Nature but the growing. The gardener manicured every corner, tended every flower with the care of a foster father, and yet, the garden had the appearance of a rainforest. Giant rattan swings, roughly in the shape of elephant trunks, hung ready to curl a couple into an intimate private space. Jenna rolled into the first swing, turned onto her side, and mulled over her conversation with Marc.

Oh my God, what's happening to me? Her lips began to quiver and she could feel her stomach tighten as thoughts flittered in her mind. *What do you want? No, not that ... I'm not even going to think it. I love you, Jack, you asshole*, she thought and could not hold back what had been pushing on her throat and pulling at her heart for the last few months. "This hurts so badly," she said aloud, finally weeping. She turned away from the trail to cover the convulsive gasps she emitted as she sobbed. She allowed the fearful crying to continue unabated until she felt drained. *If this is all about me, then all the fighting is my fault. Oh, Jack.* She lay quietly. The afternoon passed while she made decisions that she never thought she would have to face.

"My lady," a resonant voice said from behind her. "Are you okay?" A man strolled closer and asked, "Trouble in paradise? Not to worry ... no problem. The day after a storm in Jamaica is always the most beautiful, my lady," he said in a deep reassuring tone. "It clears the air and everything is brighter. Ya? Ya mon."

She brushed her hair from her face and looked at the stranger. "Are you the gardener?"

"Ya mon. Is there anything I can do for you, my lady?"

"How do I adopt the 'no problem' attitude?"

"You focus on *what is* instead of what you wish for and therefore are always satisfied."

"Huh. That makes sense."

"Anything else, my lady?"

"I think you've given me just what I needed," Jenna said. She sat on the side of the swing, preparing to stand up.

"Irie, mon. Remember, in Jamaica a problem is no problem," he said, turning to walk away.

"I'm beginning to believe that," she said and eagerly pushed out of the swing, heading straight to Jack.

Jenna knocked on the door of the room and waited. *I am so sorry*, she rehearsed in her head, *and I'll make it up to you.* Jack didn't answer. "Jack," she called. "Jack, are you in there?" She felt a rush of angst as her imagination took over. "Oh shit. Jack. Did you—"

"You shouldn't leave your key in the room," he said from behind her as he teetered up to her on his crutches.

"Jack ... Jack, listen, I am so sorry about what we've been going through," she said, holding back the tears.

"I'm sorry as well, but can I get in there and off my foot?" he said as he squeezed past her. "I want to hear all about it. Please don't leave anything out." He winced. "I swear to god, I'm listening for all its worth and I promise to do a lot more of it. Okay?" He unlocked the door and headed for the bed.

"What were you doing out there?"

"I felt like shit because of our argument. Thought I might be able to find you." He stood the crutches next to the end table and wheeled around, allowing his full weight to drop onto the bed. He lifted his leg onto the pillows and sighed.

"Oh, honey, that's sweet, but don't do that again," she said, pointing her finger at him. "We have some partying still to do and you need to get well." She helped him straighten his leg and propped it up on two pillows.

"What the hell brought you around?" Jack asked.

"I had a talk with Marc, but the clincher was the gardener. It's a long story. I'll tell you all about it later, but right now, do you think I can stretch out here next to you and we can make out a little?"

"I'm not even going to question where you got your

dope. I'm glad you did and would you mind sharing some of it?" He grinned broadly and pulled her to him.

"I realized that it was easier for me to focus on you than take a good look at myself. I'm sorry for all we've put each other through. Coming here may turn out to be just what I needed—what we needed," she said, running her fingers through his black hair.

"You're still the best kisser I've ever had," Jack said, softly touching her face. "I've missed you, missed us."

"Me, too. I love you, Jack," she said, nuzzling into his neck.

"I think I need to take a nap," he said, drawing her in close. "It's been a long day."

"Well, then let me help you relax," she said. She undressed and slid back into bed next to him. She reached into Jack's boxers, taking him completely by surprise, but he quickly responded.

"I can't remember ... the last time ... you initiated—" he muttered, nearly panting in his excitement.

As she fondled him, she gave him a wicked smile and said, "I think I owe you something." She crawled between his legs, like the vixen she remembered she used to be, and yanked off his shorts. "Seems like he's game," she said, gesturing at his erection.

"I'd say," Jack said with a funny British accent.

"Turnabout is fair play." She skulked forward and took him into her mouth.

"Oh my god, Jenna, it's been so long, I don't think it will take—"

"Just relax and enjoy."

She used her hand on his shaft, running up and down as she sucked hard on the head of his erection. Circling his crown with her tongue, she reveled in her capacity to stir Jack. Finding just the right rhythm, she felt his phallus swell.

Sucking hard one last time, she released her mouth and used both hands to bring him to completion. He ejaculated onto his stomach, grunting loudly each time he pulsed his release.

"Oh god, Jenna," he finally said.

"I think you should nap well now. I'll go grab a towel."

After cleaning up, they shared several soft kisses and then dozed off.

Jenna awoke to find Jack watching her sleep. "Hello," she said, blushing slightly.

"You are truly outstanding," he said. "I'm sorry I stopped telling you that. I really love you, Jen."

"Thank you," she said, touching his face. "Are you sure you're going to be okay with me going to the beach bash?"

"Aba-solutely," he said. "I've no problem with that. Marc and Summer will take good care of you, I'm sure."

She stretched her arms above her head and then checked the time on the cell phone. "Would you like the TV on or the radio? I need to get ready."

"No, nothing. Wait, the CD player would be great. How about some Kings of Leon?" he said and he rolled over, pressing his face into the pillow.

"I'm going to take a quick shower and get dressed. I'll be sure to be quiet when I return," Jenna said and kissed Jack on the cheek. "I'll see you in the morning."

CHAPTER TEN

As Summer and Marc approached the beach, they decided to remove their shoes. The sand surrounded their feet with a pleasant coolness as they walked among the dinner guests assembling for the evening's festivities. The sun left a warm glow over the party as it melted into the Caribbean Sea. The steel drum band played a sultry Jamaican song, inviting everyone to get into the island spirit.

The lavish buffet, lined with well-groomed suntanned couples, greeted Jenna as she approached the gala. The glow of the tiki torches highlighted the dancing palm fronds as they waved in the ocean breeze, while off in the near distance the lights illumined rows of linen-covered tables adorned with tropical flowers and sparkling water glasses set for the evening's feast.

Jenna strolled casually to the gathering, feeling lighter than she had in months. Her smile radiated her newfound resolve. She hesitated for a moment at the edge of the party, and thought, *Wow, this is a Jack party*.

"Jenna, we're over here," she heard through the crowd. "You look amazing! I love that dress." Summer threw her arm around Jenna's waist and started walking her to their table. "How are you feeling?"

"I feel better than I have in a long time."

"I can see that. You're positively glowing. My husband sure has a way with women, doesn't he?"

"Thank you for letting me borrow him," Jenna said.

"Honey, you can borrow him anytime you want to," Summer said in a sultry voice as they sauntered up to Marc.

"How nice is this? I'm blessed with my two favorite

women on the island. How are you tonight, Jenna? You look wonderful," he said, standing to embrace her.

"Thank you. I'm doing fine. I'm doing more than fine, actually. I feel great. You were great," she whispered as she hugged him.

"How's Jack doing? Is his foot feeling any better?" he asked, sitting back down.

"Well, had he stayed in bed, he probably would be feeling much better, but after our fight, he searched the hotel trying to find me."

"Did he find you?" Summer asked, sitting down next to Marc.

"He walked up behind me as I was banging on the door, thinking he'd left me and caught a flight home," she said, pulling out a chair to sit down.

"So he's in the room, now? Sleeping?" Summer asked.

"Yeah, he's in the room and forbidden to get out of bed. He was falling asleep when I left."

"Let the partying begin," Summer said, standing up. "Let's you and I go up to the terrace bar and get a drink," she said to Jenna. "Marc, do you mind staying at the table? Becky and Cliff are supposed to be meeting us and I invited two other couples from Tower Island to join us. They promised to have clothes on," she said as she took Jenna's hand and they laughed their way up the beach.

The emcee introduced the first act from Kingston, a reggae band ready to make the party jam. "The Kingston Groove, ladies and gentleman." The music beckoned those who had arrived early and finished partaking of the feast to get up and dance.

After she and Jenna got their drinks, Summer's table of friends joined the buffet crowd and piled Jamaican delicacies onto their plates. On their way back to the table, they passed the dessert bar filled with a large variety of cakes and pies.

"This is simply hedonistic," Summer said, eyeing the pastries.

"It all looks so yummy," Jenna said.

"I should have shown more discipline in my choices I suppose," Marc said. "But why come to Jamaica and behave?"

"Exactly," Summer chimed in with a big smile.

"I hope you've enjoyed the expressive style of the Kingston Groove," said the emcee. "Next up are some of our very own employees teaching you how to move through a Jamaican dance."

"Marc, come and dance with me," Summer said, pulling him up from his chair.

"I'm right behind you," he said, placing his hands on her hips. "And what a nice behind, I must say."

The party found a rhythm and a pace that encouraged everyone to embrace their inner dancer. As the night wore on and the drinks continued to flow, inhibitions loosened.

"Marc, dance with me," Jenna called over the music.

"I'd love to," he whispered into her ear.

Jenna had a hard time maintaining eye contact as they grooved to the beat. His intense stare caused all sort of feelings she wasn't ready to acknowledge. When he swung her around with a strong lead, she giggled from the feeling it gave her in her stomach. She hoped he couldn't feel her hard nipples when he pulled her in close.

They danced through two songs and returned to the table.

"I think I need some water," Jenna said, taking a sip from her glass.

"That was a lot of fun. Thanks for the dance," he said. "I'm glad you and Jack are getting along better."

"It's good. At least for now. We'll see," she said, scanning the dancers swaying to the music. She noticed Summer dancing with an older man she didn't recognized. Cast in the shadows of the flickering amber light, she watched them move together in a sexy teasing manner. The song ended and a slow song began as the man drew Summer in close.

Jenna felt the urge to escape from the scene. *Oh shit.* She glanced back at Marc who sat watching Summer gyrate. He surprised her by taking hold of her hand and leading her close to where Summer danced on the beach. As Jenna raised her eyes to look at her, she saw her kiss the man as they swayed to the rhythm of the music. As the rotation of the dance brought Marc around, she knew he would see Summer.

Jenna froze as Marc pulled her in very close. The reggae band changed to a faster beat and he released her from his grasp. Jenna, barely moving, watched Summer dance her way over to them. Believing that she'd come to dance with Marc, Jenna suffered an uncomfortable moment when she realized that Summer was cutting in to dance with her.

"What were you doing?" Jenna asked.

"I was kissing another man," she said casually, dancing to the rhythm of the steel drums.

"And Marc ... is okay with that?" Jenna asked, narrowing her eyes.

"I guarantee you, he loved it," she called out as she spun around with her hands thrown above her head.

"Wait? I don't get it. When you said you knew everything, did you mean you knew Marc kissed me?" Jenna asked, ceasing to move.

"It's hard to explain. But you'll find we're more faithful than most couples. Yes, I know about it, we tell each other everything."

"Now you really have me confused," she said, brushing her hair back from her face.

"I would never do that if Marc wasn't around. It's our agreement. He wouldn't do anything like that unless I was nearby or we had agreed otherwise."

"You weren't there when he kissed me."

"That was an error in judgment on many fronts."

"An error? Have you told Jack about it?" Jenna asked, feeling nauseous over the conversation.

"Telling Jack is up to you."

"That's a relief. Do you like seeing him with other women?" Jenna could not wrap her mind around what Summer had said.

Summer laughed. "Yes, I like seeing him with other women and we've been known to share one or two."

"Uh … I need to sit down," Jenna said, walking back to the table in a daze. As she lowered into her chair she said, "I don't know if it's the alcohol or what, but you guys are freaking me out."

Summer sat down next to her. "This is who we are and it works for us. We would never expect you to be involved in anything you weren't comfortable with."

"Who's this guy you were kissing? How do you know he wasn't cheating on his wife? This is Couples, you know. Couples!" she said.

"The two couples and the woman sitting at the table next to where we were dancing," Summer said, pointing across to a group of tables, "That is his wife and two other couples they came here with."

"Apparently there's a whole other world going on around me without my knowledge. Is this some secret swinger resort? I'm going to kill Jack."

"Not at all. There are other resorts for that sort of thing, but not here. People here are mostly just flirtatious."

"Frankly, I don't know what to make of this," she said, looking at Summer. "Are you hitting on me?"

"This is not meant to offend you but—"Marc said. "We've considered it, but you and Jack seem to have a lot you need to work out. Do we like you? Are we attracted to you? Yes on both counts. Do we think the two of you are lovely people? Yes. Do we want to get in the middle of what you're going through right now? No, absolutely not."

"Uh … hmmm. I don't know what to say. I'm at a loss. I'm not sure if I should be offended or flattered. I think I need another drink," Jenna said, putting her forehead in the palm of her hand.

"I know this can be a lot to deal with but we had to tell you sooner or later and now is as good a time as any," Marc said calmly. "We're not swingers. And really it's mostly flirtations and infatuations. It rarely goes any further than that. Although I must admit, we're willing to open our lives to other loves."

"I love Marc more than anyone in the world," Summer said. "Because of what we have, I would never do anything to jeopardize our marriage. I love the freedom to be myself and the lack of stress to freely be attracted to other people I meet and to explore those potentialities."

"What happens if you find someone you love more than Marc?"

"I don't think that could ever happen," she said, reaching across the table and taking him by the hand. "After all the people we've met, no one has ever come close to tempting me away from him. I love him tremendously and I know he loves me as well and I trust him. I don't know many couples who can say that. The idea that someone new could exceed the intimacy we've created over the years is simply not possible."

"Yeah, but why take the risk? Why be married then?"

"It's who we are. This is natural for us. Why confine ourselves to the dictates of the present culture? If I had, I would have never married Marc—I would've married a black man or a Jewish guy. Look, many people feel the way we do. A lot more than you'd think, to be honest."

"You'll have to forgive me if I seem a little discombobulated. I'm still trying to work out this thing with one person," Jenna said, breaking into an uneasy laugh. "It seems to me that it would be very complicated. Wouldn't swinging be easier?"

"It depends what you're looking for," Marc said, settling back into his chair. "I, for one, am not looking for just sex. I have one of the best lovers on the planet."

"And don't you forget it, big boy!" Summer interjected.

"But if I find somebody attractive, why not be able to tell them so," Marc said. "If the relationship evolves and grows and a deep connection is established, why not share affection through love making?"

"I can think of several reasons."

"All of which would be valid for you," Marc said. "For us, this works. This is who we are and we're thoroughly enjoying our lives and the choices we make."

"Well, you've completely thrown my mind into overload but it definitely explains the kiss. It might have been nice to know sooner so I wasn't twisting in the wind with guilt," she said, standing. "I'm leaving now. Not because I'm frightened, mind you—although I am a little—but I need some time to mull this over. I'll be in my room."

"Ladies and gentlemen, I present the bonfire…" the emcee whispered loudly into the microphone, "…where you throw your head back and let the rhythm take hold of your body."

A loud whoosh sounded and a ball of blue flame rolled into the air as the drummers pounded out an ancient native beat. The dancers rushed the area, forming a circle around the fire.

Jenna hesitated for a moment, engrossed in the energetic movement of the dancers. She broke away from the vision. She tromped through the sand, passing the many guests that by now frolicked with the enthusiasm of their college days. Thoughts darted through her mind on her way back to the room. She felt repulsed, aroused, curious, and scared all at the same time. She detected the scent of marijuana in the hallway. Unintentionally she followed the odor right up to her room door. She could smell the distinct odor of cannabis seeping through the seams. She slid in her key, entered, and walked straight to Jack.

"How did you get that?" Jenna asked, standing in front of him with her hands on her hips. "You haven't been walking on your foot again, have you?"

"Only to the door. Our bellman, Demonde, delivered it. He's a very cool guy."

"O … kay," she said as she approached Jack. "Well, I'm glad you're awake. You won't believe what I have to tell you." She unzipped her dress as she moved to sit on the edge of the bed.

"What happened?"

"God, look at the size of that thing," she said.

"I know. It's incredible, isn't it? It's some good shit, too. Want some?"

"Nah. That's okay," she said. "So you're not going to believe what I found out. Oh my god, I'm freaking out."

"Well then, spit it out already."

"I'm sitting at the table and I look over and I see Summer dancing with this older man drenched in gold, doing the bump and grind," she said, sounding very much like an excited teenager disclosing her greatest secret.

"Cool."

"Not so cool. So like I'm freaking out and Marc pulls me back to the dance area and I see Summer and this guy kissing. And I mean kissing."

"Excellent," he said, grinning and tilting his head back against the headboard.

"Then Summer comes over and I'm thinking she wants to dance with Marc and I'm about to escape but she grabs me instead and I say, 'What the hell was that about?'"

"And she said?"

"She said she was kissing another man. Just matter-of-factly, like it was no big deal."

"Very cool. I miss the best stuff."

"Then Marc and Summer explain how they're free to do what they want as long as the other is present. Marc actually enjoyed watching Summer kiss that man."

"Wow, that's some kinky shit, man. I knew those people were cool."

"Don't be obnoxious. So naturally, now I'm thinking they're hitting on me, Marc in particular, and then they tell me no. I was very confused."

"Did you say 'they're', as in they are, hitting on you. Mmm … you and Summer? Cool."

"You need to stop smoking that pot, Picasso. And wipe your chin!" she exclaimed, lightly punching his arm. "So anyway, they said we have too many problems or something like that, otherwise, they'd be interested. I felt somewhat insulted. I mean not that I would be interested or anything, but still."

"Well, speak for yourself. I'm interested."

"I'm going to assume you're either too stoned or too stupid to know what you're saying," she said, rolling onto her back away from him.

"This is making me very hot," he said with a beamy grin as he reached to touch her breast.

"Jack, would you please focus. There's something else I need to tell you."

"You could be right, I see four breasts," he said, laughing. "I think this dope is getting to me but I must say, before I go off the deep end, we should consider the possibilities before us."

"Of course you would, because you're a dog. Are you listening? Marc kissed me on the beach this morning."

Jack sat quietly for a moment and then said, "As far as I'm concerned, that makes us even. Would you agree?"

"I agree. Although a blowjob—"

"Should I talk to Marc about this?"

"Definitely not! Yes, we're even."

"Does this mean I get to kiss Summer?"

"Well I can't speak for her but—is that all you're going to say?"

"Well, have you considered it might be exactly what we need?"

"No, I don't think that's what we need. I don't think I want to see them anymore."

"I always knew those people were very cool."

"Jack, pass me the joint."

CHAPTER ELEVEN

J enna awoke with a slight headache, triggering a recall of last night's events in full living Technicolor. She stretched her arms above her head and walked out onto the balcony. She looked past the wedding gazebo to the water and saw no remnants of the beach party, causing her to wonder if it might have been a mirage. Maybe I dreamt what happened last night. *Is that Summer?* she thought. She covered her eyes from the glare of the sun, straining to see across the dazzling reflection of natural light on the sugar white beach. She focused on the figure performing yoga postures on the sand. Jenna watched Summer, who was fully in command of her slender, muscular body, move through a sequence of poses they had often executed together in class.

"What are you staring at?" Jack asked, placing his arm around her waist.

"Trying to make out if that's Summer on the beach," she said, turning into his embrace. "Hmm … look at you standing there. How's your foot feeling?"

"It's much better today but I think the shopping gig in Ocho is out. You can go if you want to," he said, watching Summer stretch.

"Oh, that's fine by me. We can get lazy on the beach."

"Right now I need some coffee. Did you smoke the rest of the joint last night?"

"No, of course not. You're not going to smoke it now, are you?"

"Uh … no," he said. "God, she's stunning."

"Yes, she is," she said, ducking from under his arm. "I wish I hadn't found out about them. It makes me see her so differently."

"Yeah … me too," he said, arching his eyebrows up and down.

"You ass," she said playfully. "I'm taking a quick shower. Do you want to join me for breakfast?"

"How about we shower together? And I'll brush my teeth before I get in."

She knew the idea of Summer had fueled his desire and although the idea of spending more time with Marc aroused and confused her at the same time, she decided to focus on the positive. "Come with me, Picasso," she said seductively.

"I'm following you."

Jenna reached in and turned on the shower, while Jack, in a surge of excitement, quickly brushed his teeth. She sauntered up next to him and laid her head against his back. She wrapped her arms around his waist and gently pulled him in close against her full breasts. "I love the way you smell."

Jack rinsed his mouth and turned to face her. He leaned in to kiss her forehead but instead found himself clasped between her hands pulling him to her lips. The release felt wonderful as they explored each other's tongues in a familiar fashion from long ago.

"That was a really nice kiss," he said.

Jenna dropped her robe to the floor revealing her want for him. Jack gently reached between her legs while maintaining eye contact and found her wet with desire. He watched as her eyes closed and her head tilted back. He nuzzled against her flesh and began kissing, licking, and biting along her neck and jawline.

"This is so good. I just want to stay right here," she whispered.

"I have other plans you might like even better," he said with a grin.

"Really? I'm looking forward to it."

They opened the glass door to the bath and stepped in. Jenna leaned back against the wall, grabbed the towel rack and mounted her left leg on the side of the tub.

"You are a mind reader," he said. He lowered himself to his knees and began a slow rhythmic tonguing of her clit.

"That's good. Just the way I like it," she said as she cupped the back of his head with one hand while hanging onto the rack with the other.

Jack then slowly inserted his finger into her wetness. "Jenna," he said.

She looked down and watched as he pushed his finger into his mouth, tasting her sweetness.

"That's so fuckin' hot," she murmured and laid her head back against the wall again. Her hips involuntarily moved in time with his ravishment.

"Turn around and spread your legs," he commanded. He then took his erection in his hand and slowly slid it into her from behind.

"Oh my god, that feels so good," she moaned.

He stroked at an ever-increasing speed until she could hear nothing but flesh slapping against flesh. She reached underneath and circled her clit feverishly as they reached the pinnacle at almost exactly the same time.

"Fuck me, Jenna, I'm going to come so hard," he called out in a strained whisper.

"Oh my god, oh my god." Jenna uttered her orgasm into the wall as she felt Jack's ejaculation fill her.

He reached around and fondled her breasts and stomach as he subsided. Jenna clung to the towel rack, drooping like a rag doll. After a few moments, they stood facing one another, staring into the eyes of their past, deeply wanting this to be a new beginning, a fresh start that would rekindle their love.

✻ ✻ ✻ ✻ ✻

As Jack and Jenna approached the Calabash for breakfast, Jenna spotted Summer and Marc.

"Let's order something to our room," Jenna said, ceasing to move forward.

"Don't be ridiculous. We can't avoid them forever," Jack said. He walked straight to their table. "Do you mind if we join you?"

"Not at all," Marc said. "Looks like your foot's feeling better. Are you guys going to go shopping?"

"We're going to skip the shopping and hang around here today," Jack said, settling into a seat next to Summer. "Foot's feeling better but I'd rather not push it."

Jenna sat down watching Jack.

"Do either of you want coffee if the server comes by?" Summer asked.

"None for me," Jenna said, standing and pushing in her chair without making eye contact.

"Yes, definitely for me, and plenty of it," Jack said.

"Try the mango," Summer said. "It's delicious."

Jack stood and followed closely behind Jenna toward the buffet.

"You know, Jack, you really piss me off," she hissed, walking away from him and picking up a plate.

"Tell me something I don't know," he said, piling on the scrambled eggs and potatoes. He reached for a smaller plate and filled it with mango.

They walked back to the table and Jenna ate in silence.

"Wow, this food is great and the coffee … have you guys tried the coffee? Here's mango if you'd like some," Jack said.

"I'm full, but thank you," Summer said with a smile.

"You know, we saw you from our balcony this morning," Jack said. "Couples should put you on their brochure. I'd volunteer to take the shots."

Marc watched Jenna while Jack talked. "Jenna, you seem a little uncomfortable. Is everything okay?"

She scooted her chair a little closer to Jack and crossed her legs. "Umm … well, yes and no. No, I'm not okay. You guys really freaked me out last night."

"Honey, it's okay," Jack said, placing his hand on top of hers. "People are just people doing their own thing."

Jenna abruptly snatched her hand away. "I feel like everybody's closing in on me … trying to pressure me into something."

"Maybe that pressure's coming from within, because I haven't heard anyone ask you to do anything," Marc said.

"Yeah, I'm not asking you to do anything at all," Jack said.

Before Jenna could respond, Kokila stepped up to their table.

"Hey there, Jenna. I'm on my way to set up the bar on the island. I'm looking forward to seeing you out there today."

"Uh … well, I'm not sure what we're doing yet."

"Gotta run," she said, tugging Jenna's hair as she passed.

They all watched her parade out of the restaurant toward the dock.

"So are you guys going to come to the island with us later?" Marc asked.

"Yeah, we'll be there," Jack said.

✳ ✳ ✳ ✳ ✳

As Jack opened the door to their room, Jenna stormed past him.

"You are unbelievable. Does nothing I say to you get through that thick skull of yours?"

"What's your problem now?"

"You don't take me and what I want into consideration.

125

You spent the entire time looking a complete fool, throwing yourself at Summer. I tell you I don't want to eat breakfast with them and you completely ignore me by getting us invited to sit at their table. Then after we discuss lounging at the beach, you tell them we're going to the island."

"I think going to the island will be good for you. It might help you to loosen up. And I wasn't throwing myself at Summer. Honey," he said, trying to encircle her in his arms.

"Leave me alone. Please just leave me alone," she said as she sat in the chair by the French doors.

"I thought we were making progress. I thought we were coming together."

"How can we come together when you don't take me into consideration? Do you even realize what you did this morning?"

"I just thought it would be better to see them sooner than later. It's not like we could avoid them forever."

"But you don't get to decide for me," she shouted.

Jack lowered himself onto his knees, placing his hands on top of her thighs and said, "You know, you're right. I shouldn't have pushed you into having breakfast with them. And the island? I'll tell them we're going to pass on going today. I know. I'm an ass," he said.

"I said you don't get to choose for me. I'm going to the island whether you like it or not."

"But I do like it. I think we'll have a great time and you'll enjoy it, after a drink or two," he said, smiling.

"You …," she said, shoving him away from her.

He snatched her up in his arms and held her close. "I love you and I want you to know my flirting is just for fun. It doesn't mean anything. And you don't have to worry about anything happening, because it won't, unless of course, you change your mind," he said, grinning.

"You know, Jack, god," she said, pushing out of his

126

embrace. "You're a dog!"

"Yeah, but it seems to me we need something to stir up this relationship."

She put her forehead in her hand and shook her head. "We have plenty of stir in this drink."

"You know what I mean. I'm not talking about fighting. It wouldn't be like we're cheating because we'd all be together and we'd both know what was going on."

"They told me they weren't interested, so it's a moot point."

"They may have said that, but the vibe is otherwise," he said, wagging his finger in the air. "I imagine they planned to tell us on this trip. They probably just didn't plan on all the fighting."

"Aren't we back to the same conversation we had before we left?" she asked. "How are they going to help us?"

"You've said several times that you wished you were more adventurous, had more lovers before we met. It seems to me, it could be a trip. What happens in Jamaica, stays in Jamaica. Unless, of course, you don't find Marc appealing and then it would be a drag for you. How was the kiss?"

"Honestly, it took me by surprise so I don't know. I do find him attractive, sort of, but not in that kind of way."

"Well, in what kind of way?"

"He's intriguing and a great listener. I guess you could say he's good looking," she said, slightly smiling.

"All things being even and you had no obligations, would you kick him out of bed?"

"Okay, I get your point." Jenna stood and walked to the French doors, breathing in the sea air.

"We don't have to decide now. Let's see how it goes. Nothing happens until we talk again, okay?"

"I'm ready to go to the island and nervous as hell."

"Want a hit of the joint before we go?"

"Yes. Hell. Sure, why not."

* * * * *

"Clearly Jack knows and Jenna seemed a bit shaken by us. Jittery," Summer said.

"Yeah, and that's too bad too, because this is the first time in a while that I've really been interested in getting closer to someone, other than you."

"So, what's the problem?" Summer asked as she packed a small bag for town.

"It seems obvious to me," he sighed.

"Fill me in then."

"What are you talking about? These guys are close to finished. It wouldn't take much to put them right over the edge. I don't want to be a part of that."

"You already are. You gave her a kiss."

"Well, I'm not sorry that I did, I just hope it doesn't have unintended consequences."

"Oh, I see," she said. She sat on his lap and put her arms around his neck. "How is it—let me see how to put this—that you can profess this life philosophy about how important it is for people to own their choices and yet, you won't let these two people make their own decisions?"

"That's not fair," he said. "Are you saying you wouldn't feel bad if Jack fell for you, causing them to break up?"

"You didn't just say that, did you?" Summer asked, astonishment flowing across her face.

"What?"

"I don't believe this," she said, standing up and putting her hands on her hips. "You wrote two books on the power of personal choice and the freedom that comes with taking responsibility for those choices."

"That's true, including my own choices. I'm not

completely closed to the idea, but I'm also not going to jump into a situation that is wrought with complications. Part of owning your choice is trusting in your intuition."

"Not to be harsh but my intuition tells me that's it's up to them to navigate their own choices in life. It's certainly not my responsibility to take care of them."

"Honey, I understand you really like Jack and would like to spend more time with him, but let's take this slowly and see what happens."

"If you don't want to follow through because of yourself, some kind of ethics or some other issue, that's fine, but don't pretend this is for *their* own good."

"Why are you so angry?"

"Your position seems paternalistic," Summer said with a wry smile. "I like Jack. I'd like to get to know him better and I don't think I should modify my behavior based on their issues. They are either going to make it or not."

"Look, I understand what you're saying and you make a valid argument. I still hold firm that entering into a relationship with a couple who are struggling with marital issues, is risky business."

"Then why in the hell did you kiss her in the first place?"

"Like I said, love, it wasn't my best moment. She looked so sad and forlorn, I couldn't help myself. That one kiss doesn't mean we are all a great match. We have to consider what kind of drama they could potentially add to our life and you know our policy on that."

"Zero drama."

"Exactly. This has definitely pushed a few buttons for you," Marc said, pulling Summer in close.

"Well, walking your talk is tough, I'll admit that, but when a person doesn't—sometimes I feel an urge to gently point that out."

"Gently?"

"Well, you know me," she said, "You can spank me later. Are you bringing cash or credit?"

"Both, one card and some cash. I'm assuming we'll be safe enough, but I don't want to take any chances. Maybe you should keep the cash in your bra?"

"Not wearing one. How about your underwear?"

"Not wearing any."

"Put the money and card in your pocket and let's go," Summer said, slapping Marc on the butt as they walked out the door.

CHAPTER TWELVE

The opulent aquamarine waters of the Caribbean Sea lay like wavy glass between the dock of the hotel and Tower Island. A small white metal dinghy jounced lazily in the gentle breeze, jerking forward every few moments while tied to the side of the dock. The onshore winds filled the cove with the scent of the Calabash and the ever-present aroma of smoky grilled jerk chicken. The landscape of the inlet beach glinted with suntanned bodies and rabid readers, laying sometimes two to a hammock.

"We're supposed to stand here?" Jenna asked, shielding her eyes, scanning back toward the dive shop.

"Yeah. There's a guy from the shop that comes out to drive us over to the island."

"Is that him?" Jenna said, pointing and then dropping her hand quickly. "He looks angry."

"Yep, that could be him," Jack said slowly, and slightly under his breath.

A tall lanky man with a white towel covering his head approached. He walked past without even the slightest acknowledgement and descended the ladder to the dinghy.

"Jack, you go first so you can help me down, please."

"Sure, okay. No problem," Jack said, and then leaned in close to Jenna and whispered, "If this guy jumps me, run like hell for the concierge of the hotel. They always know what to do." Jack stepped backward onto the ladder, made his way down to the dancing boat. He placed his hands on her hips to guide her safely into the launch.

The ferryman pointed to the rope. Jack untied the knot and pushed the nose of the boat toward the west. One strong pull on the engine cord, a turn of the gas, and they skimmed across the inlet toward Tower Island. The loud drone of the engine made it next to impossible to hear one another.

As the dinghy closed in on the drop off area, the ferryman killed the engine, allowing the rig to glide into shore. The flat metal bottom of the boat scraped against the sand and rocks, coming to an abrupt halt, throwing Jack and Jenna forward.

The ferryman stepped past them onto the shore with the skill of a tightrope walker. Holding the boat with one hand, he reached forward for Jenna. "My lady," he said, offering his hand.

She stepped from the boat into the shallow water and turned to wait for Jack. "Thank you," she said and shaded her eyes to watch him.

Jack stood unsteadily and reached for the man's hand. The hand withdrew from his reach causing Jack to stumble.

"Jack!" Jenna exclaimed, bolting forward to assist him.

"I'm okay," he said, stumbling out of the boat and into the shallow water. He limped slightly as he took Jenna's arm and started up the path. "Fucker," Jack mumbled.

The path ran between two large bushes that protected the visitors from unwanted attention. The steady increase in volume of voices alerted them to the size of the population on the tiny island.

"Oh my," Jenna said, stopping dead in her tracks. She heard the ferryman gun the engine. "Jack," she said, "I don't think I can do this."

"We can go to the private area at the other end," he said. "I can come get our drinks when we're ready."

"Where do you look when you're talking to them?"

"To be truthful, at first you keep looking at their faces. The second time you look at their—"

"Jack, knock it off," she whispered.

"Okay, look to your right and keep walking. We'll go to

the other side of the tower. There's a gazebo over there."

They made their way quickly toward the north end of the small island.

"I think I'll go topless," she said. She arranged her things on the lounge chair.

"Okay, but if you get reported, the clothes police will come and get you," he said, removing his shirt.

Jenna removed her sarong and sat down on the lounge. She spread her towel out and lay on her stomach. She untied her top and pulled it from underneath her. She then attempted to remove her bottoms without exposing her most sacred parts.

"Jack, will you help me?"

"Sure. What do you need?" He removed his swimming trunks and walked over to Jenna.

"Slide my bottoms off."

"Wow, we *are* getting along better." Jack slipped his fingers around either side and began to remove the bathing suit. "You're going to have to loosen your grip," he said, chuckling. "Relax your legs. Jenna, oh my god, you have a death grip on these. I'm counting to three and then I'm going to leave you just like this," he said, laughing at the bathing suit halfway down her legs.

She loosened her clenched thighs allowing him to remove the suit. "God, I hadn't thought of sunscreen."

"It's much easier to put on when you're naked," he assured her.

"Will you please put it on for me?"

She recalled Marc's warm, strong hands as Jack spread an even layer over her body. She shook her head slightly to rid herself of the thought.

"Are you okay?" he asked.

"Yeah, I'm fine, but I think you might be right about those drinks. Would you get me a piña colada? Strong.

Drinking before noon. What does this make me?"

"Someone on vacation in lively Jamaica, mon."

"Yeah, okay—I'll buy that."

"Be right back," Jack said as he stood and strolled comfortably around the tower and out of sight.

Jenna enjoyed the warm breeze flowing over her body. She soon realized that no one onshore from the hotel could see her and even the people on the island couldn't see her unless they walked to their gazebo. She started to relax and enjoy the newfound freedom when a boatload of tourists slowly meandered by, waving. *Ah great! Look at this, me naked, right out here, sonofabitch.* "Hi," she called out and waved. As soon as the boat was out of sight, she slunk down and covered her head with her towel.

This is ridiculous. She rolled over onto her back and sat up. *Wherein the hell is he? Why isn't he back yet?* She could hear laughter coming from the direction of the pool. She wrapped her sarong around her body, grabbed her backpack and Jack's towel, and walked toward the commotion. She approached the swim-up bar from the concrete walkway to find all eyes looking at her. From her vantage point, she could see the upper bodies—different skin tones and sizes, breasts of all shapes, but mostly she saw everyone smiling—and Kokila fully dressed, very striking, grinning at her from behind the bar.

"I'm so glad you decided to join us," Kokila said, patting the countertop as an invitation to sit.

Jenna smiled and then glared in Jack's direction. She meekly waved to Becky and Cliff, and another couple from the beach party, not quite knowing where to look. Except for her eyes that darted about to ingest the scene, she stood frozen. The naked crowd around the bar all shouted their greetings. *Move!* she commanded her body but remained as still as a mummy in a sarcophagus. *Move! Damn it!* Jack turned back around oblivious to her condition.

Kokila came around the bar and touched her shoulder, startling her. She managed to stifle a yelp, focusing on Kokila's face and the words coming out of her mouth. *I shouldn't have smoked that joint. What is she saying?* Kokila motioned for her to remove her wrap. She whispered into Jenna's ear. "Are you okay? If you're going to stay, you need to disrobe."

All at once, time fast-forwarded to normal speed and Jenna, with the same determination as a person jumping into icy water, dropped her belongings and removed her sarong in one swift movement. She descended the stairs into the water and sat on the first stool she could get to, which just so happened to be farthest from the rest of the guests. She covered her breasts with her right arm and placed her left hand in her lap. She looked around watching the laughter and camaraderie amongst the people in the pool.

Kokila brought over the piña colada that Jack had ordered and placed it in front of her.

"Thank you," she said, shifting forward to place her mouth over the straw, not moving her arms that kept her covered. She drew a long sip of the drink and took a deep breath.

Becky swam over and sat down on the stool next to her. "It's brilliant that you decided to join us. You'll see everyone's a jolly good sport. Are you okay?" she said, staring intently at Jenna.

"Yeah, another drink or so and I won't feel a thing. I know it's horrible that I have to consume alcohol to do this. Why am I doing this again?" she asked, more directed at herself than Becky.

"It'll be okay. Come over and join us when you're ready," Becky said and swam around to the other side of the bar.

"I thought you were going to pass out there for a second," Kokila said, resting her arms on the countertop in front of Jenna.

"Yeah. I don't know. This is truly strange for me. Can I have another one of these," she said, motioning with her head to her glass.

"Coming right up," Kokila said, pressing the button on the blender. "Jack's a trip. He told me he wants to sculpt me. How would you feel about that?"

"You're beautiful—Jack's a very good sculptor—seems like a good plan," Jenna said, glancing around the pool area.

"I'd be willing to do it if you're there," Kokila said.

"You don't have to worry about Jack. He's a real professional about this stuff, anything related to his art," Jenna said.

"Oh, I'm sure. But I'd still like for you to be there."

"Hi there," Jack said. "Look at *you* coming over here so brave. I'm really sorry. I saw Becky and Cliff and we started talking. Seriously I'm sorry, but, now that you're here, why don't you come over and meet some of the couples I met the other day."

"No. Not just yet."

"Jack, let her get used to it. She'll be all right after a while. Go have a good time and we'll sit here and talk," Kokila said, wiping out the inside of a glass.

"You cool with that?" asked Jack.

"For now."

The piña coladas helped Jenna throw off her inhibitions and she slowly joined in the spirit of the crowd of revelers as the music got louder and the sun got hotter. Succumbing to temptation, she stepped off the stool, and dove into the embrace of the cool water. As she opened her eyes, she found herself in the presence of the other half of the people she had, up until that moment, only seen the upper half. She immediately surfaced and went straight back to her stool without making eye contact with anyone whatsoever.

"Holy crap. I don't know how you do it," Jenna said, snickering. "Some of these guys are … you know, and then others are so … you know what I mean."

"Is this girl talk?" Kokila teased.

"I know—this is so silly," she said. "I'm kind of embarrassed."

"You should've seen me my first day bartending out here. I couldn't remember an order—even if it was a beer," she said, laughing. "Now, it's just once in a while that someone catches my eye."

"That makes me feel a little better," Jenna said, finishing her drink and nibbling on the pineapple.

"Are you ready for another?"

"How about a rumrunner this time?" she said, listening from across the bar as Jack repeated the story of their trip to the falls.

"Did you put on sunscreen?" Kokila asked.

"Only my face and Jack did my back, come to think of it."

"Here, use mine. Trust me when I tell you, you don't want to burn in the Jamaican sun. I've seen enough visitors who think they'll go home with this great tan and they end up spending half their trip in their room because of a bad burn."

"Thanks," Jenna said, taking the sunscreen and moving to turn her back to the bar. "You know what? I think I'd be more comfortable putting this on in the bathroom."

"No problem. The bathrooms are in the bottom of the tower just over there."

Jenna wrapped her sarong around her waist, and with her back to the pool area, she walked topless across the cement walkway.

"That wasn't so bad," she said aloud to herself. *What the*

137

hell, I can do this. She stood in front of the mirror and carefully spread the sunscreen over her entire legs, arms, and front.

She bravely ambled back down the path to the pool, her breasts sashaying freely.

"Jenna, cool, look at you," Summer said, approaching from the beach landing. "You are a very pretty naked girl," she called out to her.

Jenna froze. *Oh my god, keep smiling.* "Hi, when did you get back?" she asked, inadvertently covering her breasts by crossing her arms.

"How are you doing so far?" Marc asked.

"I'm getting there, two more drinks and I'll be dancing on the bar."

"Yahoo," Marc said. "I can't wait to see that."

The trio meandered down the path, sharing small talk about the shopping trip. They arrived at the bar where Kokila had placed a fresh rumrunner in front of Jenna's belongings .Jenna took her seat and untied the sarong allowing it to flow over the stool in the water.

"Marc?" Jenna said as she turned to him. "What … what?" she stammered, realizing that in a matter of seconds he stood before her wearing only a broad smile. "Would you like a drink?" she said, blushing furiously. She averted her gaze when she really wanted to take a long leisurely look.

"I'd like a rumrunner as well," he said, leaning against the bar.

"A what?" Jenna asked.

"I got it." Kokila laughed.

Jack swam over to join in on the fun at the north end of the bar. "How was shopping in downtown Ocho Rios?"

"It was alright. We bought a couple of things for the kids. Not much," Summer said.

"All this time, I didn't know you had kids," Jack said.

"Not ours. My sister's kids."

"What do you think of Jenna braving the treacherous waters of nudity and surviving like a champ?" Jack asked, reaching in front of Summer to touch Jenna's hand. "Now you get to see why I wanted to sculpt her from the first time I laid eyes on her. She's good-looking, isn't she?"

"Jack, knock it off, please."

Jack swam around Summer and up to Jenna. "I think you're extraordinary," he said. "I'm sorry if that embarrasses you."

"It does. It makes me feel awkward. Remember, I'm not a sculpture on display here, okay?"

"Okay. Hey, speaking of sculpture. I forgot to tell you my clay is in. Kokila," Jack said loudly as the music kicked on again. "When can we get together? I'd like to do a couple of sketches of you."

"Will you be there?" Kokila asked Jenna over the music.

"Sure, I'll be there."

"How about the day after tomorrow? I work, but not until late afternoon."

"Great. Say around 10?" Jack asked.

"I'll be there. What room?"

"246," Jenna said.

Kokila moved away to the other side of the bar.

"So how do you feel about Jack sketching Kokila?" Summer asked as Jack swam back over to Becky and Cliff.

"I'm fine with it," Jenna said. "You don't marry an artist who uses nude models if you're insecure. Ironic, isn't it? I used to pose nude for Jack all the time. Even posed for a few art classes in college. I guess I'm getting stodgy in my young age."

"You were in college? Where did you go to school?" Summer asked, drinking the rest of her rumrunner.

"FIU—majored in journalism. I had dreams of being an

investigative reporter and actually did my internship at a local newspaper," she said, stirring her drink with her straw. "I found that I didn't have the personality for it. You have to be really pushy and that's not my style. Then, one of the food critics at the paper was looking for an assistant. Could I eat food and be critical? You betcha. Sounded like the perfect job for me. I eat anyway, and I've been known to be critical."

"Well at least you figured it out quickly. I, on the other hand, went straight from high school to the University of Miami to get my degree in elementary education. Always thought I would love teaching."

"You do teach and you're good at it," Jenna said, patting her on the back.

"Thank you, but I thought I would educate the children of our society," Summer said. "I thought I would go into less fortunate areas and 'make a difference,' if you know what I mean."

"So what happened?"

"My internship went well enough, so I decided to push on and pursue my master's degree. After graduating, I got my first class of first graders and they kicked my ass. I held out for two more years and then I finally admitted I'd made a huge mistake. My mother was less than thrilled as you can well imagine, and to this day my father still laughs at me," Summer said, shaking her head. "It definitely clarified a few important things for me."

"Yeah? Like what?"

"I hate children," she said, laughing. "Not seriously, but I definitely decided then and there that I didn't want kids of my own. My mother is furious. She says 'I'm denying her, her right to grandmother-hood.' Marc had his children and is finished, as well. His daughter joined the military, which devastated him, and his son is—get this—getting his degree in elementary education, although, I suspect he has what it takes to teach."

"You're so funny. You do teach, just an older variety of children. I didn't know Marc had children. Or an ex-wife for that matter," Jenna said.

"Yeah. So are you and Jack going to try in vitro?" Summer asked.

"I don't want to go through all the testing and procedures. Jack says one child in our family is enough. We don't use birth control, so if it was going to happen, it would have by now."

"Are you okay with that?"

"I vacillate. Most of the time, I'm fine with it, but occasionally, especially after I've been over at my brother's, I wonder if I'm missing out. He says that I'm the lucky one. Probably the-grass-is-greener syndrome."

"How many children does he have?"

"Three. If it ever happens, one would be enough for me," Jenna said and raised her glass to toast.

"Well, thank your lucky stars; at least you don't have the scorn of being the only child without children. I'm the end of a genetic line 'for God's sake.' My mom, the drama queen."

"True enough. I like my brother but the rest, well, they're a different story."

"So you all aren't close?"

"No, not really. I've never felt like I had much in common with my family. They're alright, but I'm usually relieved when our family gatherings are over." Jenna closed her eyes and fingered the condensation on the side of her glass.

"My parents and I are very close. My father has a large family and my mother's people pretty much wrote her off when she married my father. I've seen my aunt a few times but other than that, my Dad's family is our extended family."

Jenna and Summer spent the afternoon sharing stories

while Marc and Jack vied for Kokila's attention.

"Wow, how long have we been here?" Jenna asked as Jack swam up.

"A few hours, I'm sure," he said. "Let's go back and order a late lunch to the room, take a quick shower, and eat on the balcony. Then, if all is well, let's play some more. What do you think?" He wiggled his eyebrows making Jenna laugh.

"That's a plan," she said, slurring her words a bit. "Whoa fu … this stool is a lot higher than when I sat down."

"At least one of you is higher," Marc said, laughing. "See you in a little while. You look awesome, by the way."

"Really? Do you really think so?" she slurred. "Thanks, Marc, you're a sweetheart."

CHAPTER THIRTEEN

J ack and Jenna threw on clothes, loosely resembling the two people who had arrived at the island earlier that day. They stood at the edge of the water waiting for the ferryman to come rescue them from their inebriated state.

"Oh, I feel sloppy," Jenna said lazily.

"Yeah, maybe one too many piñas?"

"I was drinking rumrunners after the first two," she said.

"Oh, mama, are you sure you can drive?"

"Oh, I don't think so. Is my shirt on backwards?" she said as she pulled her shirt out to decide.

"Here he comes," Jack said, laughing at their state. "I love you. What were you thinking getting involved with me way back when?"

"I was pretty much thinking that I loved your energy and your craziness and spontaneity. The way you just seemed to *live* your life out loud. Jack, I miss that—in me. I don't know what's happened and I'm sorry about that."

The boat slid up in front of them and a new driver got out. "My lady," he said and reached out for her hand. "Do be careful. I'll hold the boat steady." He turned to Jack and reached out.

"Fool me once, shame on somebody—fool me twice and buy me a drink," Jack said and climbed into the boat.

"I see you've had a fun day on the island," the young man said. "A little smoke will help to work this out," he said, "and some good food of course."

"I don't think I can climb the ladder," Jenna mouthed over the drone of the small motor.

"Can you get us close to shore so we can jump out?"

143

"If you jump from the boat at the dock the water is only four feet deep. Feel free to swim in."

"Excellent," Jack called out. "Will you put our gear on the dock, please?"

"No problem, mon."

Jenna and Jack stroked heavily to shore and lifted their bodies from the surf. They joined hands and tramped in silence to the front of the dock.

"Flip you for who goes to get the gear," Jack said.

"Go get the gear," she said, pointing at the barely visible bundle on the end of the dock.

Jack faltered forward to get their stuff, then suddenly picked up steam and ran straight to his sandals. He then returned with the backpack and towels. He helped Jenna to her feet and again took her hand as they labored toward the stairwell that led to their room. They slogged up the stairs and started laughing at their predicament as they lumbered to the room.

"I'll be lucky to make it to the bed," Jenna cackled.

"You'll feel better after a flower," he said and then turned back with their key in hand. "Did I say 'flower?' Because I meant shower. You'll feel better after a shower."

Jenna laughed as she stumbled against his back. He opened the door to the room and watched as she flew past him and flopped her upper body onto the bed.

"Ah, honey. This was not the plan," he said. He lifted her legs onto the bed and rolled her onto her back. "Honey? Honey? Lightweight."

Jack went to the telephone and ordered lunch for two. He then turned on the music and lay next to Jenna, spooning her body. *This is perfect. You feel so good*, he thought as he snuggled as close as he could get.

* * * * *

The knocking at the door seemed to be coming from very far away. *What the ... where ... Jamaica ... room service ... it's all coming back to me now.* Jack rose slowly and plodded to the door.

"Hi," he said. "Could you put it on the table outside, please?"

A man walked briskly through the room to the balcony and returned as quickly without making eye contact.

"Thank you," Jack said as the door closed. He turned to join Jenna in the bed and saw the motive for the bellman's quick movement—Jenna lay naked, spread eagle on the bed snoring. "Oh, lovely. I don't think I'll tell her about this one," he said as he lay next to her again and closed his eyes.

✳ ✳ ✳ ✳ ✳

A shower would be very nice right now, she thought as she struggled from the bed. Jenna started toward the bathroom and caught a glimpse of lunch on the balcony. "Oh yeah, that's a definite priority," she said as she sped to the sandwiches piled high with meats and cheese.

The sound of the shower roused Jack from his sleep. He sluggishly made his way to the shower doors, stood listening for a moment and asked, "Can I join you, please?" He leaned against the wall, waiting for her answer.

"Absolutely," she said. "Thanks for lunch."

"Lunch? Oh yeah, hang on, I'll be right back."

Jack returned with a sub in one hand and a Red Stripe in the other. "God, you look good tanned all over," he said, stepping into the shower. "Turn around."

"Jack, you're getting your sandwich wet."

"I think I'll wait to eat."

"Putting me before food, that's a first," she quipped.

Jack slid the glass door open, threw the unfinished sandwich in the garbage receptacle, and reached to place the Red Stripe on the vanity. Facing Jenna, he closed his eyes and began to run his fingers over her body, remembering her exquisiteness as a woman, her uniqueness. He painstakingly traced her from head to toe, bringing her to a heightened state that could only be quenched with the kind of lovemaking that old lovers cherished. He pushed her against the side of the shower and lifted her right leg as he thrust his manhood inside her tight wetness.

"Oh, yes," she growled. She held on to his shoulders as he shifted in and out of her.

He stroked slowly at first allowing a natural rhythm to develop. Their deep breathing blended with their soft moans. The friction escalated until Jack flipped Jenna around and she bent over at the waist. He clutched her hips, pounding into her rhythmically.

Rotating her hips back against him, she grunted with each onrush of his erection.

He reached underneath and flicked at her clit, bringing them both right up to the edge of a powerful release.

"Jack, oh Jack," she moaned. "I'm so there, come with me."

He gritted his teeth, holding back his grunts and groans. He increased his thrusts, grabbing her by the hair and letting out a long guttural sound. Jenna slowly collapsed on the floor of the shower and Jack hung onto the towel bar waiting to recover.

"I love you," Jenna said as she gazed up at Jack. "I never want to take this for granted."

"You're an incredible lover," he said, breathlessly as he allowed the shower to flow over his back.

"You're not so bad yourself," she said as she rose to join

him. She placed his hands on her breasts. "Do these still do it for you, Jack?"

"Baby, you have great breasts. I love that your nipples sit high on the curve. They always seem to be looking for attention."

"Thank you. That helps," she said. "So what do you think about Becky's breasts?"

"They're lovely," he said, mocking Becky's accent. "They're very big and round and she's pretty. Where's all this going? Am I in trouble again?"

"What about Summer's?"

"Petite breasts, flat stomach and a full round butt, that's just excellent. I'd love to cast her bottom for a wall sculpture. Am I in trouble for saying that?"

"No. I've just been thinking that I do find other men attractive, but I never say anything. Would it be okay to say that sort of thing to you?" Jenna asked, turning Jack into the water flow.

"Here's the key—you ask me first—'do you think he's handsome?' and if I say, 'yes,' then drop it. However, if I say 'nah he's nothing.' Then you can go on about him all day long."

"Do you think Marc's handsome?" she asked tentatively.

"I forgot to say that guys that are drop dead gorgeous—don't even bother to ask the question," he said with a smile.

"Listen, I know you find Summer very sexy. Hell, I find Summer sexy. I trust you to be up front about your feelings about her," she said, soaping her breasts and belly.

"What feelings? I like her, but that's it." He waited patiently for the soap.

"I know that, but she's very enticing, isn't she?" Jenna pulled the slider back after she had rinsed.

"I suppose in an artistic sort of way," he said, watching her as she stepped from the tub.

"*Jack?*"

"Okay. She has a way about her. She's fun and she likes me, I think."

"Doesn't that feel better to get it out in the open?"

"Yeah. This is sort of fun. So like you're into Marc and I'm into Summer."

"Let's not get crazy with it, just yet. Let's see what happens."

"Okay, okay. This should be interesting. I mean to be able to point out someone without getting into trouble. I think it'll be a turn on," Jack said from the shower.

"As long as we don't take it too far. No comparisons, for instance," she said emphatically. "Never use this freedom to demean one another."

"Totally agree. I'm excited! Are we expanding our relationship?"

"At this point, the honesty yes, the openness, no," she said. "We'll try this first for a while and see how it works. Then we can see where we go from there. What're you wearing for the sunset cruise?"

"I'm thinking blue jeans," he said. "After the sun goes down on the water it could get chilly."

"Hmmm. Hadn't thought about that. Jeans, white T, and my running shoes?"

Jack opened the shower door and stuck his head out. "You're so hot in that combo," he said, grinning broadly.

"Why, I think your eyes are dancing," she said as she stroked his wet face. "I'll be getting dressed now." She left the bathroom dropping her towel right as she rounded the corner.

"Tease," he called out. "I dare you to come back in here flaunting those goods!"

Jack tilted his head back to rinse his hair, allowing his body to soak up the warmth from the hot shower.

"Uh," he said, jerking suddenly. "You scared me," he said, laughing.

"Let me make it up to you," she whispered as she trailed kisses down his midsection.

＊ ＊ ＊ ＊ ＊

The couples began to stream out of the hotel exits from several different points, making a beeline for the dock. Boarding for the sunset cruise, first come first served, created a race as people glanced back and forth to size up the competition. Jack and Jenna's luxury ocean-view room, located only twenty yards from the dock, gave them a distinct advantage. They arrived first to await the vessel that would sail them into the sunset.

Clouds had gathered on the horizon promising a spectacular display for the eager seafarers. As everyone took their places and relaxed into chatting with one another, a domino effect of awe began at the front of the line and cascaded to the last person. Creating a living postcard, a seventy-foot trimaran in full sail slid effortlessly around the jetty waters and directly to the end of the dock. The crew lowered the majestic sails as they tied off the ship.

"Fantastic," Jack exclaimed. "This is just excellent."

"How far out to sea are we going?" Jenna asked. "I hope I don't get seasick. That would be embarrassing."

"We can take seats up front. You'll be fine," he said, taking his eyes off the sailboat and looking at her.

Jenna leaned around the couples behind them to see Marc and Summer. "There's Summer. See her? Hi!" She waved. "We'll have to save them a spot."

"Tell them to come on up," he said. "There's plenty of room, people won't mind."

"Marc, you guys come up here with us," she called out.

149

They started forward until they reached a man who appeared to take exception, but soon continued toward Jack and Jenna.

"What was that about?" Jenna asked while exchanging hugs.

"He recognized me from the wellness center," Marc said. "Just saying hello." He turned his attention to the snow-white vessel trimmed elegantly in hardwoods and gleaming brass. "This is one fine-looking sailing craft."

"That's totally understating it. This ship is wholly romantic," Summer said and then whispered mischievously to Marc, "I don't suppose we could have sex on that boat?"

"Not tonight, but you never know…"

After everyone boarded, the captain motored away from the dock and called for the crew to set the sails. They billowed out, picking up the speed of the wind. The captain cut the engines, so guests could better hear the yacht slicing through the ocean.

The vacationers found different nooks and crannies to settle into and enjoy the breathtaking sunset. The foursome found a cozy spot toward the front of the ship where Summer and Jenna leaned back against Marc and Jack.

"You seemed relaxed out on the island today," Marc said to Jenna.

"Alcohol induced relaxation. I do think it'll be easier the next time," she said, nodding her head reassuringly. "And the people out there were very nice and respectful, but I don't imagine I'll ever forget I'm naked."

"Well, personally, I'm glad I'll get to see you out there again," Marc said, reaching out to touch her shoulder.

"I thought you're supposed to pretend not to be looking or noticing or whatever," she said, playfully acting offended.

"Oh, there's no pretending with you, I noticed," Marc said, staring straight at Jenna who had turned around to look at him.

"Honey, you're a hottie and I'm sure every man noticed you," Jack said, wrapping his arms around her and pulling her back against him.

"And some women, too," Summer said, smiling at her. "Did you see all those men making fools of themselves over Kokila?" She glanced over at Jenna.

"Now that is a stunning woman," Jenna said. "She looks sexier in clothes than most people naked."

"The funny thing is that I think she's into women, not men," Summer said, winking at Jenna.

"Get out of here. Please, no way," Jack said, vehemently shaking his head no.

"You're usually a good judge of that, Sum, but I think you're off on this one," Marc said, kissing her neck.

"Men choose to ignore the obvious if it doesn't fit their agenda. You ever notice that, Jenna?" she asked.

"Totally," Jenna said.

"Hey, Jack, why don't you ask her on Friday?" Summer challenged. "I bet you'll find she's more into your wife than she's into you."

"You're on. All the men on the island can't be wrong."

"We'll see. So who's going to get us some drinks?" Summer asked, sitting up and shifting around to look at the men.

"Oh, nothing for me! I drank enough today for five people. Water would be nice though," Jenna said, scooching forward to let Jack stand.

"Come on," Marc said, putting his arm around Jack's shoulders. "Let's take care of these ladies."

As soon as the men were out of earshot, Summer whispered, "I think Kokila is into you."

"Get out of here," Jenna said, shaking her head.

"I bet you that's what she tells Jack," Summer said,

raising her eyebrows.

"I think she's nice to everyone and I'm sure that there are rules against employees fraternizing with the guests. I think you just have sex on the brain."

"Speaking of sex, you and Jack seem to be doing much better. Am I right?"

"Yes, actually. We're doing better than we have in a very long time. I feel more alive and freer than I have in years. It's like when we first got together."

"Glad to hear it," Summer said, reaching over to give Jenna a hug. "I'm having a wonderful time and I'm really glad we're here with you guys."

As the sun disappeared and darkness took over, the captain of the vessel surprised the guests by turning on the ship's running lights that trimmed the masts and deck. Everyone applauded. The reggae music and the flow of discourse enhanced the leisurely sail back to the resort.

Once on the dock, the seagoing guests headed for dinner or their rooms. The lights from Le Gourmet bathed the beach below in a warm glow while the thousand tiny pinpoint lights of the Bayside reflected off the water resembling an impressionistic painting.

"Who's up for dinner?" Marc asked.

"Do you guys want to grab a bite or do you need some private time?" Summer asked.

Jack stopped and looked at Jenna. "What would you like to do?"

"Let's all go change into our suits, grab a plate from the Calabash, and go over to the hot tub in the garden. It's completely secluded."

"That sounds like fun. You're on," Summer said. "Meet you in the Calabash in say fifteen minutes, maybe twenty?"

"Okay, see you then."

CHAPTER FOURTEEN

The resort became a fantasy world at night filled with lights and shadows, music, and glamour. Many of the guests dressed up for dinner and promenaded through the lobby and terraces carrying on whispered conversations.

"You're so clever," Summer said to Jenna who approached holding open her backpack.

"We filled this up with wrapped fruits and cheeses to take with us," Jenna said. "If the tub's being used, we can always hangout in the elephant swings."

They strolled through the lobby to the French doors and walked the path that led to an overgrowth of banana trees lining an even narrower stone path. The sign read 'unoccupied.'

"Excellent," Jack said excitedly.

"Last one in owes everyone a drink," Summer said as she scooted past Jack.

Marc followed behind Jenna who carried in the backpack. They made their way down the path that circled around, leading to an area with two benches on either side of a bubbling hot tub. Tiki torches reflected light off the branches of a Formosa cupola, leaving everyone in a shadowy yet romantic playground.

"Where's the light for the tub?" Jenna asked.

"Let's leave it off," Summer replied. "It's more romantic that way."

"I can see fine," Jack said from the tub, looking up at Jenna. "Are you getting naked?" he asked, completely surprised as he watched Jenna remove her suit. "May I join you?"

"Aba-solutely," Jenna said, mocking Jack. She then stepped into the tub. "I've decided to relax and have a good time this fine evening."

"Why didn't I think of that?" Summer said. She stood and stripped down, playfully throwing her wet suit at Marc. "What are you waiting on?"

"I'm stunned. You two women are so intoxicating in this light. I think it might be wise if I take my suit off in the water under the present circumstances," he said, laughing.

"Come over here and let me help you with your 'cir-cum-stances,'" Summer said sexily.

"Can we watch?" Jack asked.

"Or we could do our own show," Jenna whispered, purposely blocking Jack's view of Marc and Summer.

"You know what we should do later? We should get a few drinks and then go in the pool after eleven," Summer said.

"Why after eleven?" Jack asked.

"Because that's when it closes. If we're really quiet we can go skinny dipping," she said mischievously. "I love swimming naked in the deep end."

"Is that a metaphor?" Jack asked. "If so, I think we have something in common."

"The hot tub is so relaxing," Jenna said.

"This was an excellent idea," Marc said, kissing Summer's shoulder.

Summer turned around to face Marc and began to kiss him deeply.

Jack spun Jenna around on his lap so she could watch as the kissing played out in front of her. She closed her eyes. "Jack," she whispered, shaking her head, no, but arching to his touch. He pulled on her nipple. When she opened her eyes again, she saw Marc and Summer leisurely watching them. Jenna quickly moved Jack's hand away.

"Don't stop on our account, please," Summer purred. "That was very sexy."

"Oh … uh … I, uh, never," Jenna stuttered.

"It's okay, Jen," Jack said quietly into her ear. "What was that?"

"It sounds like people walking up the path. Did anyone turn the sign around?" Summer asked, moving off Marc's lap.

"No, not me," Jenna said as she scrambled to find her bathing suit.

"Nor I," Marc said, grabbing his shorts off the edge of the hot tub.

"Nope, I didn't either. But big deal, right?" Jack said.

"I'm ready to get out anyway," Jenna said, reaching for her coverall to pull over her head.

"Oh, *scusi*," the approaching people said, catching the foursome in a state of half dress.

"No problem ... or whatever it is you speak," Jack said. "We're leaving. Ciao."

They quickly threw together their belongings and made their way back up the path away from the small pool.

"We should probably turn the sign around for them," Jack said, flipping the plaque to the other side.

"Now it reads 'unoccupied,'" Jenna said. "They were smarter than we were. Turn it back around."

"That was too funny," Summer said, continuing to chuckle. "Did you see the look on their faces as they walked up? I wish I could've understood what they were saying."

"What do you say we save the food in the backpack for a late night snack and get a bite at the grill?" Jack asked as he reached for Summer's hand and they walked toward the lobby.

"Sounds good to me," Marc said, throwing his arm over Jenna's shoulders.

* * * * *

"Hey guys, it's eleven-fifteen," Marc said in a mock whisper. "Shall we carry out our clandestine mission?"

"We need to be careful," Summer said. "Let's go back by the sports shack and sneak into the bushes by the pool. One at a time we can slink over and slide into the water."

"Slink? What's slink?" Jenna asked, chuckling.

"No laughing or giggling," Summer said.

"By the way, I brought along a little ganja to make the night slowdown. We can light it now or when we're in the bushes," Jack said to the gang.

"None for me," Marc said. "Summer, you may want to pass. You always get the giggles."

"None for me. I've had enough to drink already," Summer said, laughing into her hands.

"Another time then," Jack said.

Jenna and Jack followed Marc and Summer down the meandering sidewalk until they reached an area where the foliage filled in, thick with growth. They scanned the area and one by one disappeared into the shrubs. After making their way to the wall of the recreation center, they darted behind a stack of unused pool lounge chairs where they quickly removed their clothes.

"I'm going over," Summer said.

"I'm right behind you," Jack said.

The two crouched down and quietly slipped into the pool. Summer flipped softly and swam to the bottom.

"Here, take my hand," Marc said to Jenna.

They tiptoed across the pool deck and climbed down the steps into the water. Light from the rec building cast soft shadows across their faces. Jack and Summer continued to play follow-the-leader underwater at the deep end while Marc and Jenna sat on the steps at the shallow end.

156

"The more I spend time with you, the more I want to know you," Marc said casually, catching Jenna off guard and causing her stomach to flutter.

Still watching Jack and Summer, she said, "I've been thinking about you as well and it frightens me." She drew her knees to her chest and wrapped her arms around them.

"Why should it frighten you?"

"I'm afraid of how it'll affect Jack and me, and I do love him," she said, turning her head sideways and laying her cheek on her knees. "It's playing with fire. I know that."

"So what do you want to do?" he said, sliding closer to her so that their hips touched.

"I'm confused."

"Jack doesn't seem confused," he said, flipping his head toward the deep end.

Jenna watched Jack and Summer holding onto the edge talking. She couldn't hear their conversation, but in the dim light, she could see the beads of water glistening in Summer's hair and Jack's bright charismatic smile. They seemed like good friends out playing, talking, enjoying each other's company. She watched Jack touched her face and Summer drop under the water in response. Jack followed and the two disappeared for a few moments only to surface next to one another again. She could hear Jack chuckling.

Marc moved behind Jenna holding her around the waist. "I'm very intrigued by you," he whispered in her ear.

She relaxed back against his chest.

"I want to know all about you. I want to know what excites you," he said, breathing warm, moist air along her neck.

"You're giving me the chills," she said, quivering in his embrace.

He pointed to the other end of the pool. "How do you feel watching Jack caress my Summer?" he asked as he felt the

157

curve of Jenna's waist and moved his hand slowly over her belly.

"It's not so bad. I like the way he lights up around Summer. She inspires energy in him … the way I used to," she said quietly.

"Summer inspires energy everywhere she goes. She's a wonderful woman and I adore her."

"That's confusing. If she is all that, then why do you need anyone else?" she said, making shallow waves in the water with her hand.

"I don't want you to think that we run around with everyone that comes along. It's not like that at all. By the same token, when we meet people we grow to have affection for and there is potential—we'll pursue it together."

"I don't know if I can ever get to that place," Jenna said. "I'm not sure Jack or I are cut out for it. I don't know if the relationship could handle it."

"We haven't found that openness makes things worse than hiding our feelings. It's the same risk for you and Jack. Be right back," he said. Marc slid past Jenna, gliding into the water. He made a short circle and returned, ending up directly in front of her. "New relationships are fun and…" he said, placing his hands on her knees to buoy himself, "if done properly and consciously can bring extraordinary new energy to your present relationship."

Jenna stared at Marc as he placed his head on her knee. She scanned him for signs of deception. She listened carefully to her own heart and mind for panic. In that moment, she felt none. It all seemed so clean and made so much sense to her.

Marc took her hand, inviting her to swim out into the water. He pulled her up to his chest, embracing her and without speaking, asked permission to kiss her again.

"Yes," she said, fully understanding a new adventure had

begun.

Marc eased closer, gently kissing Jenna's lips until all the lust and energy that had accumulated between them ignited and they both hugged each other tighter as he deepened the pressure, fully possessing her mouth and her mind. She could feel his phallus grow against her leg, startling her. As he released her from his grasp, she circled and swam back to the steps, wondering if Jack had witnessed the kiss.

Mounting the steps, she turned to see Jack and Summer engaged in a grinding kiss of their own.

"That was steamy," Summer said, but Jack was scanning the other end of the pool.

"Yeah, there's steam all over the place," he said.

"Jack, look at me," she said, placing her hand on his cheek and guiding his face to hers. "Does Marc kissing Jenna make you uncomfortable?"

"Well ... not irie mon."

Marc swam toward the two of them, pulling up behind Summer. A moment later, Jack swam back to the shallow end. He and Jenna huddled awkwardly as Marc and Summer climbed the ladder and walked to their clothes.

Summer ran over to the steps and said, "I wanted to say good night and make sure you're okay."

"I'm fine," Jenna said.

"No, I mean Jack."

"Yeah. I think so," he said, shrugging. "Thanks for asking." He turned to Jenna. "Are we finished here?"

"Or just beginning," Jenna whispered. She rose to mount the steps out of the pool.

※ ※ ※ ※ ※

Marc and Summer walked around the corner and headed up to their room, three floors above the pool area.

"I really like Jack," Marc said. "He's got this crazy energy about him—not insane, but fun loving. He's a trip to watch when he's being himself."

"That's what I was telling you. I like him for that very reason and Jenna's a beauty, both inside and out."

"I like her—a lot. I'm not sure why I have come to like her so much in such a short period of time," he said, sticking in the keycard. He pushed the door open and felt drawn to the cellphone. He pulled open the drawer. "Nothing. That's a relief. So…" he said, reaching out for Summer's arm as she passed by him, "what would you like to do now, my sexy lady?"

"Let's do something crazy," she said. "Let's go make love in a hammock."

"Have you ever tried having sex in a hammock?"

"Well, no."

"Try to imagine a monkey humping a football," he said.

She started laughing and said, "Great image. So, am I the football, because I'd love to be the quarterback. Call a few plays of my own." She placed her hands between his legs. "Hike!"

"You're so funny," he said, chuckling. "Let's go to the end of the dock."

"That could work. Or back to the Jacuzzi or let's do it on the balcony. We can close the sliders and be our own movie."

"You're on," he said as she started stripping off her clothes. "Wait. Let me do that on the balcony. Let's order a bottle of champagne and a platter of fruit and cheese. God, I love this place."

They went two different directions preparing for the up-and-coming romp—Summer to the telephone and Marc to the balcony with the blanket and pillows from the bed.

He glanced back into the room through the sliding glass door and stopped to appreciate the petite person on the phone who wielded so much personal power. He laid out the blanket and pillows so she could see the moonlit Caribbean Sea. He knew she would enjoy that.

"They're on their way. It was Daniel. He said if we were buying champagne it must be special so they would half-time the delivery. I assume that means they'll be here soon."

They made out for a few minutes until they heard a knock on the door that took them by surprise.

"Who is it?"

There was a long pause and finally, "Room service."

"I thought maybe Jenna or Jack," Summer said.

"Perhaps, hoping?" he asked playfully.

"No way," she said, opening the door. "I've got plans for you, Marcus."

Room service walked through to the balcony and placed the tray on the table.

"How did you … never mind," Marc said, smiling and handing the young man a twenty.

"Now where were we?" Summer said, strolling to the balcony hand in hand with Marc. "Turn out the lights so we can see our reflection."

"Done," he said, as he stepped inside the door and flipped the light switch.

Marc popped the champagne cork, poured two glasses, and undressed Summer slowly. She sat cross-legged on a pillow, patted the other pillow for Marc to take his place, but instead he reached for her hand pulling her up and onto his waist. He kissed her deeply as he shared his mounting desire. She threw her arms around his neck and locked her legs behind his back. As she kissed his neck, he gently caressed her back with his hands. They stopped and stared into each other's eyes and then looked at their reflection in the sliding glass doors.

Summer glanced back at Marc and then dropped

backwards until her hands landed on the ground in a backbend. Shifting her hips slightly, he easily penetrated her and rocked back and forth.

"Oh, this feels so good but I want to see your face," she said as she lifted her upper body, reaching for his shoulders. They embraced in a deep kiss, slowly finding their way onto the blanket. He rolled onto his back and she mounted him, rotating her hips for the full pleasure that comes from knowing your partner's physique and knowing what buttons to push after so many years. She bent forward, kissing his chest and hovering over his nipples.

"Stop," he said. "Not yet. Be still. Don't move a muscle."

She contracted and thrust forward, deliberately bringing on his climax. She leaned down close to his face as he growled through his release and she whispered, "I love you, I love you, I love you."

He opened his eyes. "And I love and adore you," he said. "You are a naughty vixen. I asked you to wait because I wanted us to come together in the end."

"Did you love it?"

"Yes," he said quietly, looking at her face and touching the end of her nose.

"There are other wonderful ways to bring this girl home, you know."

"It would be my pleasure to oblige," he said as he rolled her onto her back.

"No, I'm pretty sure it'll be mine," she said as he kissed her upper thigh.

Marc knew exactly the right spots to hit as he lavished her with soft kisses that caused her hips to involuntarily strain upward. He reveled in her moans and the pulling of his hair as she climbed higher and higher, losing control until she called out her orgasm.

"You, you, you are so magnificent, my sweet love," she

whispered with closed eyes and a soft smile. "Oh my god that was just excellent."

After Summer recovered, she got up and brought over the bottle of champagne. They shared a toast and a kiss. They lay quietly taking in the starry night skies and snuggled before falling asleep in the warm Jamaican breeze.

＊ ＊ ＊ ＊ ＊

Jack shut the door to their room. "I'm so freaked out. This is like some weird dream. Are you sure they're not swingers?"

"No. They aren't swingers. They are … I don't know … open is I guess the best term for it. They seem happier than any couple I've ever met. And I am attracted to them and scared at the same time."

"Scared? Like they're some kind of a cult or something?"

"No," she scowled. "Scared, like it makes so much sense to me. Like, I find it appealing to flirt in front of you," she said, turning to look at him. "I don't know … are we doing the right thing?"

"How do you feel about Marc?"

"How do you feel about Summer?"

"I asked you first," he said.

"So you like her," she said, joining him at the reading table.

He bent over, and placed his chin on his folded arms resting on the table. "Is this an open forum?"

"Yeah, I think it needs to be," she said, pulling her feet into the chair.

He laid his head on his arm and drummed the table with his fingers.

"Please don't do that," she said. "It distracts me when we're talking."

"Sorry, I was thinking," he said, sitting up in his chair. "She's cool. She's sexy. But I don't ever want to jeopardize what we have."

"I agree," she said, flipping the channel display card repeatedly.

"And what about Marc? I know you have to have feelings for him. Don't you?"

"I'm not sure how to answer that." She looked at the plastic channel display as if to read the schedule. "I find him attractive but ... not so attractive that I want to risk our marriage."

"Ground rules?" Jack asked. "I assume I have my limits but I'm not sure where they are."

"Don't you think it would be a good idea to know that ahead of time?"

"Well, let's make some suggestions then."

"Like, ah—as in no hanky-panky when we're not together?" she asked.

"Does that include kissing?" he asked, standing up and pacing back and forth.

"I don't know. I'm thinking kissing can be a free pass as long as we keep it from going any further. However, I think they already have their own rules about this. We should ask them," she said, placing the channel card down on the table.

"As for the kissing, I could live with that," he said, making his way to the French doors. "What else? Are we okay with everything else if we're together?"

"I don't know that yet. I guess we need to keep talking. Right now, I want to spend more time with them and see where it takes us. Let's make a pact that we talk about everything. Okay?" she said, watching him.

"Everything? Like specific details? 'Honey, I got a hard-on when she kissed my neck?' kind of thing?"

"Yes, that's what I meant. All of it. That way the

experience adds to our own intimacy and there are no secrets," she said. She stood up and approached Jack, taking his hands in hers. "Well, what do you think?"

Jack thought about kissing Summer and wanted more of it. He ignored the thought of Jenna kissing Marc. "I think this is fucking out of control and, well, very exciting. Okay, no secrets and we'll share everything—I think it'll work." Jack led Jenna to the bed and removed her pullover dress. "I love you so much. Let me show you," he said, lowering her body onto the bed.

Jack reached for the lotion and began massaging Jenna's shoulders, working his way down her back to her thighs and finally to her feet. "Turnover and I'll work my way back up," he said quietly. He continued to massage her feet to her moans and groans.

"Jack, come kiss me."

"Anything you say," he said as he lowered himself beside her, staring into her eyes.

"I want you to take me anyway you want," she said.

"Anyway? *Any*way I want? Seriously? This is going to be the best time ever."

Jenna closed her eyes and Jack rolled her over onto her stomach.

"If that's your thought, grab the almond oil will you?"

Jack jumped up and quickly retrieved the oil from Jenna's bag. He approached the bed shaking with excitement.

Jenna clutched the sheets in her hands and buried her face in the nook of her arm.

"Slowly … easy. Oh nice. Oh my god, Jack. That feels so incredibly good."

CHAPTER FIFTEEN

The next day, the staff prepared the pool area for the guests interested in learning to scuba dive. The foursome signed on and reported fifteen minutes early to check out the area.

"Good morning," they all said, sharing hugs in a crisscross. Their mutual excitement charged the air.

"What are we going to be doing?" Jenna asked, fingering the scuba equipment, shyly looking up at Marc.

"I've done this before," Marc said, grinning at Jenna. "It's pretty simple stuff. You put on the equipment and get in the pool. They'll teach you how to breathe and clear your mask underwater. The basics so we can go diving out in the reefs."

"Sounds cool," Jack said. "Can't wait."

"I hope I can do this," Summer said quietly. She paced nervously between Marc and the pool.

Marc captured her under his arm. "You'll be fine and if not, we can always go snorkeling instead," he said.

The guests gathered in a group at the end of the pool waiting for instructions.

"Good morning," a muscular young man said. "My name is William."

Summer leaned into Jenna and whispered, "He's looking fine."

"Killer body. And check out those eyes," Jenna said, smiling.

"The most important element in diving is the ability to focus," William said. He smiled at Summer. "It's important not to panic when confronted with a situation that's unfamiliar." He picked up an air tank with one hand lifting it and carrying it over to her. "Slip your arms through these straps," he said to Summer. "The tanks are heavy so it's important to position them correctly. My crew will assist each of you to ensure that you get it right," he said while adjusting Summer's straps. "There, how does that feel?"

"This thing is heavy!"

"You won't even notice it once you're in the water," he said, scanning the group.

The crew helped everyone on with his or her tank, flippers, and weight belt. They then assisted them into the shallow end. The sun had not yet scaled the east side of the hotel leaving the pool in the shade. The initial shock of the cold water caused a round of gasps and mumbling from the soon-to-be scuba divers.

"Place your masks on your face and adjust the strap so that it feels tight but doesn't cut off circulation," William said. "The pressure of the water will help secure the mask and prevent leaks."

"Cute, nice look," Jenna said to Marc.

"Yeah, the frogman face is big right now," he said, toying with his mouthpiece.

"Now I want you to drop into the water and look at me," William said. "When I come to you, I'll show you a thumbs up. If you're fine, you give a thumbs up—if not, a thumb sideways. If you are in trouble, a thumbs down. Does everyone understand? Let me hear you say, 'Ya mon.'"

"Ya mon," the group replied in unison.

"Irie then. Put your regulators in your mouth and breathe slowly as you go under."

They randomly submerged. William waltzed along the bottom of the pool from right to left, stopping at each person with his thumb up. After having checked all participants, he pointed to the surface and pushed off the bottom.

William removed his mask and mouthpiece. "Any problems anyone?" he asked.

"My tank keeps pulling me backwards," Jack said.

"Come over here." William adjusted his straps. "That should do it. Okay, we'll drop into the water and swim in a big circle in the deep end. Watch for others and try to swim at different levels like a school of banana fish. Okay? Everybody ready?" He tapped the first person on the shoulder who then immediately dropped and rolled forward.

"This tank still doesn't feel right," Jack said to Marc.

"It'll be weightless in the water," Marc said.

Summer stepped up for her turn and dropped below the surface followed by Jenna and then Jack. Marc eased forward into the water, almost running into Jack's flippers. He held up a moment to allow him to kick forward but Jack instead moved to a vertical position, tumbling backwards. Marc watched as Jack appeared to panic, trying to right his position, blowing huge amounts of air bubbles, and shaking his mask. Instead of swimming to the surface, he became completely disoriented and headed straight for the deep end, striking his head on the bottom of the pool just as Marc reached him. Others in the group began to take notice of the situation unfolding. Marc attempted to raise Jack, joined by two crewmembers who lifted him toward the surface.

Jenna emerged panic stricken and pulled out the regulator. She screamed, "Jack's in trouble!" Her voice echoed through the area drawing a crowd from all corners of the pool as well as the Calabash.

William immediately dropped below and swam toward the mass of bodies heading for the ladder. When they reach the side of the pool, two employees reached in and pulled Jack's limp body out onto the deck. They stripped him of his gear, laying him on his back.

"Jesus, Jack, what happened?" Jenna cried, trying to get

close to her husband.

"Hang on one second … give me room to work here. He's going to be alright." William knelt and began to administer mouth to mouth. Within a few moments Jack blew out water and coughed. The spectators clapped and several others audibly sighed out in relief. Another staff member freed Jenna from her tank and weight belt while Marc removed his own and then assisted Summer.

"You okay?" William asked Jack.

"I don't remember much," he said, rubbing his head. He withdrew his hand to find blood. "Oh that's just fucking excellent," he said. "How bad is it?"

William inspected the cut and said, "It's too small for stitches, but you'll probably have a booming headache for an hour or two."

"Let me take a quick look at that," Marc said. "Yeah, it's not too bad at all. The bump will feel huge for a while though."

"You scared me to death down there," Jenna said, sitting on her knees next to him.

"Can you stand?" William asked.

"Yeah, I think so," he said as he slowly sat up. "Whoa, this is going to hurt."

"Take your time." Jenna helped him to his feet and pulled his arm over her shoulder.

"You should at least go to the infirmary and let the doctor take a look," William said.

"Good advice," said Marc. "I'll walk with you."

Summer reached out and touched Jack's shoulder. "Let me know if I can do anything for you," she said. She leaned over to kiss his cheek and handed him his towel.

Everyone began to disperse. The rest of the scuba group returned to the pool to continue their training. As they walked past, several people patted Jack on the back and wished him good luck.

"Jenna, why don't you stay here with Summer? Really, I'm fine. Marc can walk over to the infirmary with me. You guys go to the Calabash and we'll meet you there in a bit."

"Are you sure?"

"Yes, really. I'm going to be fine."

Marc and Jack trekked through the lobby.

"This is a little embarrassing," Jack said.

"Why? It could've happened to anyone. What do you think caused it?"

"I don't know. I felt like something was pulling me backwards."

"Sounds to me like there was too much weight on your weight belt," Marc said.

"Yeah, maybe."

They passed the front desk in the lobby with its tiled floors and stepped onto the carpeted hallway leading to the familiar infirmary room. As Jack turned into the doorway, he heard the doctor's voice.

"Jack, what have you done to yourself now?" the doctor asked in a fatherly fashion.

"Attempted drowning," Jack said, chuckling. He turned to expose the cut on the back of his head.

"But I see you failed," he said. "You won't be trying that again, I assume."

"No. I think once is enough for me. I can tell you this much, I'll be taking showers from now on."

"Ah, let me see." He pushed Jack's black hair to one side and said, "You won't need a stitch, but I'm going to give you an antiseptic wash to use. Other than that, I can see you're none the worse for wear. You'll be fine. How's the foot?"

"Doing great," Jack said and then looked back at the doctor. "I guess my life was getting too quiet, not enough drama." He chuckled.

"Well if you get bored again, I'll be here to mend the broken parts."

❋ ❋ ❋ ❋ ❋

Summer and Jenna walked hand in hand to the Calabash to wait for the men to return.

"Let's sit over here. The breeze feels so nice," Summer said.

"That's fine. I don't care."

"Didn't that scare the hell out of you?" Summer asked, scooting her chair around the table to be closer to Jenna.

"Oh my god, you have no idea. He pisses me off to no end sometimes and I want to kill him, but that's my job, not his." She placed her face in her hands. "I panicked when I saw him upside down on the bottom of the pool. At that moment, I realized I could never live without him. Then when I was trying to pull myself out of the water with the weight belt and tank—Oh my god—I never want to be that scared again."

"I would be comatose for the rest of my life if something happened to Marc," Summer said. She looked back to Jenna. "This kind of situation helps you put things into perspective and get your priorities in order, doesn't it?"

"Yeah, I'm a little freaked out still."

"Here they come," Summer called out and jumped up to meet Marc. She went straight to him and threw her arms around his neck just as Jenna rushed up to Jack.

"What'd the doc say?" Jenna asked, putting her arms around his waist.

"He said there may be a slight concussion and that it'll be very important for you to nurse me for the next twenty-four hours. Hey, not my idea," he said, feigning innocence. "I tried to tell him, but … you know how doctors can be. Don't kill the messenger."

"What did he really say?"

"I'm fine," he said with a chuckle.

"You'd better be. You scared—" she said.

"Sorry about that, baby. Do you still love me?" he asked, gazing down into her eyes.

"Never stopped," she said.

Jack pulled her to him and they shared a kiss that brought a big smile to her face.

"Nice," Jenna said. "Let's have some breakfast, shall we?"

"I'd like to have you for breakfast," he whispered.

"How about an afternoon delight instead?"

"Name the place."

They joined Summer and Marc at the table and ordered their beverages. The four joined the line and shuffled through the long buffet.

"Jack, jerk again?" Jenna asked.

"Hey, when am I going to get authentic, honest to goodness jerk chicken again?" he said as he piled a leg and thigh on his plate with a huge helping of island grits swimming in butter.

"We should make a commitment to get together once in a while back in the states for an island feast," Summer said enthusiastically.

"That would be really cool," Jack said.

"That sounds like a lot of fun. There's nothing like a good feast to arouse the baser nature in a human being," Marc said with a wink.

"I could get into that," Jenna added.

"It's a date then?" Marc asked.

"A date? Maybe you and Jenna. Frankly, and no offense intended, but you, sir, are definitely not my type," Jack said, laughing.

"I'll ask Jack out," Summer said.

"Then I'll ask Jenna," Marc said. "If that's okay with you, Jenna?"

"Are we talking about here or when we get back to the states?"

"Marc, why don't you take her to the French restaurant tonight? Jack and I can find something to do to entertain ourselves. I wouldn't mind going back to the Bayside or trying the Verandah."

"Jack?" Jenna asked.

"Fine by me," Jack said, pulling out her chair and looking across the table at Summer.

"Then it's a date?" Marc asked Jenna.

"It's a date," she said. She peered up into Marc's eyes and felt her heart race and her face flush. She placed her right hand on her upper chest around her neck.

"Look at you, all blushing and everything," Jack razzed.

"Why are you saying that?" Jenna asked.

"Look where your hand is," Jack said with a teasing smile.

"Oh … uh," she said, quickly removing her hand.

"That's her nervous indicator," he said. "I can always tell when she's nervous or excited … that's the first place her hand goes."

"Thanks for giving away my secrets," she said sarcastically.

"I think it's cute," Summer said. "It fits you—sort of shy, but strong at the same time."

Jack smiled and placed his hand on the back of Jenna's neck. "I totally agree," he said.

"Jack, you're embarrassing me," she said. She placed her hands in her lap and looked away from the table.

"I don't mean to embarrass you," he said, looking at her warmly. "It reminds me of all the reasons I fell in love with you in the first place. And she's a great date," Jack said, glancing over at Marc.

"Cheers," Cliff said as he approached the foursome.

He struck up a conversation with the men and Becky squatted between the chairs of the women.

"If you don't mind saying, what're the plans for today?" Becky asked.

"We were going scuba diving but Jack had a little accident in the pool," Jenna said quietly.

"I'm sorry, an accident? Perhaps you could clarify what you mean?"

"Oh, no," Jenna said, laughing. "Not that kind of accident. He bumped his head on the bottom of the pool, cutting it."

"Oh, I see," Becky said, her hand covering her mouth. "Well now, that makes much more sense than what I was thinking,"

"What are you guys up to?" Jenna asked.

"We're taking the plantation horseback ride," Becky said excitedly. "I can't wait. It should be lovely."

"I think we're going snorkeling," Summer said.

"I'm not so sure Jack's going to want to after this morning," Jenna said and reached across the table for Jack's hand. "Honey, would you be up for snorkeling?"

"Absolutely. You guys can tie a tethered buoy around my waist to keep me from swimming to the bottom of the ocean," he said, laughing.

"What's this?" Cliff asked.

"Thanks," Jack said to the waiter when he refilled his coffee. He raised his hand to Cliff and shook his head no. "Long story."

"Okay then, we'll be off. Never been on a horse and thought it was time to give it a go," Cliff said, patting Jack on the back. "Feeling a bit John Wayne today, I suppose. Wella guess I'ma gonna go horse ridin' taday."

"John Wayne never sounded so awful!" Becky exclaimed.

"Tried to get Becky to let me practice riding last night—she'd have nothin' to do with it," Cliff said.

Becky slapped Cliff on his rump and said, "Giddy up then." She looked back at the group and everyone laughed.

"Shall we?" Summer asked.

"We're going to run upstairs for a minute and then we'll meet you guys down at the dock," Marc said.

"Cool." Jack took Jenna's hand and said, "See you in a few."

✳ ✳ ✳ ✳ ✳

The group gathered on the dock to board the boat that would take them offshore to a small reef suitable for snorkeling. The thirty-foot vessel converted to a glass bottom boat allowed guests to observe the reef from the comfort of their seats if they chose. Jack found out that if you go snorkeling, you can't drink Red Stripe until the ride back to the dock. He felt sure that actually being in the water held no advantage over drinking Red Stripe and watching the reef from inside the boat. The others disagreed and dove in. Jenna managed to swim underneath the boat at about ten feet below the surface, surprised Jack by pulling her bathing suit bottoms about half way down to moon him, and then casually swam away.

"That's my wife," Jack said proudly. "Possibly the mother of my children someday," he said, pointing toward her as she swam away.

"She seems very nice," said an older British woman. Her husband bent over the glass to get a better look at her lithe retreating form.

After exploring the colorful reefs, Jenna and Summer sat on a cushioned bench at the back of the boat, watching the wake spread over the water.

As the boat skimmed the ocean back to Couples, over the drone of the engine, Jenna asked, "While I've got you alone for a moment, can I ask you a question?" She pulled her right leg onto the bench and shifted her body to face Summer.

"Of course, you can ask me anything," she said.

"Jack and I were discussing ground rules for flirting and stuff. And we were wondering what your rules are."

"We have situation specific rules," she said.

Jenna scrunched her eyebrows. "Okay, not entirely sure what that means."

"For flirting that may include kissing," she explained, "Marc must be present, but if we're developing a long term friendship like ours, different rules apply. Like you and Marc going out to dinner tonight. That wouldn't happen with just anyone. With you guys we see long-term potential."

"Honestly, I'm taking this one day at a time. I can't think that far ahead," Jenna said as she steadied her body against the sudden turn of the boat. "So what I'm asking you—are there rules we need to know about? Like kissing or holding hands?"

"Hey guys, why are you all the way back here?" Jack asked as he and Marc made their way past several hotel guests.

"Jenna was asking me about ground rules," Summer said, patting the seat next to her for Marc to sit down.

"Yeah, Jenna and I talked about that last night," Jack said. He sat down next to Jenna.

"They're pretty basic," Marc said, wrapping his arm around Summer. "In the beginning, all activity of a sexual nature other than kissing only happens when all of us are present. If an issue arises, we deal with it as quickly as possible and no conversation is private if it concerns the four of us. Does that make sense?"

"That's pretty much what we came up with although we didn't discuss what happens if there's conflict," Jenna said, leaning back against Jack. "So holding hands and kissing is okay when we're apart? Do we care what the people here will think? I mean are we going to play platonic in public?"

"That's a good question," Jack said, running his fingers through his hair.

"I guess that's up to you guys," Marc said, looking at Summer and then back to Jack and Jenna.

"Yeah, I'm cool either way," Summer said.

"Jack? How do you feel about it?" Jenna asked.

"You know me, I don't care what people think of me. So, it's up to you, Jen," Jack said. He reached his arms around her waist and placed his hands on her stomach.

The wind caught Jenna's hair, throwing out the pin that held it in place, allowing it to fly free. She could see Tower Island in the distance dwarfed by the resort hotel that reflected radiant white. As they passed the island, Jenna waved 'hi' to a young woman sitting by herself on the lounge she had used only yesterday. It already felt like a lifetime ago.

"Well, if we're going to do it, we might as well go all the way," Jenna said, laughing anxiously about her quickly shifting life.

CHAPTER SIXTEEN

"That was fantastic. Thanks for sharing the snorkeling with me," Summer said as they walked into their room.

"Back atcha," Marc said, touching the end of her nose.

They heard a buzzing sound, but couldn't place the exact location. Each took separate paths in an effort to pinpoint the origin of the mystery. Summer slunk down next to the door of the room and listened. The hum ceased. Just as they were about to rejoin, it started again.

"It's the damn cellphone," Marc said. He stepped over to open the drawer in the end table. He picked up the phone and flipped it open. The pad indicated ten missed calls from Rich. Marc hit call return and sat back on the dresser.

Summer left the room for a shower.

"Wellness center. How may I direct your call?"

"Carol, Marc. Is Rich around?"

"Yes, sir. Hang on one second."

"Marc, I've been trying to reach you for the last few hours, man. Where the hell were you?"

"Rich, I left my phone in the room. I'm sorry. Now calm down and tell me what's going on."

"You remember Dr. Hofstetter?"

"Yes, I remember him," he said cautiously.

"He had a heart attack and went down like a ton of bricks on a treadmill yesterday. He's dead, Marc, and because he never clamped the power key to his clothes, the machine kept grinding away at his arm."

"God, that's an ugly image. Did you contact our attorneys?"

"Of course I did, but I wanted you to know what's going on."

"Sorry you had to deal with this without me. Listen, send a huge bouquet of flowers to his family on our behalf. There's not really a whole lot that you and I can do. Stay in touch as you need to and let the attorneys do the worrying, not you. Okay?"

"Okay. I wanted you to be up-to-date."

"You handled it just the way I would have. Make sure to send those flowers ASAP."

"Will do. See you in a few days."

"Okay. Bye."

Marc replaced the cellphone and crossed his arms thinking about the possible repercussions of the accident. He then lay on the bed waiting for Summer to finish her shower.

As she emerged from the bathroom, he asked, "Would you still love me if we were broke?"

"I'd still love you, but that doesn't mean I'd stay with you," she teased. She dropped her towel to the floor and held out her arms.

"I need to tell you something."

She picked up the towel and sat on the edge of the bed.

"One of our clients died on the treadmill, and to make it worse, the son-of-a-bitch always refused to wear the power key attached to his clothes so when he went down the machine ground against his arm until he was found."

"Oh my God. Who was it?"

"Hofstetter."

"No shit. What's going to happen?"

"I don't know. Rich contacted the attorneys. Now we'll have to wait and see," he said, reaching over and pulling her closer to him. "I feel bad for his family, but I don't know how they're going to react. I had Rich send them a huge bouquet of flowers. We should be okay because he signed a

179

membership agreement stating that he'd adhere to the gym rules, including wearing that damn power key."

"You know I was only kidding about leaving you. I had no idea you were dealing with this when I said it. I'm sorry."

"Come here love, I knew you were just joking."

✱ ✱ ✱ ✱ ✱

"I can't believe you mooned me and everyone else on the boat," Jack said proudly, soaping Jenna's back. "It's great to see you so alive again."

"I feel more myself than I have in a long while," she said.

"I hope this change in you isn't Marc," he said, lathering his chest and stomach.

"Jack, don't be silly. It's us," she said. She stroked his face to his chin, lifting it so that his eyes stood parallel to hers. "We're talking again ... making love again ... sharing adventures again. I'm alive again because you and I are reconnecting."

"Thank you for that." He pulled her to him and hugged her. "I needed to hear it. I feel like over the last couple of days a great weight has been lifted from us."

"I know exactly what you mean," she said. "I haven't felt this light in ages. But I'm kind of nervous about tonight."

"I'm sure," he said. "I actually feel a little weird about spending time with someone without you. That's alien, not natural anymore. Did I ever date before you? I don't even remember."

"Oh, it'll come back to you. You do fine dating as I recall," she said. She opened the bathroom door to let the cool air in and the steam out. "All those little chicks, the cool artist, the bad boy. Even now, women are still attracted to the romance in you."

"I hope you understand what I'm about to say, because

I'm not exactly sure I do, but this is like … making me want you more than ever."

"I hear that," she said as she walked from the bathroom. "I wonder if they feel this much anxiety?"

"Nah. They probably do this all the time."

"If we're to believe them, this is rare," she called out from the bedroom.

"Yeah? Really? I'm going to take a deep breath and let this take its course," he said as he stuck his head around the doorjamb. "Remember, you're the fire of my loins, the inspiration for my art."

"Come over here and kiss me like you mean it."

＊ ＊ ＊ ＊ ＊

"Hmm … I really needed that," Jenna said upon waking. She stretched her arms above her head and then curled up against Jack.

"Yeah, napping's good," he said. He wrapped his arms around her, spooning her closely. "What time is it?"

"I'm guessing around 4:00 or so. I'd get up and check," she said, nuzzling up against him, "but I'm way too comfortable."

"Yeah, me too. Do you think they're up yet?" He smoothed her hair away from her face.

"Want to call? You're closer to the phone."

"How about inviting them to play a game or two of strip pool?" he said, pulling Jenna toward him for a kiss. He grasped her gently by the chin, lowering his lips to hers. He lingered for a moment as their breath mixed a potent aphrodisiac. He broke just as gently and gazed into her eyes.

"Hmm … now, what were you saying?" she said, playing with his hair. "You've always been an excellent kisser."

"Thank you, Mrs. Harper, for that compliment and may I

181

say you have excellent lips for kissing."

"How does Summer kiss, by the way?"

"Why don't you try it out for yourself?" he said, laughing.

She playfully pushed him away. "One thing at a time, you brute!" she said. "Really now, how does she kiss?"

"This isn't a comparison question is it?" he asked seriously.

She sat up in the bed cross-legged. "Not at all. Just wondering what you think."

He ran his finger along her thigh. "She's a good kisser and Marc?"

"Did you see us kiss?"

"No actually, I didn't," he said. "I saw you break apart. I don't know how I would take it."

"I couldn't see you that well across the pool either. I'm not sure I'd like to see it up close. But anyway, to answer your question, I'd like to kiss him again tonight because both times I was too nervous, so I really couldn't tell," she said and laughed.

"Well, you're going to kiss him again tonight, right?" Jack said with a furrowed brow.

"You know I'm pretty shy when it comes to that sort of thing, I'll have to work up my nerve." She scooted to the edge of the bed. "So should I call or you?"

"Go ahead. I need to pee," he said.

Jenna sauntered over toward the telephone, stopping for a moment to look at her reflection in the mirror. She smiled. *Sun does a body good!* She pulled her hair out of the bun and piled it on top of her head, trying to imagine the best way to impress Marc. She picked up the telephone and dialed their room.

"Hello," Marc said.

"Hi. Am I interrupting anything?" she asked playfully.

"No. I wouldn't have answered the phone, believe me," he said, laughing lightly.

"Well, on behalf of the Harpers, I've been appointed to challenge you guys to a game of strip pool in the rec area commencing at five o'clock sharp and no padding allowed. What say ye?"

"You're on. And if I were you, I would pad a bit," Marc said, chuckling. "I made my way through college playing pool."

"Ha. I'm planning to wear a bikini," Jenna said.

"Fantastic."

She replaced the telephone and strolled to the bathroom door. "Honey, we've got a hot date at the pool room. Shall we go down early and get a drink?"

"Sounds like a plan to me," Jack said as he emerged from the bathroom. "Let me grab a quick smoke and get dressed, but then I'm good to go."

"Marc said we better pad up because he was a pool shark in college. I wonder if this necklace will count," she said, walking to the drawers and retrieving a short pleated skirt and a fitted spaghetti strap top. She took out a pair of thong underwear holding them up on her finger as she passed Jack.

"Going daring, I see," he said, passing Jenna on his way to the balcony.

"Yes, do you mind?" she asked. She slipped on her shirt and adjusted her necklace.

"Not if we win," he said, laughing. "No, seriously, I don't mind, just make sure you flash me at least once." He walked back to kiss her. "I like your tanned body. You look so good."

Jenna went over to the closet and looked at herself in the full-length mirror that hung on the back of the door. "I think it'll do," she said, flipping up the back of her skirt as she moved away.

Jenna and Jack casually strolled hand in hand over to the Terrace Bar. The lull of the afternoon created a relaxed atmosphere in contrast with the usual hustle and bustle.

"Can I get a piña colada and a rumrunner please," Jenna asked the bartender as he approached.

"Daniel, what's up? How's it going?" Jack said, reaching over to shake his hand. "Can I get two Red Stripes?"

"Hey mon, how are you doing this evening? Ready to do a little partying?" Daniel said with a big smile as he shook Jack's hand.

"Irie, mon. Going to play some strip pool," Jack said.

"Is this your lady? I'd be wanting to go watch this game," he said. He placed their drinks down in front of them. "Ya mon," he said, exchanging a high five with Jack.

"Thank you," Jenna said, smiling from ear to ear. "For the drinks as well."

They walked across the pool deck to the recreation room where Marc and Summer had secured a table for their games.

"Hey there," Jenna said, leaning forward to give Summer a kiss. "Got you a rumrunner."

"Thank you," Summer said. "Don't you look cute in your little skirt."

"Thank you. You must feel safe, only wearing a sarong." She peered over Summer's shoulder to see Marc in brown shorts and a beige t-shirt. She watched him inspect a cue stick and place it on the table rolling it lightly back and forth to check for straightness. Marc patted Jack on the back as he passed, making his way toward Jenna.

"Where's your bikini?" Marc asked, bending down to give her a hug.

"I see you didn't even bother to wear shoes," Jenna said.

He pointed to the black skirt slung low on her hips. "Hope you're wearing something sexy under that."

"You won't see it," she said, putting her hand on his

chest.

"I'm ready to get this started," he said with a big grin.

"Me too," she said and then sashayed over to Jack.

"Okay. Are we playing by game or by ball?" Summer asked, chalking the end of her cue.

"Oh shit," Jenna whispered to Jack.

"Get ready to get naked," Jack said. He picked a cue stick from the rack on the wall for Jenna.

"I'll use yours. Is that okay?"

"Sure, no problem. Do you feel the melt coming on?" Jack asked.

"What?" she asked.

"We've got a snowball's chance in hell of winning this game," he said, watching Summer and Marc move around the table.

"Should we lag for the break?" Marc asked.

"Is that some kind of British term?" Jenna asked.

"I hope you padded," Marc answered with a devilish smile.

"We'll break," Jack said and then whispered to Jenna, "Don't let them see you sweat." He stroked using left English, sending the balls careening off the rails in all directions, sinking both a high ball and a low ball. "We'll take low balls," he said.

"Which ones are those and why are we taking them?" Jenna asked.

"They're the solid ones and it's because there's more of them closer to the pockets than the others," Jack said with a laugh. "Good thing this is for fun."

Jack took the next shot and missed. Summer looked over the table, waved her stick, and called, "Nine ball corner pocket." A cracking sounded and the nine ball disappeared. Repeatedly she called pocket after pocket as she banked shots and combined balls for the win. "Thanks, that was fun," she said, standing the cue stick beside her.

"That was amazing!" Jack said. "I'm thoroughly impressed."

Marc and Jenna stood against the wall, waiting their turn.

"Okay. What's going?" Marc asked Jenna.

"Jack's pants."

"Hey, not so fast. I'm good for the island but—"

"Jenna, let's see some skin," Summer called out.

Jenna promptly turned around, bent over, and flipped her skirt over her waist.

"Fantastic," Marc called out. "I give. You win. Let's switch partners for the next game. It'll make it more interesting."

"Good idea. I take Summer," Jack said, walking over next to her.

"I hope you're as good as she is, otherwise we don't have a shot in hell," Jenna said to Marc.

"Not to worry my love," he said and then whispered, "I taught her everything she knows."

"I heard that! Ever hear of the pupil exceeding the teacher? We're a classic case," Summer said, chalking her stick.

"Enough talking, spitfire. Let's see what you've got," Marc said as he gathered the balls into the rack.

"Let's give them a fighting chance and let them break," Summer said, leaning into Jack and laughing.

"I think someone needs to be taught a lesson. What do you think, Jenna?" Marc said. He lined up the balls and removed the rack.

"Most definitely. That wrap needs to come off, don't you think?" she said, tossing her head in Summer's direction.

"Totally agree," he said, positioning his cue stick to break. The crack sent the balls scattering chaotically in every direction. "We're solids. I think we should trade off each shot to make the game more interesting. What do you say?"

Summer looked at Jack who nodded. "Works for us," she said. She leaned her cue against the wall and stood next to Jack. "That makes it Jenna's turn to sink a ball."

Marc loomed in close, right up against Jenna to show her the best possible shot. "Okay, you want to hit it a little left of center but not too hard," he said close to her ear.

"Yeah ... ah thanks. Speaking of *not to hard* ... or hard, could you back up a bit please?" Jenna felt her blush rush from her chest to her cheeks.

"Hey, hey, hey. Easy there buddy," Jack said, laughing uncomfortably.

Summer moved in close to Jack and whispered, "Maybe I can help *you* with your next shot." She squeezed his ass and then turned her focus back to the pool table.

Jenna bent over and took a nice easy stroke sending the cue ball toward the corner pocket. *Go in, go in, go in*, she thought. *YES!* "Woohoo," she yelled, jumping up and down. "Your turn," she said to Marc, handing him back his stick.

Marc hit a side shot into the far pocket with ease.

"I can't imagine what it's like when the two of you play each other for real," Jenna said, taking the stick from Marc. He pointed to the four ball sitting next to the side pocket. "Thanks," she said, peering up over her shoulder at him.

He moved around the table. "Focus your attention on this one spot."

The cue ball slid softly along the felt striking the four ball, barely missing the pocket.

"Excellent try," he said as she handed him back the stick. They both walked over to the bench and sat down.

Jack went first and easily sank his first attempt. Summer followed by hitting a shot behind her back.

"Does she ever miss?" Jenna asked Marc.

"Not often," he said, watching Summer move around the

table.

"Jack, go for this one," Summer said. "It should be a fairly easy shot." She then grabbed ahold of his butt and said, "I'm just holding you steady."

Jack laughed and missed the pocket, giving Marc and Jenna the chance to win the game.

They picked off the four remaining solids with ease, leaving Jenna with the last shot.

"Eight ball in the left corner pocket," she said. Carefully following Marc's instructions, she zeroed in hitting the cue ball dead center. The eight ball rolled a straight line to the corner pocket, dropping solidly into the hole. "Off with it, missy," Jenna said triumphantly to Summer.

Summer held the sides of her wrap. "You got to flash," she said.

"Fine by me," Jack said, enthusiastically.

Summer took her time, pulling open the sarong slowly, tauntingly exposing her nakedness.

"Nice," Jack said, applauding.

Marc and Jenna laughed at Summer's antics.

"What time is it?" Jenna asked.

"It's a little after six. Is it time to go up?" Summer said.

"Let's play one more game and then call it," Marc said.

Marc and Jack paired up against the women and lost on an easy shot missed by Jack. Marc kissed Jenna lightly on the lips. "I'll see you at 7:45," he said.

"Jack, come get me when you're ready. Let's get something to eat and go dancing," Summer said. She embraced him in warm hug.

"We'll figure out something," Jack said, watching her saunter over to Marc. "Are you ready?" he said to Jenna.

"Yeah, I think so," she said, glancing back at Marc as they strolled from the recreation center.

CHAPTER SEVENTEEN

"I really would prefer casual," Marc said, looking in the full-length mirror in their hotel room.

"This is casual," Summer said. "Try this together. It could be quite cool in the restaurant." She handed him a white pullover that showed off his upper arms and a black denim waist-jacket that accentuated the shape of his upper back. "Wear your black drawstring pants and your sandals."

Marc stood in front of the mirror with the palms of his hands forward. "I'll never quite get the reasoning behind outfits."

"You're not supposed to. Trust me. You look great!"

"Does my hair look okay? It's still a little wet from the shower."

"You seem a little nervous. Don't worry, I'd date you myself," she said. "Have a good time. Be nice and come home on time," she kidded.

They embraced, rocking back and forth in their own thoughts. Marc bent down and kissed her.

"Thank you for us," he said. "Have a wonderful time tonight and I'll see you later."

Before Marc had a chance to leave, there was a light knock on the door.

"Hey, Jack, are you ready for this?" Marc asked as he opened the door.

"I'm here but I'm not absolutely positive I'm ready for it," Jack said, stepping through the door. "Hi, Summer. This feels a little weird, doesn't it?"

"Yeah, a little maybe, but you guys will get used to it. Everybody's clued in on what's going on, so why not just enjoy yourself?" Summer said as she pushed Marc out the door.

"See you in a while," he said. He then blocked Summer from closing the door. "Is she ready?"

"Should be close. You guys have a good time," Jack said reflexively while starring at Summer.

She closed the door after giving Marc a parting kiss. She turned to Jack and said, "You look good." She sashayed up close to him. "What shall we do tonight?"

"I brought a bit of a joint. Thought we could smoke, maybe dance a little or if you want to and it would be my honor, I'd love to do a clay rough out of you."

"Do we have enough time?"

"Sure. It won't be totally finished, but getting the basics is no problem."

"Let's eat quickly then and get started." She untied her robe as she strutted to the bathroom and partially closed the door. "This is so cool. Will it look like me?" she called to him.

"It'll be you, only miniature. It'll end up about sixteen inches tall."

Summer pulled on a black turtleneck, a pair of blue jeans, and slipped into a pair of sandals. As she reentered the room, she held out her hand to Jack and they left.

✳ ✳ ✳ ✳ ✳

Marc stopped on the terrace to look out over the Caribbean Sea at the light show on the horizon. The lightning danced across the sky, snaking its way through the monstrous thunderclouds offshore. The crescent moon shone brightly against the clear skies over the resort. Marc greeted several familiar faces on his way to Jenna's room. He knocked and impatiently waited with the eager anticipation of a young boy

190

on his first date.

The door opened slowly and there before him stood Jenna.

"You look terrific … so radiant. May I come in?" he asked, moving forward without taking his eyes off her.

"I'm very nervous," she said. "Can I get you anything?"

"Your dress is fantastic."

"Thank you. I made it myself," she said, shaking her head as the words came out of her mouth. "Kidding around. I'm sorry." *God, relax and shut up*, she thought as she drew a deep breath.

"Well, shall we stroll over to Le Gourmet?"

"Before we leave could I ask you for a small favor?" she said, casting her eyes to the floor.

"Sure," he said, lifting her chin so he could see her face.

"May I … would you kiss me, because last night I was so … I don't exactly remember what it felt like."

"It felt like this." He wrapped his arms around her waist and kissed her fully on the lips. She melted into his embrace, relaxing into the new sensations he stirred in her. It had been so long since she felt so open, so stimulated, so alive.

She kissed him back with equal passion, savoring the uniqueness of his kiss. He escorted her on a journey of abandon, dancing his tongue around hers and she followed his lead.

"Wow … mum … nice. Very nice," she said, placing her hands on his chest to steady herself. "Thank you. I think I'm ready now."

"Then we're off," he said. He took her hand in his and led her to the door.

"Yes," she said, but thought, *I could stay here and kiss you all night.*

The line for Le Gourmet threaded into the far side of the

lobby. They fell in line, still holding hands, next to a large clay pot embellished with African figures dancing on the side. Several planters held small decorative palm trees throughout the lobby. The couples moved slowly, but steadily forward, filling the main dining area. Jenna elegantly stood, holding a brocaded clutch purse matching the slinky black dress that draped softly over her body. She adorned her slender neck with a silver necklace made of repeating hoops and her lobes with earrings to match. She decided to wear her hair up in a twist allowing wisps to frame her high cheekbones.

Jenna let go of Marc's hand, placed it on his shoulder as she raised herself on tiptoe to whisper in his ear. "I feel like we're doing something illicit, something my parents would've grounded me for," she said, laughing as her heels touched the ground and she blushed at her own silliness.

"For me, it feels right, but I've believed for a long time that I'm capable of loving more than one person," he said, resting his hand on the small of her back.

"On an intellectual level I understand that," she said. "And frankly, I've never met a happier couple than you and Summer. But this is all a little foreign to me. Exciting, stimulating, but also dangerous."

The couple behind them touched Jenna's shoulder letting her know they were next in line. They followed the maître d' to a table for two on the upper level of the restaurant near the grand piano.

"This is amazing," Jenna said, scanning the elaborate chandeliers, the linens, the fine china and crystal glasses on the tables. The tuxedoed waiter removed Jenna's napkin from her plate and placed it on her lap. He handed her the menu as the busboy filled her water glass.

"Can I order you something from the bar?" asked the waiter.

"Would you like to share a bottle of white wine?" Marc asked.

"Yes, that would be nice," she said. She stared at him as he perused the wine list.

When the waiter walked away, Marc said over his menu, "What are you going to start with?"

"The escargot ravioli." She glanced up from her menu. "What are you going to have?"

"That was my first choice, as well. Should I pick something else and we can share?"

"Yes, I'd love that." She took a sip of her water to ease her nervousness.

"What else sounds good to you? You're the food critic."

"It all sounds wonderful to me. Let's see … umm … the ravioli is a warm appetizer, let's try one of the cold ones. The Marlin drizzled with wasabi vinaigrette?" she asked, slightly shivering from the cold draft hitting her shoulders.

"Sounds great. I guess you like spicy foods, too. Would you like my jacket?" he asked as he stood to take it off.

"Thank you," she said as he slipped his jacket over her shoulders. She felt enveloped by the warmth of his trapped body heat. "I love spicy foods as long as it doesn't obscure the other flavors of the dish." She looked up as the wine steward approached to open the bottle at the table.

He presented the bottle to Marc for his approval.

"Yes, that's it," he said.

Throwing the golden napkin over his black tuxedoed arm, he proceeded to open the bottle of wine with flare. He poured a small amount in both glasses, handing them forward for their tasting. Jenna swirled the wine around the glass and smelled its fragrance. She closed her eyes and took a sip allowing it to reach all the taste buds on her tongue. She swallowed. "It's light and fruity. It leaves a wonderful aftertaste. Umm … delicious," she said, holding her

193

wineglass delicately in her hand. She opened her eyes, suddenly realizing that both men were watching her intently. She blushed.

"You're a lucky man," the waiter said.

"I know," Marc said. He reached across the table to touch Jenna's hand.

The wine steward filled their glasses, placed the wine in a bucket of ice by the table, and walked away.

She searched his face. "I can't believe all that I'm feeling in such a short time. How long have we been here? Four days?" She placed her wine glass on the table, nervously tracing the rim. "I feel ... I feel like I've lived an entire lifetime. I can't stop thinking about that amazing kiss. You know I usually don't talk like this with anyone other than Jack."

"Talk like what?" he said softly.

"Saying everything I'm thinking. I usually censor myself. I feel terrified and freed at the same time. Jack and I are doing better than we have in such a long time and then there's you. I'm overwhelmed and stimulated and exceedingly happy but apprehensive, as well. Does that make sense?"

Marc stroked the top on her hand. "Complete sense," he said. "I wouldn't say I'm anxious but I do experience some trepidation in opening my heart to you. I haven't felt this way about another person in a very long time. In fact, since the first moment we met I've found myself physically aroused and drawn to you. We've had relationships with other people over the years, but I feel that we, as a foursome, have incredible potential."

Jenna was saved from responding as their waiter delivered their appetizers. "Oh, this smells so good," Jenna said, to avoid the magnitude of his statement. "You've got to try this. The escargot melts in your mouth."

"Wow. That is delicious," Marc said, smiling. He waved

his hand to get the waiter's attention. "Could you help me move my place setting around closer to her? He settled back into his seat as the waiter walked away. "This is better for sharing, don't you think?"

"Yes, I do," she said with a demure grin.

Marc touched her face as he brought his mouth to hers. "And kissing," he said in a husky voice. He softly caressed her lips and as the intensity grew, he pulled back. He then cleared his throat and said, "Would you like to taste my dish?"

A bit dazed she said, "Oh, yes, sure," and opened her mouth for a bite.

They spent the five-course meal talking, sharing gourmet French food, and chilled wine. Jenna asked Marc about his children and shared more about her own family. They delighted in the flaming pineapple crepe as the finale to their meal.

Marc pulled out Jenna's chair and asked, "Would you like to go for a walk in the gardens?"

"Sure, that would be nice," she said. She removed his coat and handed it to him. "Thanks for the use of your jacket. I hope you weren't too cold in there."

"No, it was perfect. All of it," he said, throwing the jacket over his left shoulder and wrapping his right arm around her.

"It was, wasn't it?" she said, looking up at him.

❋ ❋ ❋ ❋ ❋

Jack withdrew the key and unlocked the door. After opening it, he allowed Summer to enter his hotel room ahead of him.

"Your place is so yellow. The yellow bedspread, and oh, look at the cool tile and yellow curtains, too. I love it. Our place is much more masculine. It's predominantly green and we have carpet. The setup's the same though, but the mirror image of ours. Wow, look at your view," she said as she walked through the open French doors. "Have you guys had the chance to watch any weddings in the gazebo?"

"No, not really. We've been a bit busy with you guys," he said, coming up behind her and wrapping his arms around her waist. "Not complaining, you understand. That's more Jenna's thing than mine. I can think of better ways to spend my time."

"Like what?" Summer asked, turning around in his arms to face him.

"Like this," Jack said. He nibbled up Summer's neck and then kissed her passionately.

"Hmm … that *is* better," she said. She threw her arms about his neck and kissed him again.

"Okay, whoa," he said, ducking out from under her arms. "That's getting me a little too hot." He sat down on the chair near the balcony table and lit a cigarette. "Would you like one?" he asked, holding out the pack.

She sat in the chair across from him. "No thanks, but I wouldn't mind smoking some Caribbean herb."

Jack stood up and retrieved the joint from his wallet. "My lady," he joked.

"Thanks," she said. She leaned forward to put the tip into the flame that Jack held for her and drew in the smoke. As she held it in, she asked in a squeaky voice, "How strong is this? I haven't been high in ages."

"Pretty strong. One or two pulls should do it," he said, taking the joint from her outstretched hand.

She blew out the smoke. "I think that will do it for me. I can feel it already. So tell me, what do I need to do to pose for you."

"Tonight I just want you to stand but in the future I would like to sketch you in a yoga pose. You know the one where you balance on one foot curling the other leg behind you? I would need to sketch it from several angles."

"It's called Nataraja-asana, The King of the Dance posture. You want this done in the nude?"

"I forgot you haven't seen any of my work. That's all I do," he said, standing up.

"Okay, so how will this work?"

"I'll show you." He put out the cigarette, took her by the hand and led her into the room. He pulled one of Jenna's scarves from the top drawer. "It's time for you to get naked."

Summer removed her clothing piece by piece as she strutted to the other side of the room.

"You're stunning," he said, walking around, observing her from all angles. He stopped in front of her and tied the scarf to cover his eyes.

"Hey, you don't need to be shy with me," she said, tugging at the material.

"I see with my touch," he said, retying the scarf behind his head. He used his fingers to caress her face softly, memorizing the contours of her features.

"Oh, so you do this with all the girls?" she asked, laughing.

"Shhh," he said gently and continued to explore her shoulders, feeling the space between her collarbone and neck. "Very nice." He moved his hands down to her breasts feeling the curve and the weight.

Summer shuddered under Jack's hand as he gently traced her areola, finally circling her erect nipples. "Oh my."

He continued to discover the hills and valleys of her body until she felt weakened by the passion he stirred within her. He removed the blindfold, and with deliberateness in his step, he stalked over to the large bag of clay on the counter, and ripped open the packaging.

"What do you want me to do now?" she asked, sitting

down on the bed.

"You can watch," he said distractedly. "I'll still need to see you but you can get dressed for now if you'd feel more comfortable." He motioned toward the bathroom without looking back. "There's a robe in there you could use," he said, sliding the plastic covering down from around the clay block.

He aptly began to mold and cut away the excess clay with a butter knife he had kept from the breakfast tray and began transferring his tactile experience into the budding sculpture. "I'll use this as a figure study when I carve you in marble or maybe granite," he called out. "The height of this counter is all wrong," Jack said angrily. "Will you help me move the clay over to the table?"

"Sure," she said. She stood, grabbing one side of the bag from the bottom. "Wow, this sure is heavy. How will you get it home?"

"It won't be as heavy after I trim away and it hardens on its own. It doesn't need to be fired. I'll ship it. Not a problem," he said, sliding closer to the edge of the table. "This height is much better," he said, quickly shaping and removing clay as he worked. "There's another pose I would like to sculpt. It's where you lie on your stomach, clasping your feet behind you and then you pull up."

"The Bow pose ... Dhanura-asana," she said. She watched Jack working skillfully and frantically, cutting away every piece that was not her, until she began to emerge from the clay.

"Can you come over here?" Jack said, scratching his nose with is forearm. "Turn around." He scanned the contours of her lower back. "Okay." He circled back around and faced the gray block.

"Jack," she said. She took his face in her hands and began to caress his lips with her own.

He gave into the kiss as he held his arms out to the side.

"I don't care if you get clay on me," she said, placing his arms around her back.

"It feels good to work," he said, his voiced charged with energy. He pressed his palms against Summer's naked body, lifting her off the floor in a deep kiss. He lowered her back down and began kissing her neck, pressing his mouth to her shoulder, making a trail with his tongue toward her breast.

* * * * *

Marc and Jenna, arm in arm, strolled out of the lobby and down the pathway to the gardens.

"I'm amazed at how comfortable I feel with you," Jenna said. She looked down at the lights that illuminated their trail.

"Why do you think that is?"

"It's so easy to talk to you and I didn't realize how attracted I could be to another man," she said. She circled to face to him.

"We've never had this much time together either."

"True. Why did you wait until now to tell us about your lifestyle?"

"Timing, I guess. We hoped you guys would be a long-term connection from the first time we met several months ago."

"You've said that before but I'm not sure we're on the same page. I mean, we found out about this a couple of days ago. This seems fun for now—for here—who knows what's going to happen once we get back home."

"I agree and that's where the risk comes in for all of us," he said. "Would you like to sit in one of the wicker swings?" He pointed to the enormous Banyan tree bathed in shadow.

"Yes." She reached for his hand as they cut across the grass.

Marc slid onto the cushion, leaning against the rattan. He held out his hand to help Jenna inside. "This is really comfortable," he said as she rested against his muscular torso. The swing swayed lazily as he lightly tickled down her arm.

Jenna adjusted her body to face him. "So you think you could love me?" she said, furrowing her brow and crinkling her nose.

"Yes, I do."

"Jack's forever telling me to live in the moment instead of the future and at this very moment I finally get it." She looked up at him. "I don't know where this will end up, but I know this is right where I want to be—right now."

"That's good enough for me." He turned on his side and encompassed Jenna in his arms. He removed the pin that kept her hair in place and ran his hand up the back of her neck into her scalp. Tilting his mouth to cover hers, he kissed her with an intensity that hinted at his building desire.

Jenna broke away abruptly as her heart began to accelerate. She breathed fast and shallow as she rested her forehead on his ribcage. "I felt that throughout my whole body," she said. She placed her hand on his chest and could feel the racing of his heart, which matched her own. She brought her lips back up to his and kissed him deeply. Her thoughts gradually ceased as she gave herself over to the experience.

He kissed her gently, suckling her lips, exploring her mouth with his tongue. He kissed her with increasing passion until she finally jerked away from him.

"No more," Jenna said, gasping. "I feel like I'm about to explode. I've got to get out." Breathlessly, she struggled to climb out of the swing. Once free, she quickly escaped to the path while Marc jumped out to follow her.

He hurried toward her. "Are you okay?" he asked.

"Yes. Well … I don't know. That was so intense and I

know it was only kissing but it felt like more than that. I hear myself, and it sounds so stupid, I'm sorry, I—"

"I understand. It's okay." He enclosed her in his arms. "It was intense for me, too."

"So what are we going to do about it?" Jenna asked. "How am I going to explain this to Jack?" She stepped away from his embrace and folded her arms around herself.

"How are you going to explain what to Jack?"

"How I'm feeling."

CHAPTER EIGHTEEN

"Whoa … wait a minute…" Summer said, pushing him away from her breast.

"This is harder than I thought it would be," Jack said, stepping away from her. "I'm sorry." He shook his head. "I … I just got lost."

"It's okay. Everything's cool." She ran her hand over his shoulder and said, "Chill, we're still good." Smiling, she sauntered to the bathroom and lifted Jenna's robe off the hook. She slid into the garment and tied the sash at her waist. After walking back into the room, she sat on the bed and watched Jack get lost in his art again. While Jack worked, Summer slipped quietly out on the porch and watched the whitecaps reflecting the hotel lights as they crested on the shore. The incessant sound of the waves softly crashing in the distance inspired her to meditate.

She filled her lungs with air. "Ohhhmmm," she breathed out. She held the tone for the length of her breath. "Ohhhmmm," she hummed, centering herself. She lowered herself into a lotus position, placing the backs of her hands on her knees. Her middle finger and thumb touched, creating a circle.

Jack continued to work with a driven ferocity while on the balcony Summer sat motionless. A knock sounded from the door and neither Summer nor Jack moved to answer it. A minute passed and another knock thundered against the door.

"Jack. Jack, are you in there?" Jenna said.

Jack looked up and felt immediately accosted by his present surroundings. To him, he had been home in his studio. "Coming," he said, quickly moving toward the door and opening it. "Sorry, I was in the zone and I didn't hear you. Where's Summ—" he started to ask but watched her enter the room through the French doors.

"Hi there," Summer said. She moved to greet Marc and Jenna.

"My robe?" Jenna said, checking out the scene around her.

"Oh, yes. Jack said I could borrow it." Summer turned to embrace Marc.

"What time is it?" Jack said. He walked forward to shake hands with Marc but laughed when he looked at his clay-caked fingers. He kissed Jenna on the cheek holding his hands out to the side.

"It's past 11:00 o'clock," Marc said. "I thought Summer and I would go back to the room and get ready for the pajama jazz party but I see she's already ahead of us."

"Cute, hon. I'll get changed," she said. She gathered her clothes together and dropped them on the side of the bed.

"May we have a look?" Marc said, pointing at the sculpture on the table.

"It's not finished but sure, go ahead," Jack said, turning to the side to let him pass. "Are you okay?" he whispered to Jenna.

She shook her head slowly and walked over to the rendering.

"Wow, this is amazing. I didn't realize it would be so big," Marc said.

"Summer this—" Jenna said, looking back as Summer dropped the robe to the floor revealing two grey hand prints on her cherry bronze back.

"The final piece will be even larger and in marble I think," Jack said. He wiped his brow with his sleeve and plopped into the chair. "You guys didn't happen to bring any Red Stripe did you?"

"No, but I do have a check for you once you're finished with this piece."

"Excellent," Jack said. "Maybe I'll do it in granite then."

Summer flounced away from the bed and said, "I'm ready." She strode over to Jack and admired the short replica of herself. "This is really cool, Jack." She gave him a hug and a peck. "It was incredible to see you work. Thanks again and see you later," she said over her shoulder as she sashayed to the door. "See you later, Jenna." She passed by Marc out into the hall.

"Thank you for a wonderful time," Marc said to Jenna and then he left the room.

"Wow, I'm tired," Jack said when the door closed.

"We don't have to go to the party." She lay back onto the bed.

"Oh, I want to. I was thinking about taking a power nap. I see your hair is down, wasn't it up when I left?" he asked nonchalantly. He uncrossed his legs and crossed them again. "So how did it go?"

She rolled on her side to face him. "Do we have to go to the party?"

"Did something happen that I should know about?" he asked. He placed both feet on the floor and leaned forward in the chair.

"I think this whole thing … us … them, it's a bad idea." She squeezed her eyes shut.

He moved over to the bed. "Tell me what happened, Jen," he said with urgency. "Did Marc do something wrong?"

"It's not like that, it's … I don't know how to say … I don't want to hurt—"

"Just say it. We said we were going to talk openly about everything, so say it."

"The kissing was—"

"Bad?"

"No. It was ... too good." She glanced up at him and pulled her head back at the same time.

"Ah, that. Well, what does that mean?" He looked down at his hands. "Damn, I need to wash up. I'll be right back."

"I thought you would be upset," she called out to him in the bathroom.

"I'm not sure yet what you mean. The kissing was too good and so—" he answered loudly.

"And so I broke it off because ... well, it felt like more than kissing." She looked away from Jack who had come back into the room.

He lay down next to her, placing his hand on her hip. "You mean you were very aroused? Wasn't that the point?" he said, scratching his head. "I'm not seeing the problem here." He propped up on his elbow and lifted her hair away from her face. "I have something I need to tell you."

"Do I need to prepare myself?"

"No. It's really no big deal but we agreed to share everything. In the middle of working, I needed to see Summer's lower back—she was still undressed—and I asked her to come over by me. She had been sitting on the bed. After I got the proportions in my head, she turned around and we began to kiss. I got caught up in the moment and kissed my way down her neck toward her breast—she did stop me though."

"When she dropped my robe I saw your hand prints on her back."

"Oh crap. Really? That's fucked up. Did that upset you? 'Cause it's hard to kiss and not have the desire for more. Is that what you were trying to tell me?"

"I don't know. It seems too complicated. I felt a lurch in my stomach when I saw the handprints. And feeling this kind of desire for another man—it worries me. Doesn't it bother you? Are you feeling the same way about Summer?"

205

"Honey, I thought that was the point. Having this adventure and sharing it with each other," he said, running his hand over her hair.

"They think we have long term potential," she said, glancing away again.

He tilted her head so he could see her eyes. "What does that mean exactly? Did Marc say?"

"It means they see us continuing this once we get home and letting it develop and see where it goes. Something like that," she said, pulling her body into the fetal position.

"I have no problem with that. I want to be friends with them when we get back. I'm not sure we're looking for the same thing, though. This is just for fun, right?"

"I pretty much expressed the same thing to Marc."

"So what's the problem, Jen?"

"I'm starting to like him more and wanting to—"

"Have sex with him?" He rolled onto his back, staring at the ceiling.

"Yes…"

"Have fun. Just don't fall for him. That's my plan," he said, rolling back toward her. He pulled her against him and kissed her tenderly.

She held his face in her hands and closed her eyes trying to push Marc out of her mind.

He sat up in the bed and said, "As long as we keep talking, nothing can go wrong. I need to wet the clay and close the bag so I can finish it tomorrow." He stood. "I'm sure the party's already started. We need to change and I need to clean up."

"Do me a favor," Jenna murmured as she scooted to the edge of the bed.

"Sure."

She turned her back to him. "Unzip my dress…"

The zipper flowed smoothly down the sway of her back

to the top of her thong.

When he finished, she said, "...and don't let Summer wear my robe again."

* * * * *

Marc and Summer left Jack's room and stepped into the pineapple-brocaded hallway of the south wing.

"So how did it go?" he asked.

"I like him. He's got passion, fire," she said. She took Marc's hand as they strolled across the lobby to the stairwell that led to their room. "What's she like in private?"

"She's excellent. She's both strong and innocent in some ways, I don't know. I like her."

They climbed in silence up the stairs and down the hallway to their room. Summer unlocked the door.

"What's he like away from Jenna?" He loosened his drawstring and walked over to the bed.

"It was incredible to watch him work," she said as she began to undress. "I didn't realize he had such a serious side. Then I made the mistake of interrupting him for a little kissy-face and he got somewhat carried away." She jumped onto the bed, extending her legs out in front of her and leaning back on her hands.

"What did he do?" he asked, dropping down next to her after removing his clothing.

"He kissed down my neck on the way to my breast, but he was in an altered state. You should see him work. It was frantic and organized at the same time. He seems like a totally different person. On fire, but in a controlled burn, if that makes sense. It's hard to explain. I was very aroused. After the kissing, I went out on the balcony and it was so peaceful I decided to meditate. I really love it here," she said, slanting her head toward him.

"Yeah, me too," he said. He placed his hand on her thigh.

"How was dinner?"

"I had a wonderful time and the food was superb. Jenna freaked out a bit at the end, though."

"She seemed a bit odd when you guys showed up. I thought maybe it was because I was wearing her robe."

He lay back on his elbows. "That may have been part of it but while we were kissing she pushed me away and said it was too much."

"You do have that effect on women," she said, throwing her head back and laughing. "Do you think they'll go to the party?"

"I don't know. If we don't get a call from them, I suspect they'll be there. What are you wearing?"

"Not much," she replied. She sat up and tugged open the drawer in front of her. "You?" she asked, slipping into her lingerie.

"How about these?" he asked, holding up a pair of silk boxers. "I could wear my robe over it."

"Sexy. How's this?" she asked. She spun around to model the blue laced v-neck babydoll with high side slits. The material held together in three places down the side with tiny satin bows that matched the straps. She wore a g-string underneath the tiny dress.

"Wow. I'm not sure you'll make it to the door without me attacking you first," Marc said as he pushed her back onto the bed. "I have some pent-up sexual tension I need to release," he rumbled, fondling his way up her body.

"Dr. Beckum, are you sure you want to expend this tension with me?" she said, laughing as she rolled him onto his back and sat on top of him.

"I'm sure."

Summer caressed his erection and used the head of his penis to rub her clit. She felt the surge of wetness flow inside her and asked, "Are you ready for this, Doc?"

"I think … that … is quite apparent," he half moaned.

She slid down his shaft engulfing the full length of his manhood. She stopped once fully seated and then slowly raised her hips and dropped again.

"This is working for me," he whispered with his eyes closed.

"Look at me," she said. "I want to see your eyes when you come you bad boy."

And with that said, Marc growled out a massive orgasm as he pounded her flesh until the very last drop of his release had been expended inside of her.

❊ ❊ ❊ ❊ ❊

Jenna stepped out of the bathroom and watched Jack raise his arms above his head to pull on a white tank top. His sinewy muscularity was still apparent with his shirt on. Pumped from the sculpting, his biceps stood out on his frame. Jenna felt sick in her stomach, remembering again the powerful allure Jack had over women.

"Look at you," Jack said. He kissed her on the cheek. "I like your hair like that."

Jenna looked in the mirror over the drawers and tightened the purple ribbon at the end of her French braid to make sure it would stay in. "Not too girly, is it?"

"No. You look very sexy. Have I seen this outfit before?" he said, messing up his hair in the mirror.

"Yes, you just weren't noticing me then," she said. She adjusted the shoulder strap on the purple camisole.

"Well, I'm noticing you now. Come here," he said. He clutched her in his arms as he lowered his mouth to kiss her.

"Hmm … better late than never, I always say," she said, kissing him back.

He adjusted himself in the boxer shorts. "Good thing

209

there's a button covering the opening on these," he said.

"You're too funny sometimes," she said, playfully punching him in the arm.

"I'm glad you're feeling better. This should be fun." He checked his hair again.

"So before we leave I want to make sure—we're doing this, right?" Jenna asked.

"You mean Marc and Summer?"

"Yes."

Jack opened the door. "Oh, yeah. We're doing it, baby."

CHAPTER NINETEEN

Jenna and Jack ambled through the lobby toward the piano bar. They could hear a slow jazzy melody floating on the warm evening air as they stepped through the threshold. In the center of the small but elegant space stood a grand piano surrounded by guests. The tall chairs were side by side in front of the alternating pale birch to dark mahogany panels giving the establishment a modern appearance. Toward the back, the dance floor lay surrounded by low tables and chairs filled with scantily clad guests ordering drinks and enjoying low, intimate conversation.

"I really like this place," Jenna said, taking in the scene around her. "I can't believe how many people are here. I thought most of the guests would have fallen out by now."

"Maybe they all took naps, like us," Jack said, leading her over to the bar. "Red Stripe and a piña colada, please."

"Instead of the piña colada, please make mine a rumrunner," she said. She sat on a stool watching the bartender make her drink, pouring rum directly into the straw. He opened the cooler and retrieved a beer.

"Here you go," he said, laying down a napkin and placing their drinks in front of them.

"Thanks," Jack said. He swiveled to face away from the bar, leaning his back against the tall chair.

"Do you see them?" Jenna asked. She shifted her legs around to the side so she could look around the bar.

"No, I don't—oh wait, there they are," he said, waving to Summer and Marc as they entered the club.

After hugging Jack, Summer immediately hopped up on the seat next to Jenna. "Love your hair like this. How's it going?" she said, placing her hand on Jenna's back.

"Thanks. Yes, I'm fine. I—" Jenna said. She glanced back at Marc who eased against the bar to talk to Jack. He looked over at her and smiled, causing her pulse to race.

"Are you sure?" Summer asked.

"Well, put yourself in my shoes for a minute. I've never even thought of doing something like this in my entire life and for you this is like an everyday thing." She swung around in her chair to face Summer.

"It's not an everyday thing for us—*not even close*," she said, enunciating the last three words for emphasis. "But I get your point, we do have some experience. If you want to slow things down a bit, if that would work better for you and make you more comfortable, then we can do that."

"No. I don't think slowing things down will make a difference. It's an either yes or no, all in or all out situation," Jenna said. She lifted her drink and held it in her hands.

"And have you decided? Where is Jack in all this?" Summer asked, flagging the passing bartender. "Can I get a rumrunner and a glass of water please?" She turned back to face Jenna. "I'm sorry," she said. "I'm really thirsty."

"It's fine," Jenna said.

"So?" She stirred the rumrunner in front of her and looked up at Jenna.

"So I've decided yes, even though on some level I'm concerned."

"Concerned with what?"

"How it will change my relationship with Jack and I'm afraid of liking Marc too much, of Jack liking you too much. I think Jack might have blinders on. I don't know—I mean on the one hand it's so incredibly exciting and I feel so alive but on the other hand it seems like the potential pitfalls are tremendous. What if we fall into one of those pitfalls and can't climb back out?"

"Life's like that don't you think? The biggest risks usually come with the biggest potential rewards, right?" Summer watched a muscular young man in very tight shorts swagger to the bar next to her. She smiled.

"Yes, but," Jenna said loudly over the music, trying to recapture Summer's attention. "It also comes with the largest potential failure. Stand up," she said abruptly. "I want to see what you have on."

"Are you changing the subject?" Summer asked.

"I am. Let's try to have fun tonight. I don't want to think anymore." Jenna stepped down from her chair. "You look … oh my god, where did you get this outfit?"

Summer stood up and strutted around. "Victoria's Secret. They have the best stuff, don't you think?"

"So what are you guys up to?" Jack asked, sliding in between them.

"Girl talk but we're done," Summer said, slowly moving to the music. "Come dance with me."

"No, I'm not dancing," he said, hopping up on a stool.

"Jack, that was not a request—that was an order. Now dance with me," Summer said, tugging on his arm.

"Fine," he said, giving in.

"Would you keep an eye on my drink?" Summer said to Jenna and then led Jack to the dance floor without waiting for her response.

Jenna climbed back up into the chair and took a sip of her rumrunner. She looked over to her left at Marc who stared at her intently. She waved him over.

"I wasn't sure you were going to talk to me," Marc said, moving closer and reclining against the bar next to her.

"I'm still talking to you," she said, smiling. "I'm sorry I walked away like that. I was a little overwhelmed. I … can we pretend it didn't happen?"

He touched the ribbon in her hair. "No, but we can try

again," he said, smiling. "Can I kiss you?"

"Here?" she said, glancing around.

"Yes, here." He shuffled behind her and pulled out the chair to make it easier for her to get down. As soon as she stood, he embraced her in a warm hug. "I was hoping I would see you again tonight," he whispered, capturing her mouth with his. They began to kiss slowly, softly until the intensity of their passion took over. When they were in the throes of a fiery kiss, Marc stopped because of a tap on his shoulder.

"I'm thinking you've made a mistake, mate. This is not your wife," Cliff said with raised eyebrows and a confused expression.

Jenna quickly stepped back, crossing her arms in front of her.

"Oh shit, you're right," Marc said, squinting his eyes under the pretense of seeing Jenna better. "Sorry, ma'am, I don't know what—"

"Hey, Cliff," Summer said. She paraded toward them holding hands with Jack and winking at Marc.

"Oh, I see—wife swappin'. As long as everyone's on the up and up. Should warn the missus though, not sure how she'll take to it. Do carry on. See you all on the island tomorrow?" Cliff said, speaking rapidly.

"Not until the afternoon for us," Jack said. He glanced over at Jenna and she nodded.

"Not sure for us either," Summer said. "I want to sleep in but we're definitely going out there tomorrow afternoon. Right?"

"Sounds good to me," Marc said.

When Cliff moved away Jack said, "Honey, you look pale. Are you okay?"

"I guess. That was a pretty weird experience," Jenna said. "Actually I think it was harder on Cliff. He handled it well but you guys didn't get to see the look on his face when he first came over."

"Yeah, I wasn't sure if he was going to fall over or hit me," Marc said, laughing.

"That's not true," Jenna said, narrowing her eyes. "The falling over part, maybe." She laughed. "I can't believe I'm laughing about this. My life is so surreal right now."

"What did you say to him?" Summer asked Marc. "I saw you throw your arms in the air."

"He was telling me that Jenna was not my wife and I said, 'Oh shit, you're right." Marc and Jack laughed.

"Poor man," Summer said. "If we're lucky he'll be too drunk to remember."

"Well if he was drunk, he sobered up very quickly," Marc said. "Wouldn't you say, Jenna?"

"Oh yeah. He seemed wide-eyed to the extreme. But I imagine he was shocked to see you cheating on Summer," she said, poking Marc in the chest.

Jack strained his head forward and pursed his lips. "What about you cheating on me?"

"Oh yeah, that too," she said. "I need another drink after all that excitement."

"Let's dance some more," Summer said. She quickly took a sip of her cocktail and then pulled Jack back toward the dance floor.

"Okay," Jack said and looked over at Jenna, shrugging his shoulders with his palms up.

Marc placed a new rumrunner in front of Jenna and said, "So?"

"Oh, thanks. So..." she said, making eye contact.

"How was that for you?" He took a swallow of his scotch.

"You mean before the Cliff episode?" she asked. She leaned back in her chair and took a deep breath.

He came closer and ran a finger down her thigh.

"Before," he said.

"Stop," she said, catching his hand in hers. "You're giving me the chills."

"Would you like to go for a walk?" he said, flipping her braid.

"Yes, I think I would." She picked up her glass to take a sip.

"Be right back." He kissed Jenna on the top of her head as he passed.

She watched him walk over to Jack and Summer who were gyrating slowly to the jazzy Reggae beat. She could see them shaking their heads and then Jack waving.

As Marc returned he said, "We're free to travel." He finished his drink and then helped Jenna from her chair.

She took another pull on her straw and left her drink on the bar. "Where are we going?" she said. She felt his hand clasp hers.

"I told them we'd be down on the beach."

They walked out of the bar and into the lobby.

"So?" Marc said.

"So," she repeated.

"So you didn't answer my question," he said, staring down at her.

"I know," she said, chuckling under her breath. "When we were kissing, I forgot where we were, and I was startled back into the bar with Cliff's interruption."

"And?"

"And...?" She smiled. "You were looking for something else?"

"*Jenna*?"

"It was amazing. Is that what you're looking for?" she said as he led her down the steps.

"It's ... well ... how am I supposed to reconcile that I'm more aroused by you right now than my husband?" She stopped by the palm tree and continued, "It's confusing and I don't want to spend my time analyzing it but I don't know. I'm perplexed."

"Try to keep it in perspective. This is new and so it's exciting. A lot of what we're feeling is chemistry, not the longevity you have with Jack, or I with Summer. They're two different animals. Try to enjoy it for what it is—a beginning," he said. He gestured to the hammocks. "Want to try them out?"

"Sure, okay." She climbed in while he held down the netting for her.

"Scoot over," he said. He sat on the edge and then brought his legs around. When he lowered his upper body, Jenna rolled into him.

"Do you have enough room?" she asked, laughing as he jostled the hammock around trying to get settled.

"There," he said, finding a comfortable position and reaching out for her. He wrapped her in his arms, enjoying the swinging motion. "Is this good for you?"

"As in, am I comfy?" She laid her head on his chest and sighed.

"I meant emotionally," he said, twirling the end of her hair.

"I'm working my way through it, slowly but surely. Let's talk about something else or..."She tilted her head up to look at him.

"Or?" he said as he moved in to kiss her.

As their lips touched, he pulled her on top of him. The hammock swayed back and forth matching the rhythm of the crashing waves. She could feel his arousal beneath her and an energetic surge coursed through her body. She didn't stop. She continued to allow her arousal to build until he finally pulled away.

"I need a breather," he said, rubbing his forehead. "Let's

try talking for a little while." He rolled her to the side of him.

"Oh?" she chuckled. "I see, so *we are* having the same experience."

"I think I've said as much, have I not?"

"You always seem to be totally in control. I see myself as being a basket case by comparison," she said, playing with the soft hair on his arm. "It's reassuring in an odd way."

"I can assure you I'm feeling everything you are. Maybe more because I'm hoping for more."

"What do you mean, hoping for more?"

"I mean everything. I mean living and loving and being in each other's lives from now on. The four of us."

"Do you think that's possible?"

"Just as possible as any two people getting into a relationship."

"Only way more complicated," she said, gazing up at the stars. "It's so nice out here. This was a great idea." She laid her head back on the hammock.

"It doesn't have to be complicated," he said. "The best solution for complication is open communication. Four people can talk just as well as two."

"Or there can be twice as much fighting."

"That's true, I suppose. We'll have to wait and see where this takes us."

"What about the women in your past with Summer? Why aren't you still together?"

"There have only been a few. Two lasted for over two years. One woman actually lived with us for a while and it was wonderful while it lasted. I don't have any real explanation for why it didn't last, other than in the end they wanted different things." He moved a wisp of hair behind her ear. "We're still close with them. There was one other couple but we realized early on that they were dealing with some serious psychological problems."

"Oh, and we're not?" She laughed. "So you've never really had a relationship with another couple."

"No, we haven't, but we *have* flirted *a lot*," he said, chuckling.

"Why not look for another woman instead of a couple?"

"Depends on what you're looking for."

"What do you mean?" Jenna asked.

"Summer enjoys a woman every now and then but would really prefer a couple."

"That's certainly understandable. That would be my preference."

"So, how about women?" he asked, placing his hand behind his head as a pillow.

"Women? What are you talking about?"

"Do you like them?" he said, raising his eyebrows.

"I experimented in college with a roommate of mine and kissed a couple of her girlfriends, too, but it didn't do it for me." She shifted her position onto her back.

"Details please," he said, smiling broadly.

She hit him on the arm and quipped, "No, but I will say that women do not know how to kiss. What's with the scrunched up mouth and keeping their lips tight. It wasn't like I was attracted to my roommate. I did it for the sake of experimentation. And the going down thing, I love to receive it but don't send me down there. On a man, any day but—"

"Let's not go there just yet," he said, playfully covering the front of his pants. "Have you ever been attracted to a woman?"

"Yes, once, but she was very muscular with extremely short hair but an attractive, feminine face. I'm not sure it counts. Besides, I like it when the man takes the lead. Passivity is not a turn on for me."

"I can assure you, there are a lot of aggressive women out there."

"I'm sure there are, but can they kiss?" she said, laughing. "I like how *you* kiss."

He wrapped his left leg around her thigh and shared a torrid kiss, pulling her into him. Time ceased until they heard the voices of Jack and Summer calling their name. Jenna knew her neck must be red from arousal and her hair had to be a mess. She worried how Jack would react to her appearance.

"Over here," Marc called out, his voice husky with arousal. He sat up and smoothed his hair. He swung his legs back over the side and helped Jenna out of the hammock. "How was it after we departed?" Marc asked, standing up and steadying the net.

"It was fantastic," Summer said, walking up the beach with Jack. "You guys missed a good time. The place really filled up after you left."

"Looks to me like they had some fun of their own," Jack bristled, observing Jenna straightening her clothes and hair.

"Why don't we all go back to our room for a while?" Summer asked.

"Okay by me. Jack?" Jenna asked. She scanned Jack's face and then glanced back at Marc.

"Okay," Jack said, taking a deep breath.

"Sounds fine to me," Marc said.

The foursome rambled silently to the north side of the resort up to Marc and Summer's room. Marc walked over to the nightstand to check his cellphone. No messages. Summer sat down on the bed and Jack moved over by the TV propping his arm on top of it. Jenna stood by the door with her arms crossed in front of her.

"Well, aren't we all being quiet," Summer said. She patted the bed beside her for Jack to sit.

Jack shuffled over to the bed and asked, "So how's this supposed to work?"

Marc came back around the bed toward them. "We can figure that out now."

"I have an idea," Summer said.

"Okay," Jack said. "Tell us."

"Why don't we take turns watching each other kiss? That way it's done and it's out there," she said, glancing around at everyone.

"I'm assuming you mean more than a peck," Jack said.

"I mean a real make-out session, at least a couple of minutes. It's up to you and Jenna," she said to Jack, "because this is for you guys. I've watched and enjoyed Marc kissing other women. I thought it would help break the ice. Yea? Nay?"

"What do you think?" Marc asked Jenna.

"Jack?" Jenna said, shrugging.

"I think we should do it. At least here, away from the other guests, we're prepared for watching the kiss instead of being surprised by it somewhere else. Okay?" he said to Jenna.

"Okay," she said, taking a deep breath. "You and Summer first." Jenna moved over by Marc and prepared herself to watch them. Marc took her hand and she smiled up at him. "Okay, I'm ready," she said, squeezing his hand.

Jack took Summer in his arms and tentatively began to kiss her. Summer stepped it up by placing her hand behind his head and putting her tongue in his mouth.

As they made out, Jenna relaxed. She found it much more pleasant than she had anticipated. Summer was shorter and more petite, making Jack appear taller and larger. Marc stroked Jenna's hair as she watched, looking down to see her reaction. She couldn't be sure how long they kissed but she could see the look of concern on Jack's face when they finished.

"I'm fine," Jenna said, smiling at Jack.

"Are you sure?" he said hesitantly, searching her face.

"You look really good together," Jenna said. She stepped forward and reached to touch his cheek.

"That's a relief," Jack said. He stood up to move away from the bed.

"Your turn," Summer said, trading places with Marc.

Jenna sat down on the edge of the bed and Marc moved her over so that her legs crossed over his. She closed her eyes when he began to kiss her slowly and tenderly. The heat of their kiss quickly accelerated, wiping out any thought of Jack and the room they sat in. When Marc finally pulled away, Jenna hesitated before opening her eyes. When she did she saw Jack staring at her.

"That wasn't as bad as I expected," Jack said stiffly, shaking off the experience. "Although, Summer kissing you would be much hotter."

"I would love to kiss Jenna but I don't get that vibe from her," she said, messing up Jack's hair.

"Jenna doesn't think women know how to kiss," Marc said, winking at Summer.

"Oh, I believe Summer can prove you wrong," Jack said with a big grin.

Marc got up from the bed and Summer dashed for his spot. Before giving her a chance to think it through, Summer grabbed Jenna's face in her hands and planted her lips on Jenna's. She initially resisted but succumbed to Summer's skill in a matter of seconds. They stayed in that spot, locked together in a smoldering kiss. Summer moved her hands to the nape of Jenna's neck as Jenna buried her hands into Summer's wild, frizzy hair. After another minute of sumptuous kissing, Jenna pushed her away.

She leaned over, placing her hands on her knees to catch her breath. "Okay, I give. You win."

"That was amazing. You guys are totally hot. Do it

again!" Jack said with boyish glee.

"It's time to call it a night," Jenna said, making eye contact with Marc. "We have to be up tomorrow before Kokila arrives in the morning. Thank you for an overwhelming and exciting experience. Today, I think, has been one of the longest days of my life and not in a bad way." She turned to Jack and said, "Say your goodbyes and let's go."

Marc followed Jenna to the door, leaving Jack the opportunity to say goodbye to Summer.

"This was an amazing day. I look forward to what tomorrow brings," Marc said. He hugged Jenna and gently kissed her goodnight.

Jack shook Marc's hand on his way out.

Marc closed the door behind them and settled himself on the end of the bed.

"I could be wrong but Jack seemed to tense up when you guys first started kissing," Summer said, joining Marc on the bed.

"Really? He looked fine when we finished."

"Yeah, maybe I'm wrong."

✳ ✳ ✳ ✳ ✳

"That was incredible," Jack said enthusiastically once they were out in the hall.

"Jack, people are trying to sleep. Keep it down."

"That was incredible," he whispered. "Did you enjoy it?"

"Stop it!" she yelled in a whisper.

"Come on, you can tell me. Did you like it?"

"What are you turning me into?" she said, shaking her head. "Yes. She's an incredible kisser. Do I enjoy it as much as I enjoy kissing you or Marc? No. It was different but not in a bad way. My head is reeling and I really need to get some sleep. Can we talk about all of this in the morning?"

"Yes. Have I told you lately how much I love you?"

"You just like me right now because I kissed a woman in front of you," she said, going around the corner of the lobby.

"That was an added bonus I must admit, but that has nothing to do with my love for you. I love you, Jenna. We can talk tomorrow."

"Yeah, I think we should," she said quietly.

CHAPTER TWENTY

"Was that the door?" Jenna said. She opened her eyes under silent protest.

"Yeah," Jack said. "It must be the breakfast I ordered."

Neither moved to get the door. The knock came again, a little more insistent this time.

"Jack!" she said, pushing him out of the bed.

"Alright, alright already." He stumbled to the door as he pulled on his boxers. He turned the knob, pulled the door open, and leaned facing the wall, resting his forehead on his right hand.

The bellman marched over to the inside table and encountered the mounds of clay. "Ah, excuse me, sir. Where would you like for me to put this?"

"Here on the bed," Jenna said, sitting up with the sheet tucked under her arms.

The bellman turned his face away as he placed the food in front of her.

"Thank you," she said.

"Enjoy your day." He avoided looking directly at her. "Irie, mon," he said, passing by Jack who still held the door.

"Oh, I need some coffee," Jack moaned. "What time is it?"

"We're in Jamaica, Jack. It doesn't matter, remember?"

"Yeah, I know. I was thinking I need to take a quick shower though, before Kokila shows up. You're still okay with this?"

"Drawing Kokila? Sure, why not?" she said, handing Jack a cup of coffee. "I'd love to have a sculpture of her in the house. Even in her clothes her body looks very womanly, very curvy and sensual."

He placed his coffee on the end table. "Speaking of very womanly, my sweet," he said as he fell forward on the bed.

"Hey, be careful you're going to spill breakfast all over me."

"So anyway, as I was asking, what's the state of affairs, no pun intended, with you and the kiss," he said, grinning.

"I loved it, Jack. I loved the feel of her soft lips," she cooed. "I could feel her erect nipples through her shirt and it turned me on to know you were watching intently. By the way, would you like some of this sweet melon," she said, holding out the plate to him.

"Oh my god, you're not doing this to me, are you?" He laughed. "You so had me going. Now tell the truth."

"It was an interesting experience but I still prefer men," she said, smiling. She got up from the bed, letting the sheet drop. "So, would you ever kiss Marc for me?"

"Hell no!"

"Then don't expect me to fulfill your fantasies," she said as she strutted to the bathroom.

"So you're saying if I sleep with Marc, you'll sleep with Summer? Damn, I guess I never will get to see you play with Summer then," he said, laughing. "But you did like it right?" he asked through the bathroom door.

"Just so we can keep your fantasies alive; I did like it, Jack." She emerged from the bathroom.

"So women are definitely out then?" Jack asked, following her to the bed.

"She would have to be someone very special and even then I don't see the necessity of sleeping with her except that you want me to."

"You would do that for me?"

"I might consider it, who knows."

"You're killing me here," he said, chuckling.

"Do you think you could be satisfied with only me ever again?" Jenna asked. She sat on the edge of the bed peeking up at him.

"Are you serious?"

"Very."

"Do you want the short or long rambling answer?" he asked.

"It's the gentleman's choice."

"Honey, nobody's ever going to take your place."

"That doesn't answer the question. We've opened this box and I'm not sure we can close it again."

"So maybe I should ask you the same question."

"We can stop now, right here," she said. "And not go where we both know we're heading."

"Is that what you want? Don't you think the fantasies will plague you? The 'what ifs?'"

"Maybe." She cut the cantaloupe from the rind. "I believe we're into this for two different reasons."

"How's that?"

"Jack, for you sex is for fun. You love the rush, not that it's not a rush for me, but for women it's about the emotional attachment as well. Feeling safe."

"So you're saying you don't feel emotionally attached or safe with me?"

"Jack," she said, exasperated. "*I do* feel safe with you and I love you. I just don't want to jeopardize what we have, and I'm not sure you're seeing past your goal of simply getting off. My emotions are involved here. It's not just for sport."

"I thought we agreed we wouldn't fall."

"I'm not in love with him, but I'm becoming emotionally attached."

"Aren't we all becoming better friends? I think if we stick to the ground rules, we'll be fine. Keep talking," he said as he reached out to touch her face.

227

"And listening, Jack. That's very important in this process." She stood up and walked to the closet. "Are you going to shower now?"

"I think I'm going out on the balcony to have a smoke."

"Well, I'm going to shower then. Listen for the door, okay? Are you okay, Jack?"

"I think so," he said, walking toward the French doors. "I sort of have that feeling in my stomach that I get whenever I'm about to get on a rollercoaster."

"I know what you mean," she said as she strode to the bathroom.

"We're going to be okay in this, aren't we, Jenna? Jenna," he called out. He could hear the shower running.

✳ ✳ ✳ ✳ ✳

"Hang on a sec, I'll be right there," Jack called as he briskly strode through the room. He reached the door and found Kokila standing before him in a flowery sarong and a bikini top. "Kokila, hey, babe, how are you? Wow, I think I need to get this look on paper," he said, moving to the side allowing her to enter into the foyer. Jack followed her into the room admiring her assets.

"Jenna's in the shower?" Kokila asked.

"Yeah, she'll be out in a second. Then if you don't mind, a real quick shower for me?"

Kokila sat in a chair studying the clay figure on the table. "Is this my destiny?" she asked. "This is pretty remarkable."

"That's where you'll end up as a middle stage. I'll probably finish you in marble."

"So will I get to see the finished product?"

"Only if you come to the states or I could email you a photo."

"Hi, Kokila. How's it going?" Jenna asked, wrapped in

228

one towel and drying her hair with another. "Caught me at my best." She pulled open her top drawer and chose clothes for the day.

"You look great to me," Kokila said, stepping out onto the balcony.

"I'm going to shower," he said. "See you in a minute."

Jenna dressed and joined Kokila watching the resort come to life. The hotel staff quickly arranged flowers in the gazebo for a wedding later. A table filled with assorted appetizers sat just below their balcony.

"Amazing how much goes into a wedding," Kokila said.

"Yeah, Jack and I had an unusual one. The best man was a male figure in papier-mâché wearing a tux," she said. "Jack's idea of fun."

"That is funny." Kokila turned her back to the resort and leaned against the railing. "I'll bet that made some memories. He seems like a fun guy. He's always happy and energetic."

"He's a lot of different things. He's wonderful and a pain in the ass sometimes, and I assure you he's never, always."

Jack stepped through the French doors. "Can I join you two? Are you ready to get started?"

"That was fast. Sounds good to me," Kokila said. "Where do you want me?"

"Come inside and I'll make a place for you to pose."

Jack moved the rattan chair occupying the corner of the room to the center and opened the blinds enough to filter in the light he needed for sketching his preliminary drawings.

"Normally, I would be blindfolded. That helps me shape you in my mind, but I'm going to have to work from the drawings when I get back."

"What do you mean?"

"He uses his hands—running them over your body to get a feel for your contours," Jenna said.

"I see. You could still do that if you think it would help,"

Kokila said, grinning.

He unpacked his sketchpad and drawing pencils and sat comfortably in the rattan cushion chair.

"Could you remove the top and sarong? And stand right over there in the light."

"Right here?" she asked as she pulled the string to the bathing suit top allowing her full breasts to find their natural place.

"Hang on a sec, leave the sarong on for a moment and go up on tiptoe on your right foot," he said. "Yes, like that. Good." He worked quickly with broad strokes. "Gauguin would be proud. You're lovely."

"You really are," Jenna said as she pulled up a chair from the table to watch.

Jack smiled as he laid down the first of many pencil strokes capturing as much of Kokila's native body as he needed to produce a finished work of art.

"How long have you been married?" Kokila asked as she held her pose. She piled her hair on top of her head with both hands, allowing a few strands to fall that partially covered her left breast. "How's this?"

"Excellent. Jenna, how long have we been married?"

"Nine and a half years."

"But we met four years before we were married, right?" Jack said. He switched to a pencil with a sharper point.

"Right," Jenna replied.

"So how did you guys meet?" Kokila inquired.

"There was a show of all the art students' work at the end of the semester. My college roommate and I went over to check it out. I saw Jack from across the room but we didn't meet then. My roommate and I ended up at the local pub for a drink. What was it called, Jack?"

Kokila and Jenna looked at him.

When he didn't respond, Jenna continued, "Anyway, a

bunch of the artists came there after the show and the place was pretty rowdy. I decided to go outside and get some fresh air and I ran into Jack, literally. I knocked his drink out of his hand and all over his coat. I was expecting him to be furious but instead—"

"I asked her if she would model for me," he said. "I was very enthusiastic."

"Yeah, he was jumping around like a little boy. It was rather cute. I knew I was in trouble," she said with a laugh.

"I pretty much moved into her apartment after that. She had more room and let me turn the den into a makeshift studio."

"When he first told me about his technique, I thought he was bullshitting me. So, here's the guy saying, 'I'm going to put on a blindfold and run my hands over your body to get a feel for your proportions' and I said, 'yeah right.'"

"But you've got to admit it's a pretty good line," Kokila said.

"Yeah. I gave in and let him do it. His first completed sculpture of me made me cry. I couldn't believe it was me—how he saw me. It was an incredible experience."

"How'd he ask you to marry him? Or did you ask him?"

"No. He asked me. He had this art showing up in, where was it?"

"Chicago."

"Right and I couldn't go because I was finishing my semester exams right before graduation. When I got home from school that day I found an envelope placed against a small sculpture of us I'd never seen. The letter said, 'I always thought I could live my life alone and be happy with me and my art, until I met you. Because it wasn't until us that I truly came to know what happiness is. Lift us up as you always do and find what my heart has for you.'"

"How romantic."

"It gets even better. I'm sitting on the couch studying for my last exam and I keep thinking. Lift us up. Lift us up? I go to the statue and lift it up and underneath I find a ring. An antique ring we saw one day when we were exploring the town. I slipped it on and began to cry," she said, looking over at Jack. "So I'm sitting there all misty eyed and he comes strutting through the door and scoops me up in his arms."

"But I thought he'd left?"

"So did I, but his flight wasn't until that night, so we spent the rest of the day making love. He had to race to the airport, barely making the flight."

"Wow. That *is* a cool story."

"Kokila, could you drop the sarong and turn your back to me? Strike that same pose, pulling your hair up. Yeah, just like that," he said as he began to draw again. "Fantastic. You have a magnificent butt and legs, if you don't mind me saying."

"Not at all," she said. "So rumor has it, you guys are playing with the other couple. That's pretty cool."

Jack looked over at Jenna.

"That's a very recent thing and we're still figuring it out," Jenna said, shifting uncomfortably in her chair.

"I love that you're so open and willing to try something new," Kokila said.

Jenna and Jack looked at each other again.

"Is there a question in there?" Jenna asked.

"Could you turn to the side, just a little bit more. Okay, right there."

"I suppose if I were to ask you a question, it would be how open are you two?"

"What do you have in mind?" Jack asked as he flipped over the page to a clean sheet.

"I was wondering if Jenna would mind posing with me," she said. "Don't you think we would look good together?"

"That's an excellent idea! Jenna?" Jack said. He touched her shoulder.

"Umm ... I haven't ... in a long time," Jenna said. "I don't know, Jack."

"Come on, Jenna," Kokila said. "You look great!"

She shook her head and said, "This trip is really pushing my limits." She hesitated and then said, "Well, what the hell." She rose to her feet pulling her shirt over her head. She stepped out of her shorts and panties and stood in front of Jack. "Where do you want me?"

Jack moved around the table taking Jenna's hand in his. He led her over to Kokila. Glancing from Kokila to Jenna, he saw the artistic potential but realized he would have difficulty separating the art from his arousal.

"Wow. What a killer contrast. I haven't felt inspired to paint in years. I wish I had my palette and a canvas here," he said excitedly as he moved about posing the two women. "Jenna lay your head against Kokila's shoulder, and Kokila bring your arm about half way up her back. Let your arms entangle. Jenna, close your eyes. Kokila, you do the same. And tilt your head back just slightly. There that's amazing. Perfect. The contrast is excellent. I can't stand it. Where's the camera, Jenna? Don't lose the mood please."

"It's in the top drawer I think," she said, her eyes still closed.

Jack ran to the drawer and snatched it up. He turned and began to frame the women in the window of the digital camera. "Oh my god, you're not going to believe how pretty this is." Jack snapped three photos. "Change positions. Let it flow. Hang on, I'll put on some music." He flipped the switch on the CD player and Jill Scott began to sing. "This is great. Just go, more ... move, oh yeah, man, that's fantastic." He continued to frame and photograph their bodies moving and touching and sliding against one another.

"Jenna, turn your back to Kokila. Kokila lean against the wall. There, now Jenna drop back on her. Oh yes." Jack hammered picture after picture with stills and sculptures flashing through his mind as he directed the pair.

Kokila began slowly moving her hands over Jenna's waist and across her stomach. Jenna closed her eyes, getting lost in the rhythm of the music as they continually shifted positions. She heard Jack command, "hold it right there." She opened her eyes to see Kokila only a breath away from her lips, leering steadily into her eyes.

"God I love your eyes," Kokila whispered. Moving her face close to Jenna's ear she said softly, "You take my breath away."

"Keep moving," Jack said as he gracefully and intuitively darted around the room. He jumped onto the bed to shoot from above. "Kick your head back Jenna and let Kokila kiss your neck. Get a little more aggressive," Jack said strongly. "Let me see you two let go—go with what you're feeling."

"Stop! I can't take this," Jenna said, pushing Kokila away. "No offense, Kokila but I'm really aroused at the moment and I need to back off."

"Did I do something wrong?"

"No, not that. I was getting too—"

"Come on Jenna. What happened to my crazy girlfriend?"

Kokila unabashedly approached Jenna, taking her by the shoulders and kissing her generously on the lips.

Jack forgot about the camera, as he stood on the bed mesmerized.

Jenna broke off the kiss and they all stood there in silence.

He shook his head and said, "Okay. That's a wrap." Stepping down from the bed he uttered, "You guys are so sexy."

"Yeah, I think we are," Kokila said and winked at Jenna

as she reached for her sarong.

"I'm spinning," Jenna said and then laughed at the weird expression on Jack's face. "You okay, Jack? You look positively spent."

"I'm ... I'm feeling the heat," he said, reviewing the shots on the digital camera.

Jenna reached down to pick up her clothes as Kokila nonchalantly eased up in front of her. Jenna raised her arms above her head to slip on her shirt. The next sensation almost made her collapse as Kokila sucked her nipple into her mouth, biting down slightly.

"Ahhh ... I can't take this," Jenna cried out. "Oh my god, we have to stop. I know this is going to sound crazy, but we're somewhat committed to someone else. Jack, I feel like we're cheating."

"What?" He wheeled around almost dropping the camera.

"On Marc and Summer," she said.

"You've got to fucking be kidding me," he said, running his fingers through his hair.

"Whoa, I think I'm going to go now," Kokila said. "Maybe we'll do this again. Come see me tonight at the terrace bar. Jack, thanks for everything. I look forward to seeing your work."

"Yeah, not a problem. I was looking forward to seeing your work, too."

"See you guys later," Kokila said, leaving the room.

"What the fuck, Jenna? What's the problem?" he asked, crossing his arms in front of him.

"Jack, not now."

"What not now?"

"It's hard to explain. I'm so conflicted. I can't even think about sex at the moment."

"You've got to be kidding. It's all I can think about. Wait a second. You can cozy up with Marc but when we have an

235

opportunity with Kokila, you back off? Are you even listening to me?"

"Yes, I am," she said, bringing her gaze from the outside terrace back to Jack. "I'm sorry. I'm just a little confused right now."

"Shit, I'm going to have to take another shower—a cold one."

CHAPTER TWENTY-ONE

"**S**o how'd the posing go with Kokila?" Summer asked as she and Marc approached the dock where Jack and Jenna stood.

"It was cool, it went okay. Got some great shots to work with when I get back," Jack said as he hugged Summer.

"Can we see them?"

"That wouldn't be ethical," Jenna said abruptly. She walked into Marc's embrace and hugged him. "I mean without Kokila's permission." She sat down on the edge of the dock to wait for the ferryman.

"Do you plan to sculpt her?" Marc asked. "Summer says you have great technique. Very sensitive."

"I try," Jack said. He smiled at Summer, pointing in her direction. "Thanks for the compliment."

"It was my pleasure—no, seriously—it was my pleasure," she said, holding out her hands in front of her. She closed her eyes and began to feel around as if blindfolded. "Jack? Are you there, Jack?"

"You're getting warmer. Follow the sound of my voice."

Summer placed her hands on his chest and face. She then took his hand in hers and began to stroke it from the wrist to the tip of his middle finger and said, "Proportions, got to love them."

Jack snatched his hand away from her and stuck it in his pocket.

"Good day. How is everyone doing?" said the ferryman as he climbed down into the small boat.

"Off to the island of iniquity." Jack winked, pointing out toward the coral isle.

Everyone climbed on board for the short trip across the bay.

"Thanks," Jack said, upon arriving. He stepped off the boat into the water and helped Jenna steady her footing. He reached up to help Marc step from the boat and then lifted Summer under her arms over the rail.

Summer decided to wrap her legs around Jack's waist to avoid getting her Capri pants and shoes wet. Jack lost his balance, causing them both to fall back into the water.

"Thanks," she said sarcastically. "We need to work on that."

"What the hell was that?"

"I thought you would catch me," Summer said, laughing.

"You could have at least warned me." He chortled, wiping the water from his face.

"God they sound like an old married couple, don't they," Marc said to Jenna as he led her toward the pool.

Summer and Jack stayed in the water bantering.

"Look at my clothes, they're soaking wet," Jack said.

"So take them off for god's sake and lay them in the sun. Hello! We're on a nude island!"

"Would you do my laundry for me?" he said, feigning innocence.

"Shut up and get naked!" Summer ordered. She stood up and climbed out of the water, disrobing and hiding behind the bushes to wait for Jack.

"Hey fella," she said, jumping out onto the path in front of him. "Need a date?"

"You're in big trouble," he said, chasing her down the path. "I'm going to spank you!"

"Well then, I'll stop running so fast." She turned around and tossed her clothes to him and said, "Catch."

Jack managed to collect all the clothes in his arms.

"Could you hang those up for me? It is *your* fault, after

all, that I got soaking wet."

"That is so flawed, Summer! It was completely and totally your fault, but I'll hang them up, just for you," he said, maneuvering the clothes to one arm and reaching to spank her naked butt.

"Too slow," she said, skipping off toward the pool.

Summer joined Jenna who was already at the swim-up bar. "Hi Cornelius, how's it going?"

"Ah, my lady, I'm doing fine on this lovely island day. Shall I pour the rum shallow or deep my lady?"

"Let's start in the shallow end, Cornelius," Summer said as she got settled on the stool next to Jenna. "Take good care of me, will you? Don't let me go into the deep rum too soon."

"Ya mon. Not like your husband, he's strong," he said, smiling a toothy grin. "Dat mon can handle his rum."

"Yeah well. He has this ability to stop before it gets out of control."

"That's a good thing," he said. "Keeps ya from trouble, irie."

Jack swam up next to Summer placing his chin on her shoulder.

"Jack, did you find a clothesline?" she asked. "You did rinse the clothes in fresh water in the bathroom didn't you?"

"No. Why?"

"Our clothes will dry into salt packs, Jack," she said, rolling her eyes. "Show me where you hung them up."

They left the pool for the gazebo on the north end where Jack had laid the clothes over the sparkling white rails. After a rinsing and letting the garments flap in the breeze, Summer cornered Jack against the outside tower wall.

"You did such a good job, I want to give you a little reward." She pressed her naked body along his, wrapping her arms around his waist.

"Can we do this here?"

"Shut up and kiss me," Summer said.

Jack circled his arms around Summer, pulling her breasts firmly against his chest.

"I think you like this, Jack." She could feel him hardening against her mound.

"Shut up, Summer," he said and then kissed her fervently.

When they finally came up for air, Summer said, "Now that's what I'm talking about."

"Come here you," he said, turning her to smack her bottom.

She bent forward, smiling over her shoulder, and then quickly trotted away.

Jenna joined Marc against the wall of the pool. "Marc, I need to say something to you and you need to tell me if this is part of the experience you and Summer have had." She took a deep breath.

"Sure, what is it?"

"This morning Kokila came over and one thing led to another and I mean nothing, well something, I mean nothing big happened but I was like freaking out that we ... I mean, I was being unfaithful to you and Summer. Or more to the point, you."

"That's interesting," Marc said as he dropped into the pool to cool off. He came up wiping the water from his face. "Well, we're making progress if you feel like you're cheating on us," he said with a smile.

"Don't be smug."

"No, really. I love that you thought of us, but what if Kokila is a person that you should get to know better, not necessarily sexually but as a person?"

"I only know her sexually so far and that's pretty intense but not really sexually. I mean we didn't ... oh god, this is ridiculous. I don't even like women. What's gotten into me?"

"It sounds to me like you're opening up to different possibilities. There's a lot more out there than maybe you've come to know so far."

"That's an understatement," she said, as she dropped below the surface. She blew out her air and sat on the bottom in the quiet of the water until Cliff trudged through the pool stepping a mere foot from her face. She shot up from the bottom and said loudly to Cliff, "You should warn a girl when you're coming up on her like that."

"Sorry, didn't see you there. I often get that reaction. In the beginning Becky would say 'what am I going to do with this thing?' and smile. Now she says 'what the hell are we going to do with this thing?'"

"Cliff," Becky shouted from the bar, waving for him to come back.

"Be back in a few. Sorry again," Cliff said as he swam to meet up with Becky, Jack, and Summer.

"What do you think about me and Kokila?" she asked after Cliff swam out of earshot.

"Do you want to spend time with her?"

"No, I want to spend time with you. Jack wants me to spend time with Kokila. This is getting very complicated."

"It's only as difficult to sort out as you make it, and believe me, people can make it *very* complicated. I think Kokila is intriguing and you know how I feel about you. My thought would be that all of us should get together for dinner at some point."

"That's not helping," Jenna said, lowering her shoulders.

"Why? It's the truth. I think it would be fantastic with all of us. Summer thinks Kokila is very pretty and I think you're delicious. I get the feeling that Jack and Summer knew each other in another lifetime," he said, chuckling. "So how bad could it be to get together and see what happens?"

"God you make it sound so ... simple."

"And you make it seem very perplexing."

"I think I should talk to Summer about this."

"That's a good idea."

＊ ＊ ＊ ＊ ＊

"What's up?" Summer asked, taking Jenna's hand as they strolled down the path.

"I'm having a hard time making sense of everything that's happening. On the one hand, I want to let go and enjoy everything and then—like I was saying at the bar—it all seems so problematic."

"Did something else happen? Is this about our kiss last night?" Summer pointed to the lounge chair under the gazebo.

"No. It's about this morning and Kokila," Jenna said. She sat on the lounge and looked out over the ocean.

"Kokila? Oh my god. What happened? I'm so jealous."

"Well you know she came over this morning to pose for sketches."

"Right. And?"

"Well, it was going pretty normally. She's gorgeous."

"Yeah, I know."

"So I watched Jack sketch her. While she was posing, she asked us some questions, like, how we met and—"

"Yeah, I'd like to hear that story."

"—and then the conversation turned to her hearing a rumor that the four of us were playing together."

"Yeah and?" Summer said, sitting on the edge of her seat.

"And she told us how cool she thought we were 'cause we're so open,'" Jenna said and laughed. "Then somehow it led to her suggesting that I pose with her."

"So you posed with her? Naked? Oh my god! Why didn't I come by this morning?"

"So Jack puts on music and starts taking pictures of us in different poses. Skin touching and all. Then I got so turned on."

"You're turning me on..."

"Then she kissed me and I lost my mind. I was so into it. Me? I don't know who I am anymore."

"Is there more?"

"Yes. So then we stood there looking at each other," Jenna said.

"So what happened?"

"Jack said it was a wrap and so we stopped."

"You stopped?" Summer said, slapping her knee.

"Yes. She got dressed and I picked up my clothes to get dressed. As I slid on my shirt she sucked my nipple in her mouth and bit it lightly."

"*Oh my god*, girl. I'm going to come right here."

"Would you focus! I feel like I'm talking to Jack."

"Sorry, you're right," she said, crossing her legs. "So finish."

"So, I started to wonder if this meant I was cheating on you guys."

"Oh, Jenna, you think waaay too much. So was that it?"

"Yes. That was it and then she left."

"Seriously, if that would've been me!"

"Can't you pull yourself out of your sex chakra for one minute? Maybe talking about this was a bad idea."

"No. Honestly, I'll behave, but you've got to promise to answer all my questions when we're through. Okay?"

"Okay."

"So what's the problem, other than you stopped?"

"There's so many things. First of all, how does all this fit with the four of us developing a relationship? What are the parameters? And then, what the fuck is going on with me? I'm not into women and yet I've kissed two women in less than 10 hours?"

"What are you thinking? We're just starting our—whatever you want to call it—friendship, relationship. We haven't established any type of commitment. So you're free to do as you please."

"I see," she said, biting her bottom lip.

"Your second question is something you have to figure out for yourself, love, but let me ask you something—how long have you and Jack been together?"

"About fourteen and a half years."

"So it seems to me a whole new unexplored world is opening up to you. If Jack's into it, I say go for it."

"I don't recognize myself anymore and I'm starting to feel like I don't want to go back to who I was. I don't think that I *can* go back."

"Look, you've been through a lot lately. Think about it. You just recently found out you can't have children, your mother almost dies, you and Jack have been distant for a while now, and you have a crazy couple stalking you in Jamaica." Summer laughed.

"You know what, you're right. I *have* been through a lot. I don't know why I'm beating myself up over this," Jenna said, shaking her head.

"Then, I suggest you just enjoy yourself. Why do any of this, if you're only going to torture yourself the whole time? Make a decision and see where it takes you. I think you'll like what you find, but you have to make a decision one way or the other."

CHAPTER TWENTY-TWO

After their lunch arrived at the island, the foursome settled in under the south end gazebo twenty feet above the jetty. The waves gently splashed against the coral, while the warm afternoon winds inspired a nap. The group finished their lunch and curled up together on the lounge chairs.

"Marc, that was really sweet of you to share your food. That guy looked like he needed it," Jenna said.

"Hey ... it was my idea," Jack said.

"So sweet you are," Summer said. "Come over here and give me a hug."

"I could really use a shower," Jack said.

"That's no excuse for not giving me a hug. Let's shower together," Summer said gleefully. "Jenna, you up for that?"

"Three of us in a shower would be kind of tight," she said, laughing.

"What do you mean the three of us?" Marc said. "You're not leaving me out of this."

"Then we need an awfully big shower," Jenna said. "I can just picture all of us like a can of sardines."

"If we were at our house in Hollywood, we'd all fit comfortably," Summer said. "Hey, I've got an idea. Nobody's ever in the gym showers. We could go there and have some fun. Marc, you go upstairs, or I should say, *will* you go upstairs and get the shampoo and stuff?"

"Sure, no problem," Marc said.

"I'm game!" Jack nearly shouted.

"Are you sure we won't get caught?" Jenna asked.

"No, I'm not sure but think about it, women's prison in Jamaica, that could be cool," Summer said, laughing.

"Don't do that to me," Jenna said, trying to hold back her smile and maintain a serious exterior.

"Come on. Have I gotten you into trouble yet?"

"Hell yes! I'm definitely not going," Jenna said, laughing at herself. "What happened to naptime, anyway?"

"Nap, snap, we have better things to do. Alright people, let's board the boat," Summer said.

※ ※ ※ ※ ※

"We'll be right back," Marc said.

"And don't forget the conditioner," Summer called out.

"The conditioner?" Kokila asked.

"You don't want to know," Summer said.

"So how are you doing?" Kokila asked Jenna, leaning on the bar in front of her.

"I'm working it out," Jenna said.

"Well, if there's anything I can do to help. Let me know," she said. "The usual, ladies?"

"Surprise me," Jenna said. "I'm in the mood for something different."

"How about an Orgasm or Sex on the Beach?" Kokila said.

"You're killing me here," Jenna whispered, lowering her head into her hands.

"Tell me which you'd prefer," Kokila said. "You need to make up your mind." She touched Jenna's hand before she walked to the other side of the bar.

"You know what, she seems a little possessive," Summer said. "I'd be careful if I were you."

"But I thought everything was so simple," Jenna said sardonically. "Just make a decision and all that." She sat back in her chair and watched Kokila prepare drinks for the other guests.

When she came back to stand in front of them, she said, "So did you make up your mind?"

"I'll take the usual," Summer said.

"Jenna?"

"I think I'll stick to a piña colada for now. Maybe try something different later."

"There's no adventure in drinking what we're used to," Kokila said, throwing pineapple, rum, and coconut milk into the blender.

"Hey there guys," Jack said, walking up with Marc. Marc carried a small duffle bag and Jack carried several towels over his shoulder.

"Are you ladies ready?" Marc asked. "Hey there, Kokila. How are you?"

"Doing well. Can I get you something to drink?"

"Not for me. Jack?"

"Sure. A Red Stripe would be great. Thanks," Jack said, perching against Jenna's chair.

"So are you girls ready to go?" Marc asked.

"Let's do it," Summer said, standing. She grabbed her drink and led the group to the gym.

"Wow. I didn't know this was back here," Jenna said as they walked into a large tiled bathroom with lockers and a wooden bench.

"You would have if you'd taken the tour, my lady." Summer laughed and took Jenna's hand. "See, what did I tell you? Nobody's here. We've got the joint all to ourselves." Summer undressed and opened the duffle bag filled with soaps and clothes for them to change into. She tossed the small plastic bottles of shampoo and conditioner to Marc. She handed the soap to Jenna. "Jack, grab the towels, will you?" she said, walking into the shower area. "Think this is big enough?"

"Ah ... this is strange. I get it now," Marc said. "The

men's side has stall showers. I like this wide open stuff."

"Okay, let's steam this place up," Summer said, turning on one of five showerheads.

"Honey, this is too hot," Marc said, moving out of the water flow.

"I like it hot," Jack called out.

"Well then, come over here," Summer said.

"Jenna, can I shower with you?" Marc asked.

"Don't wash her hair," Summer said. "I want to do that."

"Can I wash you?" Jack asked Summer.

"You want to wash my body?" she said teasingly.

Jenna threw a soapy washcloth at Jack. "You're such a dog," she said, laughing.

"Hey, that's a fine thing to say coming from a woman who's standing naked in the shower with one of my friends and oh my god that sounds so cool," he said. "I am a dog. I am."

Jenna stood for a moment watching Jack and Summer play in the flow of the shower. She could see the water beading up on Summer's back and trailing down over her firm buttocks and legs. "You know what?" Jenna called out to Jack and Summer. "I enjoy watching you two." She smiled. "I thought I would share that." She felt Marc's arms coming around from behind her, wrapping her upper body securely in his grasp. She relaxed against him, raising her arms above her head to wrap around his neck.

"Are you ready?" Summer asked as she filled her hand with shampoo.

"This is a little weird," Jenna said.

"I'm only washing your hair," Summer said. "I'm not going to bite you unless you want me to."

Jenna stepped away from Marc and tilted her head back. Summer worked the shampoo into her hair. She then moved around to the front of Jenna and continued massaging her head, making slow circles around her temples. Summer guided her backward into the water, and then lightly ran her hands over her nipples, causing them to peak.

"Oh," Jenna moaned as she rinsed the soap out of her hair. After she finished she gave Summer a light kiss on her lips.

"She's all yours, Marc," Summer said, still holding eye contact with Jenna. Summer walked back to Jack who was rinsing off his body.

As Marc soaped up the washcloth, Jenna said, coyly, "You know, this isn't the first time you've had your hands on my back."

"I know. That first day on the beach is when I felt sure we might have a chance with you guys."

"How's that?" she said, lifting her arms.

"A feeling ... chemistry. I could feel you watching me." He chuckled. "Spread your feet apart so I can ... there." Marc squatted behind her, washing the back of her legs and around her thighs.

When Marc stood and Jenna turned around, she was confronted with his desire. "Oh," she said, stepping back and admiring his full body. "Do I get to wash you, too ... all of you?"

"Every last inch," he said, smiling.

After Jenna rinsed, she lathered the washcloth and started on Marc's back, trailing down across his buttocks to his thighs. Spinning him around, she took her time washing until she reached his erection. She cupped his balls and stroked his shaft with the cloth.

"If you keep that up…" he said, bringing her hands up to his chest.

"Sorry, I got a little carried away." She glanced over at Jack to see if he'd been watching and he had an odd look on his face.

Summer brought everyone's attention to her when she called out, "So, what are you guys up for tonight?"

"Do you mean us as in—?"

"As in, you and Jack. What are your plans? Wait, listen ... shhh," Summer said, putting her finger to her lips. "I hear women's voices."

"Oh shit," Marc said, covering his erection.

"No way," Jack answered dismissively.

"I don't hear—oh, they're coming." Jenna giggled and froze when they entered.

Marc and Jack stood looking at one another as three women walked into the shower. They continued to speak in a language only they understood. Each walked up to a showerhead taking very little notice of the men. Marc casually walked away from the shower.

"Ladies," Jack said politely, tipping an imaginary hat as he passed each one.

They smiled and returned to their conversation.

Summer and Jenna looked at one another and chuckled.

"Let's get dressed and get out of here," Jenna said.

✳ ✳ ✳ ✳ ✳

"Marc, you looked like a boy caught doing something naughty," Jenna said as she passed him entering into his room.

"Yeah, well, I have to admit I panicked a bit and the erection didn't help matters. It's that one way in, one way out thing," he said, shaking his head.

Summer dropped her things on the bed. "Every time I think about Jack tipping his imaginary hat—" she said, breaking into laughter again.

"That's my job, keeping you folks entertained," Jack replied. He plopped into the high-backed wicker chair in the corner.

"What a gorgeous afternoon. Look at this view," Summer said. She opened the glass sliding doors to allow the breeze to flow through the room.

"I love it here." Jenna stepped onto the balcony followed by Summer.

"This has been a great week so far. Are you guys having fun?" Summer asked.

"Yeah," Jenna drawled slowly. She took a seat in the lounge chair. "I mean yes, of course, but the rollercoaster, oh my god. I'm going through a boatload of changes. I never expected this trip to be so intense."

"So it's working out for the best?" Summer asked, sitting next to her.

"I hope so. I feel like it is, but—"

"I think you guys are great. I think you needed a trip like this to get it back together. It's hard in the States. A lot of demands on your time and health. The everyday stress is good for my business, but I'd rather be teaching yoga here."

They sat quietly for a few minutes until Jenna spoke.

"Summer, what's the deal with you and women?"

"The same as me and men. If I really like someone, expressing my love shouldn't be limited as long as everyone knows what's going on. I don't want you to get the wrong idea either. There have been only three women in my life. All are still good friends of mine, but sex is no longer a part of our relationship."

"Why? I mean why even start then?"

"It just evolved that way," Summer replied honestly "Not every relationship is meant to be long-term. When you open yourself up to something new, the experience finds you. That's why it's so important to be cautious. Make sure it's a direction you can live with in the end."

"But isn't that counter to what you said earlier?"

"No. What I was saying to you is that it doesn't make sense to choose a direction if you're going to give yourself a hard time all along the way. If you make a decision, make it clean."

"Okay. I get it," Jenna said. She looked out at the beach. "Can I ask you another question?"

"Shoot."

"So how is it different being with a woman?" Jenna glanced back at Summer. "I experimented a little in college but I wasn't attracted to her in that way so I don't know."

"It's definitely different. It's softer, though not necessarily less passionate or forceful. They feel completely different and I find women spend more time touching and enjoying foreplay than men. Is that what you were asking?"

"Yes, that's what I meant."

✳ ✳ ✳ ✳ ✳

"Oh hell," Marc said.

"What's wrong?" Jack asked.

"My phone is flashing. It's probably Rich. I wonder when he called." Marc dialed and waited. "No answer," he mumbled to Jack. "I hope everything's okay."

"What's up?" Jack said, moving onto the bed closer to him.

"Someone died while on one of our treadmills."

"No shit. Was there something wrong with the thing?"

"No, no. He died of a heart attack. He'd been taking heart medication for a long—"The cellphone rang and Marc walked into the bathroom to take the call.

Jenna and Summer walked back in the room when Summer heard the ring. She filled Jenna in and they all waited on the bed for Marc to emerge. He stepped from the bathroom with a concerned look on his face.

"The police now believe it was murder," Marc said, rubbing his chin.

"What?" Summer said. "Do they know who did it?"

"I couldn't get much out of Rich. He's not handling the news very well. I need to make some phone calls and find out what I can," he said rather calmly, given the situation.

"This is messed up," Jack said, standing up. "We'll go back to our room so you can take care of it without the distraction."

"Thanks," Marc said. He sighed and Jenna could see the tension in his shoulders.

"Let us know if we can do anything," Jenna said. "Call us if you still feel like going to dinner later."

"I will," Summer said, leading them out.

After the door closed behind them, Jenna said, "That is so bizarre, don't you think?"

"Yeah, but Marc seems pretty calm about the whole thing. Either he's incredibly stable or a phenomenally good actor," Jack said as they made their way down the stairs. "I'd be totally losing it, but then again, I can't imagine running a business."

"We *have* a business, Jack."

"Yeah, but you take care of all of that. I'd be lost without you and you know it," he said as they stepped into the lobby. "Want to go by the bar and get a drink before we go back to the room?"

"Umm ... do you think Kokila will still be there?"

"How would I know? Why?"

"Well, she was hitting on me pretty hardcore earlier when Summer and I were at the bar."

"Cool. And you have a problem with that?" he said, chuckling.

"I ... well ... I'm not sure I'm up for more than a little flirting or—"

"I'm up for anything and I really think you should go for it, too. We're here to have a good time." He rubbed his hands together sporting a mischievous smile.

"Well … I—" Jenna said, taking his hand.

Jack eagerly pulled Jenna along with him. When they arrived at the crowded bar, Kokila busily made drinks for her customers. Her eyes locked with Jenna's as she sat down in the swivel chair next to Jack. Jenna quickly looked away as she felt the jolt of energy pass between them.

"I don't know about this," she said uneasily.

"Let's invite her back to our room when she gets off," he said, placing his arm around the back of her chair.

"What will you be having tonight?" Kokila asked as she sidled up. She looked directly at Jenna.

"An Orgasm, for Jenna, please," Jack said.

"What?" Jenna yelped.

"In the liquid form or otherwise," Kokila said, still staring at Jenna.

"The drink," she said, surprised at her own reaction.

"Red Stripe for me," Jack said, laughing.

Kokila sashayed away to fetch their drinks while Jenna and Jack watched her without speaking. When she returned with the beer and cocktail, she inclined forward and whispered, "Does this mean a decision's been made?"

"Oh … um … I—"

"I wasn't kidding when I said you take my breath away. I get off at nine o'clock," Kokila said, scanning the bar for new customers. She strode over to the man waving at her.

"That was so hot," Jack said excitedly. "She really has it bad for you."

"Stop drooling." Jenna felt turned on but befuddled at the same time. *Could I do this for Jack?* she wondered. Pulling herself out of her thoughts, she asked, "How often do you think she does this sort of thing?"

"Does what?"

She leaned toward Jack and whispered, "Fools around with the guests."

"Why don't you ask her?"

"Yeah, okay," Jenna said sarcastically, looking apprehensive.

"No, really, ask her. But I don't think she's into me," he said. He glanced over at Jenna who stared at Kokila.

"We should definitely call it off then."

"It's not a problem for me," he said. "As long as I can watch, that is."

"You have to be able to watch because that's the only reason I'm even considering this. For you, Jack." She pulled her attention away from Kokila and faced him. "Don't you feel like we've been here forever? So much has happened in such a short span of time."

"Yeah. I'm glad we still have a few more days but I must admit I'm excited to get back and create. You and Kokila together were—"

"Did I hear my name?" she asked, sliding up in front of them. "How's the drink?"

"Delicious."

"You're delicious," Kokila mouthed quietly.

"I have a question for you," Jenna said. She waited until the bar-back passed with a bin of ice. "How often do you do this?"

"I'm not sure what you're asking. Are you asking me about my sexual orientation?" Kokila whispered, bending over so Jack could barely make out what she said.

"No, but I want to know that as well," Jenna said as she stood. She hovered over the bar and whispered, "How often do you fraternize with the guests?"

"Never," she said. "Well, at least not until now."

"Never?" Jack and Jenna said simultaneously.

"I've been working here for five years," Kokila said in her normal voice. "Never."

"Oh," Jenna said.

Jack furrowed his brow trying to figure out how he felt about her response.

"And the other question?" Jenna asked.

Kokila leaned over again and whispered, "I'm attracted to whom I'm attracted to. Sometimes it's a man but most of the time, it's women."

Jack sat up and glanced over at Jenna. She appeared befuddled.

"I see," he said. "Can you come by after you're done here?"

"I would love to." Kokila moved away holding Jenna's gaze until she had to turn around.

"Are you okay with her coming over?" Jack asked, swiveling back around to look at Jenna.

"It would have been nice if you'd have asked me first, but I'm fine. Let's grab our drinks and head back to the room. I think I'm going to have to get myself psyched up for this."

❋ ❋ ❋ ❋ ❋

"What time is it, do you think?" Jack asked. He sat smoking a cigarette on the balcony across from Jenna.

"Not sure. Eight-thirty or so," Jenna replied, stretching her arms above her head and rolling her neck. She closed her robe over her crossed leg.

"How was your nap?"

"Wonderful. Did you nap for long?" she asked.

"No. I just needed a fifteen-minute power nap." He tapped out his cigarette. "Marc seemed okay at dinner, don't you think?"

"Yeah," she said. "He said his partner is handling it well and there's nothing more he would do even if he was there." Jenna moved to the railing, looking out at the ocean and the night sky. "Have you decided about the horseback riding excursion tomorrow? It sounds like fun but I'm fine hanging out here."

"I'm thinking we should stay here. It'll give me a chance to finish the sculpture and ship it home. I don't want it to get dried out before I can complete it. We can go early next week."

"Okay," she said, turning around to face him. "Jack, I'm nervous. I'm not sure we should even play with Kokila. I mean, I know Marc doesn't have an issue with it but—"

"I think you should be more worried what I think," he said, crossing his arm in front of him.

"I do, I am. I just don't know what to do and I don't know what to wear tonight."

"Come here," he said, opening his arms.

She sat on his lap and toyed with his messy hair.

"Enjoy yourself. You look great together. I wish I had a video cam—"

"Jack!" she howled indignantly, slapping his arm. She rose from his lap and headed for the closet, still feeling unsure of why she even agreed to have Kokila over. Part of her was curious but she also realized that she wanted to please Jack and push her growing feelings for Marc back to a safer distance.

"Hey, a boy can dream can't he? How do you feel about photographs?" he called out as he followed.

"Please, Jack! Come help me pick out something to wear."

"Does it really matter? How long do you plan to be clothed?" he teased as he approached. He pulled her close and kissed her neck.

"It matters to me."

"Okay." He opened the middle drawer and pulled out a fitted tank top and a pair of boxer shorts. "Here," he said, holding out the clothes.

"Are you sure?"

"Definitely. Get dressed. I'm going to smoke a little ganja on the balcony."

Jack walked outside and Jenna went into the bathroom to dress. While brushing her hair and trying to decide how to wear it, she heard a knock. She stepped out of the bathroom and opened the hotel room door. Kokila immediately stepped inside, dropped her bag, and pushed the door shut. She pressed Jenna against the wall, pinning her arms slightly above her head.

"I've been thinking about this all day," Kokila said, her face close to Jenna's lips. She placed her knee between Jenna's legs and kissed her ardently.

Jenna moaned when she pulled away. "Jack," she said.

"Jack will find us soon enough," Kokila said, breathing heavy from the kiss.

"Why is your hair wet?" Jenna asked.

"I showered off the day. I wanted to smell sweet for you." She lowered her head and began kissing Jenna's neck. "I haven't felt this aroused in a long time," she said, planting small kisses all over her face. "I really had trouble focusing tonight. All I could think about was kissing you ... sucking your—"

"Sweet déjà vu," Jack called out as he reentering the room. "May I join you?"

"No, sir. Why don't you sit on the bed and watch us," Kokila said, relegating Jack to the front row voyeur's seat. She let go of Jenna's arms and cradled her face in her hands. "You are so lovely."

Jack circled to the side as Kokila pushed Jenna back and fell on top of her onto the bed.

She trailed her hand up Jenna's waist and pushed her top up to expose her breasts. "Ohhh," Jenna groaned. "That feels—"

"There's so much I want to do to you," Kokila said, tickling her hand down Jenna's stomach.

Jenna closed her eyes and found herself imagining that she was feeling Marc's large hands caressing her hips, moving slowly up her inner thighs. When Kokila's mouth descended on Jenna's protruding nipples, her body twisted and convulsed. She knew they both stared at her but she tried to lose herself in the fantasy that played out in her mind.

"Look at me," Kokila demanded as she reached down and drew her finger through Jenna's wetness.

She opened her eyes as she groaned out. Her body responded fully to Kokila's administrations but her heart did not.

Just as Kokila started to circle her clit, Jenna sat up and said, "I'm sorry, I just can't."

Kokila said, "Excuse me?" at the same time Jack said, "What?!"

Jenna scooted to the end of the bed and said, "I didn't mean to lead you on and every touch felt amazing but—"

"Then what's the problem?" Jack asked, almost yelling.

Jenna shook her head and said, "I don't know how to say this other than to share the truth. I'm not feeling it here." She pointed to her chest. "You are a lovely and sexy woman but—"

"I understand," Kokila said. "Hopefully we will have time to try again … after you—"

"I don't get it, Jenna. I thought this was just for fun."

Jenna rose from the bed, embarrassment filling every pore. "Can you go so Jack and I can talk?"

"Of course." She scooped Jenna up in a tight embrace and whispered, "I don't give up easily." Kissing her softly, she sucked in Jenna's bottom lip, making Jenna gasp. "Have a great night," she said as she sashayed out the door.

"What the hell was that?" Jack asked as he paced back and forth.

"I thought I could do it for you and it might be fun, but I—"

"Is this about Marc?"

"Partially, yes. My emotions are wrapped up in what we are forming with Summer and Marc and it seems wrong to muddy it with Kokila."

"But they said that they don't care," Jack whined.

"But I do," Jenna replied with resolute firmness.

CHAPTER TWENTY-THREE

Jenna tied her floral wraparound dress at the waist and slipped on her sandals. Jack buttoned and zipped his white linen pants that he had rolled up three turns at the bottom.

"That looks really good together," she said. "I like the turquoise and palm trees on the shirt. You look so islandy."

"Are we supposed to bring drinks with us?" he asked.

"No. Summer said she was taking care of it. Is it time to go?" She checked herself in the mirror and added some lipstick.

"No, we have a few more minutes. Come join me on the balcony. I think I'll roll a joint to take with us."

"Okay," she said, following Jack through the French doors. "Let's not mention Kokila tonight."

"Why not?" he asked.

"I want tonight to be about them and not about that."

"What are you saying? Just say it."

"I don't want you to think when we get home that we're going to be looking for women to—"

"Jenna, I don't and I won't. But please explain to me what that has to do with tonight."

"I don't want to bring what happened with Kokila into the relationship we're developing with our friends," she said and moved over to the railing. "That's private and kind of embarrassing to me. Do you get it?" She glanced back at Jack trying to gauge his reaction.

"Yeah I get it. Okay. Can I just say again that last night was incredible until you stopped things?" he said, shrugging.

"Let's drop it for now, okay?" she said, sitting down.

"Okay, but one last question and then I'll leave it alone. If we did find a woman that you could feel something for—" he said with a cheeky grin.

"Jack! Cut it out. I love you but don't be such an ass." She stood up. "Are we ready?"

"As ready as I'll ever be, I guess," he said, taking her hand.

❋ ❋ ❋ ❋ ❋

"So am I going to talk to Jenna or are you going to talk to Jack?" Summer asked, standing in front of the bathroom mirror using her hands to tease out her hair.

"You and I know these arrangements are always made through the women," Marc said as he walked into the bathroom. "You look fantastic." He swept her up in his arms. "Have I told you lately how much I simply adore you?"

"Yes, but I never tire of hearing it." She nuzzled her head on his chest and said, "Are you excited about tonight?" She moved from his embrace and walked over to the closet.

"Yes. I missed them today. I had a great time but—"

"I know what you mean. How's this?" she asked after she donned her spaghetti strap sundress.

"Very nice. So did you decide on champagne or—"

"Champagne and Red Stripe. Jack doesn't seem like the champagne type. The drinks should be here any minute." She sat on the end of the bed and slipped on light brown sandals that crisscrossed under her calf. She hopped up and slid her large hoop earrings through her lobes.

"How's this?" he asked, turning to face her.

"Wear this out," Summer said, untucking the shirt from his beige Chinos. "There. The blue in the shirt really makes your blue eyes stand out. She'll love it."

There was a knock on the door.

"I'll get it," he said. He strode to the door and let the

262

bellman into the room.

"On the table is good," Summer said. "Thank you."

"Enjoy your evening," the man said as he departed.

"They should be here shortly. Come give me a kiss," Marc said, pulling her onto his lap.

They heard a second knock and broke away from each other.

"I'll get this one," she said, jumping from his lap and flouncing to the door. "Hey guys." She kissed Jack and hugged Jenna. "Look at you two! You look fabulous!"

"You guys look great," Marc said, kissing Jenna lightly on the lips. He shook hands with Jack, pulling him into a hug. They slapped each other on the back and smiled.

"You, too," Jack said, walking over to the table and holding up a beer. "Thanks." He sat in the chair next to the table.

"Should I open a bottle of champagne?" Marc asked.

"Not on my account," Jenna said, standing by the dresser. "I need to eat something first."

"The bottles are on ice, we can wait until after dinner," Summer said, sitting down on the bed.

"Any word on the guy who died?" Jack asked.

"Looks like we're off the hook completely," Marc said.

"That's so great," Jenna said. "That must be a huge relief."

"Yeah, it is," Summer said. "They arrested his wife."

"His wife?" Jack and Jenna said in unison.

"The police believe that his wife found out about an affair he was having and replaced his heart medicine with sugar pills," Marc said.

"It turns out he was having an affair with another member of the wellness center," Summer said, shaking her head. "Why is it so hard for people to be honest? It always amazes me how invested the world is in monogamy when it fails

263

more times than it succeeds."

"But you and Marc are married," Jenna said as she settled in the wicker chair by the balcony.

"That's true. We like the benefits of marriage, but don't confuse that with monogamy," Marc said, resting against the wooden poster of the bed.

"What is it then?" Jack asked.

"We don't really call it anything other than being open," Summer said.

"Some people call it polyamory which means being able to love more than one person," Marc said.

"How's that different from swinging?" Jack asked.

"The primary focus of polyamory is love and relationship. Swinging is more or less just about recreational sex," Marc said. "Not that I have anything against sex, you understand."

"But come on ... this here ... us ... it is about sex," Jack said. "Friendship also but don't tell me it's not about sex."

"Well, I think you're sexy," Summer said as she walked over and put her finger on his chest. "But I also like you a lot. And if we never have sex, Jack, I'm still going to like you a lot."

"Sex is not fundamentally necessary in polyamorous relationships," Marc said, sitting back against the edge of the dresser with his arms folded in front of him. "In fact we prefer sex not be the primary focus. For us the primary issues are honesty and intimacy—being able to share affection in an honest way."

"There's a lot of freedom for me knowing that Marc can spend time with Jenna, like her very much, have a good time, and I totally trust him in that situation," Summer said.

Jenna turned to Marc and asked, "Do you and Summer kid around the same way that she and Jack do?"

"Not really," Marc said. "That's why Jack is so

appealing. He brings something different and you, Jenna, you bring something different, too."

"This is all starting to make so much sense to me," Jenna said, excitement rushing through her. "I mean, it's helping me to understand you guys much better." She back stepped for Jack's benefit.

"That's good," Summer said.

"I'm a little slow on the uptake," Jack said. "So, where do these things end up?"

"Like any other relationships. Jack, this is not *the* answer, it's just another lifestyle choice," Marc said. "It leaves more room for others."

"I still don't see how it's any different from swinging," Jack said.

"Because it's more than just a physical excursion, it's also about connection." Summer stepped toward Jack but sensed his defensiveness. "We're not going to ask you to marry us. Not yet anyway," she said and winked.

"Listen if this is—" Marc started to say as he got up.

"No, it's cool," Jack said, waving his hand for Marc to sit again. "I'll figure it out. It's just that I'm an experiential learner, and sometimes I need to be walked through things."

"That's understandable," Marc said, pushing away from the dresser.

"Shall we go to dinner?" Summer asked.

"Does anyone object to the Veranda?" Jenna asked.

"Not at all," Summer said. "That sounds great."

"Fine by me," Jack said, taking Summer's hand.

Marc held the door as they filed into the hall, heading to the lobby.

After arriving at the Veranda, they took their seats and ordered dinner.

"I'm going to the powder room," Summer said as she stood up. "Coming?" she asked, looking back at Jenna.

"Sure." She rose and followed Summer toward the bathroom on the far side of the lobby.

"Jenna," Summer said, placing her hand on her shoulder, bringing her to a halt.

"Is something up? What's going on?"

"I'm sorry?"

"You have this funny expression on your face," Jenna said, laughing.

"Oh ... no. It's just that Marc and I were planning to ask you guys if you wanted to change partners for the night, tonight. All of us, in our room. But I was thinking that with all we've been talking about, maybe we should do it some other time."

"I don't know. I'm up for it. I'll ask Jack but my guess is that he's up for it, too. It's the whole 'relationship part' that he doesn't get, although I think he understands it better now. So do you actually have to go to the bathroom or was this a ruse?"

"It was both, actually," Summer said. "Let's hurry."

✱ ✱ ✱ ✱ ✱

"That was a delicious meal," Marc said as they left the restaurant.

"You guys up for a short walk on the beach to give our food a chance to settle?" Summer asked.

"That sounds like a great idea," Jenna answered, taking Jack by the hand. She pushed through the French doors leading off the terrace.

The sun had set and the evening sky had turned magenta over Tower Island contrasting beautifully with the lime green of the shallows. Two twin-mast sailboats, heading for the harbor, sailed silently past the coral isle.

Summer and Marc lagged behind to give Jenna the

opportunity to talk with Jack.

"When I went to the bathroom with Summer, she asked me something and I want to check it out with you."

"Okay," Jack said, looking out over the ocean.

"Let's stop for a minute, okay?"

"What is it, Jenna?" he said with impatience.

"They had planned to ask us if we were interested in switching partners for the night. We'd all stay in their room."

"You said they had planned but—" Jack said with an expression of confusion.

"Well they did, they have. Summer expressed some concern over the timing because of the earlier conversation."

"Oh, I see, okay. So what did you say?"

"I said I would talk to you about it. So what do you think?"

"Did they mean sex? Intercourse and everything?"

"I assumed that's what she meant," Jenna said, resting her hands on his chest.

"I don't have any condoms," he said, running his fingers through his hair.

"Is that a yes?"

"How do you feel about it?"

"I'm not sure. I mean I want to, but again I think we're crossing a line and I don't know where it will lead us. You?"

"Yes, I want to. Summer … well you know…"

"I understand," she said.

"How would it work?" Jack asked. "I mean ... I wouldn't want to do it on the same bed or anything like that."

"I'm assuming we can work all that out. The condom issue would have to be resolved before I'd be willing."

"They probably have them in the store," he said, running his fingers through his hair again.

"Right. So are you sure? Because—"

"I'm sure. I'm a dog, remember? What about you?"

"I'll have to wait and see how I feel at the time." She searched Jack's face intently and wondered if they were making a huge mistake.

He wrapped his arms around Jenna and they swayed gently for a few minutes. "Let's go find them," Jack finally said. He took her hand in his, giving a gentle squeeze, as they set out to find Marc and Summer.

"You guys in there?" Jack said as they approached the hammock.

"Here," Summer said, waving as she sat up.

They climbed out of the hammock and stood in front of Jack and Jenna.

"So," Summer said. "What's been decided?"

"It's a go but we need to find condoms," Jack said, smiling.

"Excellent," Summer said, winking at Jack.

"We have them," Marc said, assessing Jenna's mood. "Shall we go open some champagne to celebrate?"

"Good idea," Summer said, grabbing Jack's hand and walking ahead of Marc and Jenna who stood locked in a stare.

"Can I kiss you?" Marc asked, moving closer to her. "I missed you. I've been thinking about kissing you all day."

Jenna moved into his arms with her face tilted up. "I missed you, too." She could feel her legs begin to tremble. As he touched his lips to hers, they quivered slightly. She closed her eyes—swirling—she could hear his breathing through his flared nostrils as she melted into the strength of his arms, taken by the care in his kiss. When the kiss ended, they had difficulty breaking away from each other to walk side by side up the beach.

"I have to tell you something. I wasn't going to," she said, walking toward the stairs with him, "but I feel I have to if we're going to ... you know ... sleep together."

"Make love," he said, peering down into her eyes.

"Right, well," she said, glancing away. "Kokila came by last night and we—"

"Made love?"

"No ... well ... we started but it was just sex. Good sex but there was no love there so I stopped it. I couldn't get you out of my mind."

"And Jack, was he there?"

"Yes, he watched."

"Summer will be so jealous."

"I know you tell her everything, but can this wait, please? I don't want tonight to be about that."

"I completely understand," he said.

"So it's okay? You're okay with what happened—didn't happen—with Kokila?"

"For now, yes."

"What does that mean?"

"I mean I still have no say about what you do, but maybe in the future—"

"Oh, I see," she said, bringing her hand to her lips. "I'm nervous. Really nervous. It's been a really long time since I was with another man besides Jack."

"It'll be okay. We have all night and we'll take it slow," he said, stopping in front of his door. "Kiss me again before we go inside."

Jenna wrapped her arms around his neck, decidedly uneasy. She glanced at the door of the room.

Marc gently cradled her face in his hands and kissed her forehead and eyes. Lifting her chin, he lightly kissed her lips. He then bit her bottom lip gently, breathing her in, pulling her hair forward to smell her fragrance. Gripping her firmly behind the head, he circled his other arm around her waist lifting her off the ground. The heat between them sparked a fire as their fervor escalated. She became lost and found again

269

in his arms as they solidified their connection. A bit dazed and high from the kiss, they joined hands and entered the room.

CHAPTER TWENTY-FOUR

Marc and Jenna found Summer and Jack on the balcony smoking the joint Jack had rolled earlier.

"Would you like a hit?" Jack asked, holding it out to them.

"None for me," Jenna said.

"I'll pass for now, too. Should we open up a bottle of champagne?" Marc asked.

"That would be wonderful," Jenna said, stepping through the sliding glass doors and following him back into the room.

"It's going to be hard for me to wait," Marc whispered, passing close to Jenna, trailing his hand along her back. He picked up one of the bottles of champagne and removed the foil.

"I wish ... no ... never mind," she said, shaking her head.

He put the bottle down and took her hand.

"Tell me."

She looked to the balcony and back to Marc and silently mouthed no. He walked her away from the table and away from Summer and Jack.

He held her and said, "What is it?"

"It's stupid," she whispered.

"What is? Tell me," he whispered back.

"Here we are about to ... you know—"

"Make love and?"

"I don't know how to say it. We're ... ahhh—"

"Just say it."

"We're about to have an intimate experience that's really between the two of us, no matter how you look at it, but we'll be doing it in front of them. I don't know how to communicate what I'm feeling. It feels weird, unnatural."

"Last night you—"

"That was completely different," she said, wrapping her arms around herself. "Believe it or not, I'm beginning to understand the difference between enjoying sex and what you and Summer are looking for in a relationship. If this was about just sex for you—and I don't think it is—I couldn't do it. I value our friendship and my relationship with Jack far too much for that. It's hard for me to contemplate being with you while the two of them watch, even as much as I love them. It's like ... it's like having an intimate moment, but having to share it. Do you understand? Am I making any sense here?"

"I think I understand. Will it help to know that Summer and I discussed one couple being on the balcony and the other being on the bed?"

"Where's the champagne?" Summer asked, coming into the room from the balcony. "Oh I'm sorry, if you're talking, I'll grab a couple of beers." She took two Red Stripes and slipped back outside.

"That helps a little," Jenna said, stepping in close. "I guess I'll have to see how it goes. I'm sorry for being such a pain in the ass. I swear I don't mean to be."

"The only pain I'm feeling right now is having to wait to touch you," he said, bending down and giving her a hug. "Let's have some champagne and relax, shall we?"

He walked over to the chair next to the table and sat down, placing the champagne bottle between his legs and untwining the metal cap. He looked up and smiled. "Here goes," he called out. He placed a thumb on either side of the top and popped it. Champagne immediately welled over the long narrow neck, spilling onto the carpet. Jenna held two glasses at a time for him to fill. "It's a celebration of love," he called out to Jack and Summer.

"Thank you," Jenna said, before walking outside and

handing Summer a glass. Jenna moved to go back inside but Summer caught the hem of her dress.

"Is everything alright?" she asked. "He sounds awfully happy."

"Yes, yes he does." She smiled through the sliding glass door at Marc.

Marc joined them on the balcony offering Jack a glass of champagne.

"Sure," he said. "Thanks."

"I would like to make a toast," Marc said, leaning against the railing to face the group.

Jenna moved over to the lounge chair and lay back with her legs outstretched.

"I would first like to say that this trip has been incredible so far and I have no doubt that the good times will continue. I've also enjoyed getting to know you both better. So, let's drink to our friendship," he said, holding up his glass.

"To friendship," Jack said, raising his glass and then taking a gulp.

"To friendship," Summer said, looking to Jack and then smiling at Jenna.

"To friendship," Jenna said, catching a wink from Marc as she looked around at everyone.

"And here's to logistics," Summer said.

"Here, here," Jack said. "So are we taking the balcony or the bed?"

"What's your preference?" Marc asked.

"To get started," Jack said, wrapping his arms around Summer and kissing her on her shoulders and neck.

Marc and Jenna took that as their cue and walked into the room, closing the door behind them. A few moments later the glass sliding door opened about two feet and a blanket, pillows, beer, and the open bottle of champagne surreptitiously passed through, unnoticed by Jack and

Summer.

Summer cooed in Jack's ear stroking his back softly. "I really like you, Jack."

He beamed.

"Oh my god and that smile—I love your infectious smile."

"Stop it," he said, feigning embarrassment. He covered his face. "I have so much fun with you, too. So sexy and playful, I want you so badly I can taste it."

"Anytime you want," she said sexily.

Jack pulled her to him in a frenzy of wanton lust, pushing hard against her lips as if to merge with her. He growled his aggressiveness as he picked her off the floor and held her tight against his body. "And yes, 'I'm glad to see you'," he said as rubbed his erection between her legs.

"It would seem so," she said as she took his hand and placed it on her breast. "I like it a little rough ... yeah, oh ... but not too hard," she gasped.

"I'm sorry, I just feel so intoxicated by you, like I don't know where I am," he whispered against her neck, reeling. "It's been so long since I've felt such heat." He held onto her as if she would float away, pressing her against the wall of the balcony to keep her in place. "Is this better? Oh please, let this be better." Fondling her breast and nipples, he gauged his pressure by her verbal reaction.

"Jack, open your eyes and look at me," Summer said.

"This is ... I'm—" Jack laid his head against her shoulder and tried to steady his breathing. "We should make arrangements."

They worked in tandem to spread out the quilt and set the pillows. He opened a beer and poured Summer another glass of champagne while striking a match to rekindle the joint they had shared earlier. They lay beside one another looking up at the stars.

Jack turned on his side to kiss her full lips. He moaned as he increased his pursuit.

"Hang on a sec," Summer said as she sat up and stripped out of her sundress.

Jack straddled her waist, fondling her breasts and tugging on her nipples.

"Yes, perfect," she moaned, as she greedily thrust her hips up into him and reached up to pull his lips to hers.

He kissed her back, getting lost in the sensation of all things Summer. He trailed his fingers under her panties, capturing her wetness on his fingertips. Bringing her essence up to their mouths, they shared her taste in a steamy kiss that escalated their desire to the boiling point.

He began to lightly touch and kiss his way down, savoring every inch of her body.

"Jack, I can't take it," she said, nudging him toward her most concentrated desire.

He seized the moment and pulled her panties to one side, exposing her ache. He teased with small kisses, increasing, tasting, and enjoying her fleshiness, basking in her womanhood as he gave of himself selflessly, anticipating her arrival at the peak of release.

"Sweet god," Summer cried out, clamping down on Jack's head with her thighs and pulling him in tight against her body. She convulsed and jerked as her orgasm exploded and then subsided with unusual aftershocks. "What the fuck was that?" she said muffled by the blankets that twisted about their bodies in a tangled mess. "Jack, what have you done to me?" She laughed, pulling her legs to her chest and wrapping her arms around them. "Is there more?"

"I think that can be arranged," Jack said. "More champagne?"

"Absolutely," she said, jumping to her feet and throwing her arms above her head basking in the ocean breeze. "Jack, that was amazing."

"Thank you. But I have to tell you, you completely jazz me." He lay back on the pillows, observing Summer. "Your ass is so round. I love the curvature in the small of your back," he said, throwing off the blanket.

"Well hello there," she said, hungering after Jack's arousal. "One good turn deserves another." She knelt on the blanket between Jack's legs. "Shit." She sat up straight.

"What's up?"

"Condoms ... they're inside. It's your fault you know," she said softly as she kissed his face. "I'll sneak in and get them. Be right back."

✱ ✱ ✱ ✱ ✱

"Why are you standing all the way over there?" Marc asked after he moved away from the glass sliding door.

Jenna stood by the dresser, holding the empty champagne glass in her hand with her arms crossed in front of her.

"You have me all to yourself now," he said, advancing to where she stood and taking the champagne flute from her hand.

"I'm struggling." She released her arms and let them hang to her sides, palms out.

"Come here and stop worrying," he said, enveloping her in his embrace. "It's just us. Let's enjoy each other. Kiss me, Jenna."

She could feel the blood pulsing in her body. She gazed into his eyes, which were illuminated by the light filtering through the small opening in the glass doors off the balcony. She closed her own and rose up to kiss him.

"Jenna, please look at me. Be with me, here and now," he said softly.

Her eyelids fluttered open as he began to kiss her with an urgency that caused her to cry out. He possessed her with his very kiss. Guiding her away from him, he then untied her halter.

She stood there with her dress hanging from her shoulders aching for his touch.

"So, so, beautiful," he whispered. He turned her around and from behind, he gently caressed the dress off her shoulders, letting it fall languidly to the floor. He lightly bit his way down her neck and wrapped her in his arms as he pressed his body against her back. "I've thought about this moment a great deal over the last couple of days," he whispered. He stepped back and helped her slip out of her panties, immediately scooping her up in his arms. Carrying her toward the bed, he lowered her to stand in front of him. He pulled his shirt over his head, not taking the time to unbutton it.

"I've wanted to touch your chest since—"

"Since the beach," he said, grasping her hand and drawing it to his upper body. He curved his arm around her back. "Do you remember when we were in the water?"

"Yes," she said, lowering her head against him. "Yes," she said again and began kissing his chest. "Hmm ... you smell wonderful."

"What happened to you that day before you looked away?" he said, invading her hair with his hands. He moved her mouth over his nipple. "Gently." He threw his head back and moaned, "Ahh ... yes." Moving her face to his mouth, he sucked her tongue into him. He pushed himself against her and they fell back on the bed together. "I love how you kiss me ... it's so good yet it's so excruciating." He leaned on his arm over her and said, "So tell me."

"It was like you sent a white hot electric bolt of energy through my body," she said, laying her arms back above her head. "I didn't know what to do. It scared me but then afterward I convinced myself it didn't really happen. Did you do it on purpose?"

"No. The same thing happened to me. Only I knew right away what it meant," he said, trailing his finger between her breasts.

"You're causing me to shiver," she said, arching her back slightly. "What ... oh what ... did it mean for you?"

"That I wanted you and you wanted me," he said, circling his nail around her areolas. He traced her left side, working his way down the outside of her leg. Tickling under her foot, he caused her to squirm. He then trailed up her inner thigh, liberating a loud moan.

"Wait," she said, lowering her hands to stop him.

He took the arm that he had been leaning on and used it to hold her wrists above her head.

"Oh god," she growled as he drew his finger up and around her mound. "I can't take it anymore."

He held his finger slightly above her belly button looking intensely into her eyes.

"Don't stop," she whimpered.

Gripping her arms above her head, he began kissing down her neck, biting and suckling as his mouth migrated lower. He licked around her areola breathing in the air around it. The anticipation burned through her body, eliciting moans of want in a way she'd never had before. He sucked her nipple into his mouth, using his free hand to clutch the other nipple. Increasing the pressure on both, he bit down, causing Jenna to writhe under his attention.

"Oh my god," she uttered in tortured ecstasy.

Marc tracked his hand with his mouth traveling slowly down her body.

Jenna moved involuntarily until she felt his touch on her nether lips.

"Ahhh..." she groaned.

"You're so wet." He let go of her hands and tilted his head to taste her. "Oh my god, you taste so sweet," he whispered.

Jenna clutched his head against her. "Oh, Marc. Oh … yes … that feels … so good   so good. Oh … don't stop," she moaned as he softened the pressure of his tongue and then increased it again.

He stopped and rested his head on her stomach letting his hand become acquainted with her. "So wet," he said again. He peered up at her. "You're exquisite … so lovely."

She stared back as she arched and moaned to his touch. "Oh, please Marc," she said as he increased the speed and pressure.

"I want to see your face when you come for me, Jenna. I want you to see me when you explode," he said, laying his head down next to her. He kissed her while he alternated between slow soft circles with his fingers to a firm fast pitch.

"Oh, I can't take it," she said, clutching his hair. "Don't stop, Marc, don't stop … oh please…" She pushed herself into his hand and came with the crazed delirium of a freed prisoner. She held his arm to stop his touch. Unacknowledged tears ran down her cheeks. "Marc," she whispered, finally closing her eyes.

He touched her face, softly tracing her features. He kissed her tears and stroked her hair back from her face. "Are you okay?" he asked, staring down at her.

She engaged his gaze and felt the arresting desire to touch him, to be filled by him. She reached up and caressed his face. "Thank you," she said. "I'm not okay by any stretch of the imagination. I'm dissolving in my desire for you and I don't know if I'll ever be okay again. Please take off the rest of your clothes and lie against me. I want to touch you." She watched him undo his belt and remove his pants.

Marc lay down beside her and covered her with his body. He kissed her, owning her with his mouth and his touch in tandem.

"Let me see you," she said, rolling him on his back. "Look how hard you are. What a gorgeous head." She groped her way down his body. Jenna opened her mouth to receive him, stroking up and down as she twirled her tongue around the bulbous end. The intensity of connection had her swaying back and forth, hoping to please him.

"Stop," Marc whispered, bringing her back to him. "I want to make love with you, Jenna." He sat up on the bed and retrieved a condom from the end table drawer. He slipped the condom on and rejoined her on the bed. He lay on top of her as she spread her legs to allow him passage.

"Easy," she said as he attempted to push all the way in. She had to adjust her body to accommodate him.

As he rocked back and forth, tears began anew for Jenna when the agony of her desire surpassed anything she had experienced before. They crashed together like the waves on the shore, trying to get past skin and flesh and as deep into one another as possible, experiencing the surge of undeniable suffering of passion.

"I can't get close enough to you," Jenna whispered, wrapping her legs around his back.

CHAPTER TWENTY-FIVE

Summer slid through the open door and felt her way to the end table where they kept the condoms. She could hear the sounds that Jenna and Marc made in the throes of their abandon. She reached the door again and looked back to see Jenna's legs curled tightly around Marc with her toes pointing at the ceiling. She slipped easily back onto the balcony in silence.

"How are they doing?" Jack asked as he reached to aid her onto the blanket.

"They're getting along fine," she said and they both started to laugh. "Shhh ... you've been smoking too much dope." She lay next to him again, pulling the covers up to her breasts. "Here, I'll put this on after I play for a while." She ripped the package open and pushed it under his left shoulder. She flipped over and eased her way under the blanket. "Jack, tell me what you want me to do," she said from under the tented covering as she grasped Jack's erection in her hand and introduced him to her oral skills.

"Oh fuck ... Summer ... oh yessss."

She took her time stroking and sucking, but finally interrupted her play. "Now lay back and enjoy the ride," she whispered from under the cover. After a minute, she threw the blanket off and reached for the condom.

Jack, stunned and mesmerized, closed his eyes. He could see in his mind's eye her unrolling the condom down his shaft. He knew, in that moment, he wanted her more than anything in the world.

"Jack, this is for you, baby," Summer said as she adjusted her body over him and sat on his hard phallus, causing an arch in Jack's back.

He grappled for her, wanting to kiss her, knowing he was about to explode in a moment that would be completely out of control. They disappeared for an eternity, holding on tight to each other's body, rocking together in ecstasy. Back and forth, Summer shifted her hips and ground against his hardness. She strategically hitched her clit against his pubic bone on each thrust and just as she felt him enlarge, his release carried her over the edge with him. They exploded together in rapture, crying out into the night.

Jack opened his eyes to see Summer poised against the balcony rail. "How embarrassing." He rose to his feet. "How long have I been out—" he asked but was interrupted by the sound of Jenna intensely crying out, "Oh god ... yes, yes ... ahhh ... YES!" followed by a deafening silence. Jack looked from Summer to the darkened room and back.

"Sounds like she's having a good time," Jack said pensively. "I guess they're getting along well."

"Come here, give me a kiss," she said, reaching for him.

"No. I don't think so," he said, defiantly turning away. "She hasn't screamed like that for me in years." Jack immediately began to pull on his pants. "I had a feeling." He slipped into his shirt and sat on the side of the lounge, running his fingers through his hair, his eyes darting back and forth. "How long do we wait before we can interrupt?"

"This was for the night," Summer said, reaching out to touch his head in an effort to comfort him.

"No. Don't," he said, pushing her hand away.

"Okay fine. Do you want me to break this up?"

"And make me look like a fool? I don't think so. I'm fucking trapped here on the balcony, twenty-five feet from the door," he groaned, looking over the side of the rail.

"Listen, let me put a stop to this and you and Jenna can go home."

"Home? There's a lot of explaining..." he trailed off.

* * * * *

"Oh god ... yes, yes ... ahh ...YES!" Jenna screamed, feeling the pulse of Marc's orgasm merging with hers.

"Jenna," he whispered and then kissed her softly.

They held each other tight as they floated in the bliss of their lovemaking, coming back to earth ever so slowly.

Marc pulled out of Jenna and removed the condom. "Oh shit."

"What?"

"The condom broke," he said as he placed it on the end table.

"It's okay," she whispered. "Don't worry about it."

They climbed under the sheets wrapping themselves around each other. He caressed her back as she played with his hair. Neither spoke. They lay there while Jenna fell into a quiet sleep.

Marc disentangled from Jenna when he heard Jack raise his voice. He slipped on his pants and walked over to the open balcony door.

"Excuse me," Jack said as he pushed past. "Jenna," he said, rocking her body back and forth. "Jenna, let's go."

"Okay. What's going on?" she asked groggily.

"Get dressed and let's go," he said, fighting to control the fear that raged through him.

"Jack, what's happened?" she asked, sitting straight up in the bed. She looked toward the glass sliding doors recognizing Summer and Marc's silhouettes.

"Jenna, please. I'll talk to you about it when we get back to the room. Get dressed," he said, pacing back and forth. "If you're not dressed in the next thirty seconds, I'm leaving without you." He tramped over to the door and placed his hand on the knob.

"Damn, alright Jack. Can you at least turn on the light?"

"No," he said, bending down to collect her dress and sandals. "Here, here's your stuff."

She got dressed glancing back, time and again, at Summer and Marc who stood motionless, watching them. She slipped into her sandals and looked back one last time as Jack pulled her from the room.

"Jack, let go of me. What the hell has gotten into you? What's happened?" she said, struggling to keep up with him.

"We can talk about it when we get back to our room," he said, stomping hurriedly across the lobby.

They slogged down the hallway to their room in outward silence. Jenna's mind filled with a jumble of thoughts but could not fathom what had happened. Her breathing became heavy from the speed at which they walked and because of her ever-growing anxiety. Jack opened the door, walked straight to the balcony, and lit a cigarette.

"What the hell happened?" she said, following him. "You scared the shit out of me and I'm imagining all kinds of things. What the fuck?"

"I heard you," he said, looking out over the balcony and exhaling smoke.

"What? Heard what, damn it?"

"Heard you. Heard you with him. I haven't heard you cry out like that since, so long ago."

"That's what this is about? You heard me come? Give me a break. What were you doing on the balcony, Jack?"

"That's completely different."

"Excuse me?"

"I wasn't into it like you were."

"I see, so you didn't sleep with her, right?"

"No. I did."

"What the fuck? I don't get this. You wanted this. You

even pushed for it to happen and now what? You hear me come and that's it?"

"Yes, that's it. No more. I don't ever want to see them again."

"You're being totally ridiculous. I know you, let's not forget—you come quietly. So was it good for you? Huh?"

"Yes, but—"

"Yes, but nothing. This is so completely fucked up. Jack, listen to me. I've never felt so open and connected to you. You've got nothing to worry about. We're doing this together. Come on. I love you and that hasn't changed except that the love between us has become stronger. You can't compare what we were going through now, to me and Marc. Jack, look at me, for Christ's sake."

"I can't look at you. I won't look at you. Don't you see, Jen? It's over for us with them."

"That's not being fair to me or even to them. Shit , look at me, damn it. I love you. I have no intention of ever leaving and you wanted this. You, Jack. YOU! Have you forgotten that you talked me into it? Have you?"

"It wasn't like it was hard to convince you," he said, lighting another cigarette.

"I can't believe this is happening. What happened to everything will be okay if we talk about it? If we share everything? Please don't do this. Please. They're our friends and this whole experience has changed me, changed *us* for the better. I've never felt so open and free, and I thought, connected with you."

"Maybe too free."

"God," she said, laying her head in her hands. "Jack, please." Tears streamed down her face.

Jack grabbed one of the chairs by the table, shoved it into the corner of the balcony and sat down.

"What are you doing?"

"I'm sure they can probably see us from their balcony," he said, gesturing toward the main building of the resort.

"Do you want to take this inside?"

"I probably owe us both an apology. You were right. We should've never gotten involved with this to begin with."

"So where do we go from here? You tell me. You've got all the power right now."

"I'm very confused and hurt. Whether you meant to or not, it was devastating to hear you."

"Whether I meant to? You're not going to make me responsible for what you're going through. I went with the program, Jack. Reluctantly at first, but I'm in now and if you're not, then we need to work this thing out."

"I don't know if I want to work it out."

"That's your ego talking. I think you need to sit here and think this through. I'm going to take a shower and then I'm going to bed."

As she brushed her teeth, she stared at her reflection in the mirror. *Oh god, Marc, I'm so sorry. I don't know if I can say goodbye.* She took a quick shower, put on her pajamas and lay down, turning her back to Jack's side of the bed.

❋ ❋ ❋ ❋ ❋

The door shut and Marc and Summer moved off the balcony into the room.

"What happened?" he said, taking Summer into his arms and holding her close.

"He heard her cry out and he lost it," she said, resting her head against his chest. "Do you want to help me bring the stuff in from the balcony?"

"Sure."

"I'm completely confused," she said, gathering up the blanket off the ground. "We had an amazing time together and we were just hanging out at that point." She handed the blanket and pillows through to Marc.

He placed the pile on the chair in the corner of the room. "I was afraid of this in the beginning but I thought…" he said, gazing up at Summer with sadness in his eyes.

"You really like her," she said, passing by him into the room. She touched his cheek tenderly. "I need to shower."

"Let's shower together," he said, following her to the bathroom.

Summer set the temperature and they stepped into the tub. She let the water flow over her face, washing off the night. "How are you feeling?"

"I'm confused," he said, lathering a washcloth with soap. "I knew there were risks going in, but this was a hell of an unexpected reaction. You?"

"I don't want it to be over because I really like him. He's a kick," she said, raising her arms for him to wash her. "Is that a worried look on your face? Are you falling for Jenna?"

"Yeah, I think so. Tonight certainly pushed that along. I really do feel at a loss at the moment," he said, making small circles with the washcloth on her belly. "I really don't even know what to say."

"Well, you still have me," she said, reaching up to touch his face.

"You're my rock," he said, pulling her into his arms.

"Are you giving up?"

"It might take a while but I haven't totally given up on the idea that it might still work out."

"Yeah, but you didn't see his face," she said. "It's over."

CHAPTER TWENTY-SIX

W hen Jenna opened her eyes in the morning, she could see Jack still sitting on the balcony right where she'd left him. She lumbered to the bathroom and leaned on the vanity. "Oh," she breathed, looking at herself in the mirror. She brushed her teeth while staring into her own distant eyes. She dreaded another confrontation with Jack and didn't want to face all that had happened and what it ultimately meant for them—the four of them. She slipped into her robe, tying the sash as she walked to the French doors.

"Is it safe to come out here?" she asked from the doorway.

"Yes. Please come and sit with me," he said meekly, peeking up at her.

She moved the second chair closer to him and sat down crossed-legged, folding the robe over her legs.

"I'm sorry. So sorry about last night. I don't know if it was the pot or that I'm an incredible jerk but please forgive me, Jenna." He reached out and touched her hand.

"I'm so relieved to hear you say that," she said with a slight smile. "Did you sleep at all last night?"

"I dozed on and off."

"You never came in?"

"I took a quick shower and used the bathroom but otherwise—"

"Oh," she said, not sure what to think. "So where do we go from here?"

"I thought we could call them and ask them to lunch. It'll give me a chance to apologize," he said with a sigh.

"Where does this leave us?"

"In regards to what?"

"In regards to us and them, I mean you said it was over. Is it over with them?"

"Do *you* want it to be?" he asked.

"I don't know how to answer that question. I really wish we'd never started but now that we have, I want to see where it could go. Having said that, you and me," she said, gesturing her hand back and forth between them, "is my main concern right now."

"I think you're telling me the truth, I just don't believe you."

"What? Jack, I'm tired," she said, waving her arms above her and shaking her head. "You must be completely exhausted..." She turned away mumbling to herself, "...because what you just said was totally fucked up."

"You know, I don't need much sleep."

"Tell me what we're doing, Jack."

"Like you have no say in it?"

"Do I? I don't think so."

"I'm willing to try again, if they're willing."

"They'll be willing," she said, feeling utter relief but staying low key. "I wonder what time it is." She stood. Her tight hamstring from last night's rendezvous caused her to falter on the way to check the time on her cell phone. "It's almost eleven o'clock already," she called out. "I can't believe I slept this late." She bent over to stretch her legs.

"Call them."

"What time should I say?"

"Two o'clock," he said, rising to his feet. "I'm going to the store, I'll be right back." He traipsed to the door and opened it. He turned around and said, "Just tell them everything's alright, okay?"

"Yeah, I'll tell them," she said, sitting on the bed by the telephone. She watched the door close and then picked up the receiver. Her heart began to beat fast as she waited for an answer on the other end.

"Hey. I've been hoping you would call," Summer said before she had a chance to speak.

"How did you know it was me?"

"Who else would be calling us on this phone?"

"Right, sorry, I'm not quite with it yet."

"So, how's Jack?"

"He told me to tell you guys everything's alright. Can you guys meet us for lunch at two o'clock? He wants to apologize."

"Marc," Jenna could hear her say, "lunch at two okay?"

"Sure, can I?" Marc said in the background.

"Marc would like to speak to you. Here you go," Summer said and then Jenna heard him take a breath.

"How's Jack doing? Are you guys okay?"

"He's in a funk and I'm in a fog. He did reach out to me, though. I don't know."

"Last night meant so much to me," he said softly. "Although it had a bizarre ending. I was looking forward to holding you all night."

"Oh," she sighed. "I know. I was already asleep, so content. I felt so warm and protected in your arms."

"Are we all going to get beyond what's happening for Jack?"

"He says yes but—"

"But you're not sure."

"No, I'm not. Last night he said it was over and Marc, oh this is so fucked up, if this is over I don't know what I'm going to do."

"We'll figure it out."

"I should go," she said, tears welling in her eyes. "I'll see you at two o'clock."

"Okay. Take care. Call us if you need us."

"Okay, bye," she said, breaking down as she hung up the phone.

She shambled to the bathroom and closed the door. She sat down on the toilet lid, cradled her head in the palms of her hands, and cried. "This is so fucked up," she howled.

When her crying subsided, she heard Jack return. She turned on the shower, peeled her robe away, and stepped into the water. Afterwards, she wearily plodded to the bedside and found him fast asleep.

Jenna quietly dressed and moused her way to the balcony. She had the impulse to smoke a cigarette, but instead chose to watch the wedding taking place right below where she stood. She leaned on the railing and watched an elderly couple exchange wedding vows. *Jack wanted us to renew our vows*, she thought.

The marrying couple faced each other under the flower-filled gazebo. Just them. No family or friends. Jenna didn't know why but it made her feel like crying again. She heard the bathroom door shut and turned to see that Jack was out of bed. Falling back into the chair behind her, she pulled a cigarette out of the pack. She lit it and inhaled, immediately feeling lightheaded. Resting her head back, she blew out the smoke. Startled by the door, she turned to see Jack staring at her with an incredulous expression.

"What are you doing?" Jack said, running his fingers through his hair and squinting into the light of day.

"I ought to think it would be obvious," she said, inhaling again.

"Jenna, come on. Don't," he said, taking the cigarette away from her and putting it out. He lifted her to her feet and hugged her tight. "I'm sorry. I got so scared I was losing you. I couldn't handle it if you left me. You're mine to lose."

"You're not losing me, Jack. I love you," she said as the tears began anew.

"You know I can't handle it when you cry. It's all going to be fine. I promise. Come with me," he said, leading her back into the room over to the bed.

They lay in the bed together kissing and trying to reconnect.

"I don't want to lose you. I love you," he said.

"We're going to be okay," she said, but she was not completely sure she believed her own words.

CHAPTER TWENTY-SEVEN

They had moved the tables from the middle of the Calabash and in their place, a huge block of ice sat melting ever so slowly, sweating its life away. In a matter of moments, an emcee introduced a member of the hotel staff that doubled as an ice sculptor. The guests had crowded around, blocking the view of the patrons that had chosen their lunches and sat at the periphery of the show.

"Ladies and Gentleman, we'll provide a free lunch to anyone who can guess the final piece of sculpture," the emcee announced.

The audience laughed and applauded. Jack made his way to a point where he could observe the action that was about to take place. A loud burst came from the chainsaw and the ice submitted itself willingly to the skill of the artist. He eyed the block and then charged with vehemence causing ice to fly.

"It will be a dolphin," Jack yelled, cupping his hands around his mouth.

The artist looked toward him, let the chainsaw die down and broke into a warm white-toothed smiled, "Ya mon. You be the winner."

The crowd applauded Jack as he made his way to the table. The artist took ten more strokes with the saw and left a glistening spectacle for the crowd to admire—a four foot Dolphin.

"The artist is great." Jack smiled as he approached the table. "Listen," he said, directing his attention to Marc and Summer, "I want to apologize for losing it last night."

"How are you feeling today?" Marc asked.

"Jenna and I have a few things we need to work out,

but—" Jack said, flexing the muscles in his jaw. "Can I get a couple of Red Stripes over here?"

"Perhaps we could help," Marc said.

"I don't think so," he said, through gritted teeth, body tense. He took a deep breath. "But if you guys can forgive last night's performance, then let's have a good time today." He reclined in his chair in faux relaxation.

"Sounds good to me," Summer said, placing her hand on his shoulder. "Are you guys going to the island this afternoon?"

"I'm not sure," Jenna said and glanced at Jack. "I'm thinking we need to pass."

"Nah. We should definitely go get naked," he said, shifting in his seat.

"Really? If you're up for it," Jenna said. She avoided making direct eye contact with Marc.

"Summer, come look at the dolphin with me," Jack said, pulling her away from the table.

"What happened last night?" Summer asked, turning to face him as they approached the ice sculpture.

"I don't know. It was hearing her and being with you. You and me—fuck, I don't know. It started out as a lot of fun then went psychotic on me."

"What does that mean?"

"I didn't think about her being with Marc. I just knew I wanted to make love to you. I guess what's good for the goose is not necessarily good for the gander in my mind."

Summer assertively took him by his shoulders and said, "She loves you, Jack."

"I thought we were under an exclusive contract."

"Jack, you and I had sex last night, too."

"That's why it's all so fucked up for me right now. And I would do it again if I could but I don't think I could handle Jenna with Marc," he said, glancing back at the table. He saw

294

Jenna lightly place her fingers on top of Marc's hand and then remove them quickly when she noticed Jack looking at her. She immediately placed her right hand on her upper chest around her throat. "I can't fucking do this," Jack said, pushing Summer's arms away and storming back to the table.

Summer ran after Jack and arrived at the same time. "Jack, calm down," she said, trying to grab his hand.

He shook her off and said, "You know what? Fuck you."

"Let's slow down here," Marc said. "Let's try and get it together." He rose slightly in his chair.

"Fuck you, Marc. Who died and put you in charge," Jack said directly in his face.

"Jack, what the hell? What's gotten into you?" Jenna said, standing and throwing her hands up in the air.

"Don't pull that innocent shit with me, Jenna. I saw you!" he growled, shaking his fist. "God damn it."

"I'm going back to the room," Jenna yelled in a whisper.

"Don't bother. I'm going," Jack said as he ramped away from the table.

Jenna bit her bottom lip hard enough that she could taste blood. "Excuse me," she said to Summer and Marc as she rose to leave.

"Jenna," Summer called. "He's very angry. Let him have some space."

"I hate this," she said as she slowly returned to her chair, scanning the direction Jack had taken. "He seems so out of control."

"He's scared, Jenna," Marc said. "He's afraid of losing you. He's alarmed by the feelings that he sees growing between us."

"But he's doing the same thing with Summer! I don't get it," Jenna said, shaking her head in frustration.

"He's feeling threatened because he thinks he's losing you to me. He no longer feels like the top dog and doesn't know how to handle it. He's in an awkward situation for a man."

"So now with the shoe on the other foot he's having a reaction? We've had a really good relationship up until recently. I just ... well, I've gone through some changes and I need for us to—" Jenna trailed off.

The three sat in silence for a few moments.

"What do you want to do, Jenna?" Summer asked, reaching and touching her hand. "What do you really want to do right now?"

"What I want I really can't have, so what it comes down to, is choices, doesn't it, Marc? I have to choose."

"There really isn't a choice, is there? You and Jack have spent fourteen years together. Most of it, great. We ... we've only just begun and that doesn't make a lifetime," Marc said, sighing. "Who knows what will happen in the future, but for right now, is there really a choice?"

"Aren't you the one who told me there's always a choice? You're the one who helped me see why I fell in love with Jack in the first place. There's a real irony here. I feel devastated that we can't continue what we've started," Jenna said, placing her palms on Marc and Summer's hands. She looked out over the water and then back to Marc. "But I do understand what you're saying. He can be such an ass sometimes but I really do love him and can't imagine my life without him."

"We're here if you need us," Summer said, standing to give Jenna a hug.

"Thank you so much," Jenna said as she hugged them both. "I need to go find Jack."

She walked briskly through reception with sadness in her heart but clarity of mind. She crossed the lobby to the hallway that led to her room. She didn't notice Jack, to her left, in the concierge's office as she passed.

✳ ✳ ✳ ✳ ✳

"Hi," Jack said, smiling, controlling his rage with every ounce of his mettle. "Could you tell me when the next flight to the states takes off from Montego Bay?" He tried his best to sidestep his anxiety.

"Let me check for you," she said as she punched the keys, bringing up the Air Jamaica flight schedules. "There's a flight to Miami at 4:55pm.I would offer to get you a ticket but it's sold out."

"I need to leave today," Jack said, inclining on her desk and dropping his head.

"Try standby." She smiled. "You'd be surprised the number of people that book another few days."

"Excellent. What's the fastest way to get there?"

"Now? You'll be needing to take a taxi. That's going to be a bit expensive."

"I don't care. Can you call someone? Please, someone you know and trust."

"I'll call my cousin. Seriously, you'll be in good hands."

"You're a godsend. Thank you."

"Are these your bags?"

"Yes."

"I'll have someone bring them to the front of the hotel."

Jack pulled open the back door of the taxi and immediately smelled the pungent odor of old smoke. The taxi driver reeked of marijuana. He looked back over the seat and smiled, "Where to, mon?"

"Montego Bay Airport," Jack said, settling in for the ride.

"Ah yes," he said. "Now I remember. No problem."

The taxi jerked forward and stalled. He cranked it again and they were off with a jolt. Jack looked back at the diminishing hotel façade as the driver sped down the hotel drive. The stop sign flew past as he careened around the corner onto the highway.

"I'd prefer to arrive alive," Jack spoke loudly competing with the reggae music on the radio.

The driver looked back at Jack. "Did you say something?"

"No," he said, pointing to the highway.

"Would you like a smoke, mon?" the driver called out in a friendly voice.

Jack gave him a 'thumbs up' and perched his arms on the back of the front seat. He watched the driver—all with one hand—pull a large paper from a pack, fill it with sticky grass, roll it and lick the edge while still driving the taxi.

"That was amazing," Jack said. He accepted the joint and his lighter. He drew on the marijuana, filled his lungs and passed it back.

Jack laid back and closed his eyes, dozing for a while until he jolted awake from the images of Jenna and Marc together. He sat up straight, staring out of the window at the poverty squatting no more than twenty feet from the road, rising up and dappling the mountainside. He rolled down the window slightly to allow fresh air on his face.

"How much longer?" he asked only half expecting the driver to answer him.

"Not that far now," he said as he swerved to miss a pedestrian, his expression never changing. "About five minutes up the road."

"Thank god."

"Ya mon, every day."

The driver turned into the Montego Bay airport driving slowly to the entrance. "Air Jamaica, mon. You have a nice flight home."

Jack reached into his shoulder bag and produced the fare

and a handsome tip. "Thanks for the ride. Good things will come to you."

"Ya mon, and you as well."

Jack shuffled through the throng of passengers waiting for customs. People stood in the parking area, in a makeshift line. The building cut off the ocean breeze, which left the hapless travelers enduring the hot sun. The crowd seemed jovial considering the circumstances. He waited alone, scuffling forward a few feet at a time, mulling over the last twelve hours. He felt conflicted, angry, sentimental, anxious, tearful, and hopeful. He finally made it to the window. "I need to fly standby for the next flight to Miami," he said calmly. "Here's my other ticket." He handed it to the clerk.

"Mr. Harper, this flight is booked solid right at the moment. If you'll take a bench right over there, I'll call you if a seat becomes available. I'm expecting the usual two to four no-shows."

"Thanks," Jack said, picking up his shoulder bag. He plodded over to the nearest bench and sat down. *Will she or won't she? I'm thinkin' no fuckin' way,* he thought. He threw his gear down on the end of the seat and laid back. After removing his sunglasses, he pulled his straw hat over his eyes, laced his fingers behind his head, and waited.

❋ ❋ ❋ ❋ ❋

Jenna accelerated her pace across the lobby, heading for their room. She scaled the steps to the second floor charged with anxious energy. The hallway seemed unfriendly and foreboding as she concentrated on the doorway of 246. She knocked and immediately called out with her ear against the door to listen carefully for any signs of life.

"Jack," she called out. "Jack, if you're in there open the door." She turned her back to a couple passing. "Jack, I forgot my key," she said meekly. She scurried back down the hallway and into the lobby, hurrying back to the Calabash.

"God, fuck, where is he?" she exclaimed, looking around. She rushed to the patio bar where Cliff sat chatting with Kokila. "Have you guys seen Jack?"

"No. Are you okay?" Kokila asked.

"No. He's not in our room and I don't know where he might be."

"That's a bad bit," Cliff said. "I'll go look around and see if I can find him."

"Thank you," she said with a slight smile.

"I'll tell Jack you're looking for him if I see him," Kokila said.

"Okay," Jenna said, sighing with her head in her hands. She sat alone at the bar, trying to decide what to do. Kokila walked near and Jenna asked, "Do you have a phone back there?"

"Sure," Kokila said, snatching the telephone from under the bar and placing it in front of her.

Jenna dialed Marc's room and listened as it rang. On the fourth ring, Summer answered the phone. "Hello?"

"Summer, I can't find Jack and there's no answer at the door."

"Why don't you get a key from the front desk and see if he's in the room. Maybe he's on the balcony and he can't hear you."

"Of course. I'm a wreck. I'm not thinking straight. Thanks," Jenna said, hanging up the telephone. "Thanks, Kokila." She hurried from the bar, taking a bead on the front desk and never losing sight of her goal. "I need an extra key to my room, please, right now."

"Mrs. Harper, that's not a problem at all. You seem panicked."

"My husband … I forgot my key," she said.

"Here's another."

"Thank you," she said abruptly and walked briskly back to the hallway that now seemed like a long tunnel from out of a nightmare, keeping her from her hotel room. She couldn't get there fast enough. She opened the door and took in the half-empty closet and the pulled out drawers. "Oh no," she cried. She sat on the bed and called Summer again. "He's left. All of his stuff ... it's gone. Oh my god, what have I done! I can't breathe."

"Calm down, we'll be right there," she said.

"Hang on. I heard a knock at the door." Jenna put the phone down on the bed and ran to open it. "Jack," she said as she pulled on the knob.

Instead of finding Jack, the concierge stood with an envelope in her hand.

"I've been trying to find you, Mrs. Harper. Mr. Harper left this note for you. He asks that you meet him at the airport."

She ripped open the note.

> *Jenna, I love you so much. I know I've been a complete ass but I'm not sure that I'm cut out for this lifestyle.*

She could see where he had scribbled through— bullshit—and wrote 'lifestyle'.

> *I know I pulled you into it, but I can't sit back and watch you fall in love with Marc. I can't lose you and I can't stay. I'm sure they'll never want to speak to me again anyway. You were right about everything. I shouldn't have invited them. I thought they would distract us from ourselves. And they did, didn't they? I understand if you choose to stay but just remember it's you and only you that I love. Lift us up, Jenna, one more time and I promise I'll make it up to you. If I don't see you at the airport, I'll know*

your decision. I love you and only you.

He had underlined 'you' twice.

She wadded up the note and ran to pick up the phone again. She lifted her hand intending to throw the note in the wicker wastebasket but instead slipped it into her pocket. "He left me a note," Jenna said, looking at the mess around the room. "You know, he wanted this. Shit, I knew this was a bad idea."

"So maybe you know him better than he does himself," Summer said.

"You know what, I've come to realize I really do love him," Jenna said, squeezing the phone cord in her hand. "Damn it, I need to get to the airport quick."

"We'll meet you in the lobby," Summer said.

Jenna slammed the phone down, grabbed her backpack, room key, and cellphone and hurried after the concierge, remembering what Jack had once told her, 'They can handle anything.'

"Listen, can you help me?" she asked as she caught up with her.

"How may I help you?"

"My husband ... he has ... did he ask you about flights to the US?"

"Yes. He's on his way to Montego Bay now to fly standby for the 4:55pm flight to Miami."

"Oh my god, I'll never catch him. It's 3:55 now. What am I going to do?"

"Call him on your cell phone."

"I have our only cell phone. What's the fastest way to Montego Bay?"

"Taxi, but you won't make it," she said, nodding her head. "There's a small airport one mile down the road. I could call my uncle. He has a small two-seater."

"Are you kidding me? Oh my god, how long does that

take?" she asked, knowing she really didn't want to hear the answer.

"Twenty-five to thirty minutes, depending on the winds."

"I'll be right back. Call your uncle and see if he's available. Find out how much in dollars." She hurried to the lobby where Marc and Summer stood by the front desk. She showed them the note and told them about the small plane.

"I don't think I can do it. I can't even stand the big ones."

"You can do it, Jenna," Summer said.

"Have a couple of quick drinks," Marc said.

They ran to the terrace bar where Kokila came from around the other side to meet Jenna. "Did you find him?" she asked.

"I need a couple of good drinks to get my butt on a two-seater," Jenna said.

"No problem. Mango martini," Kokila said. "Two of them coming up."

"Not good terms to use at this point," Summer said wryly.

"We'll go with you to the airport," Marc said.

"That'd be great. I don't know if I can get on a little plane," she said, wringing her hands. "Thanks, Kokila." She took a drink in each hand and without a blink downed them back to back. "I don't feel a thing. Maybe I should take a hit?"

"No. You'll be feeling these in a few minutes," Kokila said. "These drinks are really called 'Captain Courage' in the islands."

"I'm going to need it," Jenna said. "I need to get going. Thanks, Kokila."

"Jack has my information and I hope to hear from you both," Kokila said. "You take good care of yourself."

"Okay, let's go," Summer said as they left for the office of the concierge.

"My uncle says he can take you for two hundred American and you should be in Montego Bay in twenty-five minutes. If you leave now you'll make it there ten minutes before the flight leaves for Miami."

"Let's go," Summer said, pulling Jenna toward the lobby.

"There's a taxi waiting for you. He knows what's going on."

They jogged to the rotunda where a taxi waited.

"Daniel, is this yours?" Jenna said surprised.

"Ya mon," he said. "I'm told to help you get to Jack," he said as he quickly opened the door. "Get in." He slammed the door shut.

The taxi pulled away defying the laws of physics and blended into the traffic on the highway, ignoring the blaring horns and the near misses. Suddenly Daniel wheeled into a small parking lot with a two-room cinderblock building.

"Your pilot is right over there," Daniel said, pointing to a very tall lanky man with dreadlocks piled on top of his head.

"No fucking way am I getting on that plane," Jenna said, peering out the back window of the cab.

"He's a good pilot. The best runner between the islands there is."

"I'll go if you want me to," Marc said.

"That's not even a good idea," Jenna said, feeling a little numb.

"You can do this," Summer said supportively as she pushed Jenna toward the pilot who was smoking a huge doobie.

"Don't worry about your stuff. I'll take care of it," Summer said, hugging Jenna tight.

"You guys are the best. Here's my room key. Thank you and I'm so sorry about everything," she said and turned toward Marc.

"We never meant to come between—" Marc said, sadness infusing his expression.

"I know," she said, walking toward him. "I wish it wasn't ending this way."

"Me, too," he said, enclosing her in his arms. "I'll miss you … I miss you already, Jenna. I know it's been fast, but you've touched me in a way—I still hope…" he said, shaking his head and struggling to hold back the tears. He kissed her ever so gently, not wanting to let her go. Despite all he felt, he said, "You're doing the right thing. Go fight for him. He loves you."

"Thank you." She touched the tear in the corner of his eye, mirroring her own. "I've got to go." As she hurried toward the plane, Summer following closely behind, she called out, "If I die, take care of Jack." She had begun to feel the effects of the mango martinis. "Oh, I can't do this."

"Jenna, get ahold of yourself. You have to go to Jack and this is the only option." Summer held her by the arm, pulling her up to the pilot. "She's very afraid of flying," she said, standing next to the wing of the plane.

"No problem. Everyting's going to be alright." The pilot helped her aboard and said, "Here, my lady, take a short toke on this, not too much now. You will be enjoying this flight. I'll show you all the places of interest on the way."

"That'll be good," she said, managing a small smile. She piled into the passenger seat with the grace of a football player tackled from behind.

"Are you okay, my lady?"

"Yes. Maybe I should've only had one Captain Courage," she said, holding up one finger to the pilot. "I can't see out the front."

"You will when we take off." He turned over the engine causing the propeller to spin. The engine choked, backfired and then died.

"I'm getting out, right now," Jenna said, pulling on the door handle.

"No, no. That happens all the time," he said, taking her by her arm. "This time she will whine like a sewing machine." He turned over the engine again fulfilling his prophecy. The engine whirled loudly and the plane began to taxi. Suddenly her ears filled with a loud roar as the plane sped down the airstrip gaining speed, bobbing back and forth.

As Jenna waved frantically to the rapidly shrinking Summer and Marc, her heart lurched in goodbye.

The plane floated and tilted to the side, curving around to fly a path along the coast. "Shall we fly back over your friends?"

"No," she said with her eyes closed, gripping the sides of her seat. "Are there any in flight instructions?" she asked, cracking her left eye to look at the pilot.

"No," he said. "If something goes wrong we can land on the highway or try the beach."

"Oh my god," she said, burying her face in her hands.

"So you're trying to catch Jack?"

"Yes. Does everybody know about this?"

"Just the cousins. Jack's a nice man. Look down there, that's Sandals and over there is something else, I don't remember," he said, trailing off as he looked out the window.

Jenna lay back in her seat, crossed her arms and closed her eyes. She tried to convince herself she was just in a car on a bumpy highway.

She zoned out until they hit turbulence, causing the small plane to drop and then float. She put her right hand on her upper chest around her throat and said, "Please, how much longer?"

"Ten minutes till we are on the ground," he said and radioed ahead. "This is not good, my lady. We will have to circle the field because Air Jamaica is ready to fly."

"Shit," she said through clenched teeth. "I can't believe I missed him." She peered out the window, straining to see the jet poised for takeoff.

The pilot circled as he descended to the landing strip at Montego Bay. He made his adjustments, lined up the small craft, and landed as Air Jamaica ascended from the other end of the tarmac.

"My lady," he addressed her, "remember the islands are for restoring your soul. You must keep the faith. Ya mon?" The pilot jumped out of the plane and hurried to her side to assist her.

She thanked him profusely as he helped her out of the plane. She trudged to the terminal, pushing through the glass doors. Searching the measly crowd for Jack, she came up empty. She walked around for a moment and sat down to call Summer and Marc.

"After all that, I didn't make it in time," she said as her voice cracked under the strain. "God damn it."

"Are you okay?" Marc asked.

"No. I can't believe that this is so screwed up. I miss him already," she said as she began to break. She laid her head back against the pew in an attempt to gain control of her feelings. "I love him so much. Why didn't he believe that?"

"You know … if we sell another sculpture, we can come back here and do this right," Jack said from the other side of the bench.

Jenna didn't know whether to laugh or cry. As she tried to gather herself, she said into the phone, "You're never going to believe this … I've got to go! I'll call you back in a few."

"Pick up a little ganja, go to the nude island, eat until we're fat and make love," he said, sitting up and looking over the pew-styled bench. He smiled the toothy grin Jenna had fallen in love with the very first time she laid eyes on him.

"To each other—exclusively, if you don't mind—for an entire week. What do you think?"

"I don't know whether to hit you or to hug you but I must admit, that sounds pretty good to me," Jenna said, shifting around to face him. "But don't you ever do that to me again. I got on a small plane for you and I'm not totally sure you deserved it!"

"You have every right to be furious with me. I should've listened to you from the beginning. I was a complete ass and I plan to spend the rest of our lives making it up to you."

"Really? Starting with some counseling when we get back?"

"If that's what it takes."

"In that case…" Jenna said and hesitated. She pulled Jack's straw hat off his head and placed it on her own. She flounced around the end of the pew and said, "Move over, Picasso."

AUTHORS' BIO

Dana and Blakely Bennett love to explore stories outside the realm of what society deems "normal." They find relationships and love to be a fertile ground for exciting intrigue. Their first writing project together happened way back in 1996, which, in their own words, was "dreadful", but solidified their dream of writing fiction for a living. They now write collectively and individually and love to support each other's projects.

Dana and Blakely are very happily married and have been together for nineteen years. The time has flown by quickly for them and life's twists and turns have made their journey all the richer.

Blakely is the published erotic suspense author of the My Body Trilogy and is currently working on her next erotic romance series. Dana is finishing up the first book in his Jones Whitman, Time Traveler, and historical romance series.

You can find out more by going to:
Blakely: http://www.blakelybennett.com/
Dana: https://www.facebook.com/GearedToThePresent

Thank you so much for reading The Demarcation of Jack. If you enjoyed our writing style, we have other books available.

By Blakely Bennett:
Bound by Your Love Series (erotic romance)
Stuck in Between
Bittersweet Deceit
Blue Persuasion
My Body Trilogy (dark, erotic, suspense)
My Body-His
My Body-His (Marcello)
My Body-Mine
My stand-alone romantic comedy
The Second First Chance
Co-Authored with Dana Bennett (romance)
The Demarcation of Jack

From Dana Bennett
Jones Whitman Time Travel Series
Geared to the Present
Geared to the Past
Geared to the Future